MAIDEN'S BLUSH

KAYLA LOWE

Cover designed by Virtually Possible Designs

This book is a work of fiction. Names, characters, places, and incidents
either are products of the author's imagination or are used fictitiously.
Any resemblance to actual persons, living or dead, events, or locales is
entirely coincidental.

Visit my website at www.kaylalowe.com

First Printing: 2007

❀ Created with Vellum

For Jen

*Thanks for all your encouragement and laughs without which
this book would not have been possible*

CHAPTER 1

*T*error filled her as she ran, stumbling across the snowy terrain. Her arms and legs stung from the icy wind whipping across them. She cried out as something sharp struck her. Pushing past the thorny branch, she felt the cut now upon her visage. As the tears trickled down her face, she felt the salty burn of them upon the fresh gash across her right cheek.

A roar sounded behind her, and she turned as the red Lexus skidded to a stop. A new panic seized her as she heard the door slam shut and saw the figure racing toward her. She turned and fled, faster than before, hoping she could make it to the road just ahead.

Hearing the deafening thumps of the steps getting closer, she hazarded a look back. As she turned, the strap of one petite heel stuck on a low-lying branch, tripping her. She smashed to the frozen ground—hard. Jerking her foot from the shoe, she scrambled up, her hands stinging against the cold snow.

Halfway up, she felt a fierce tug from behind. Harsh

hands gripped her waist. "Where do you think you're going?" The dark voice rasped in her ear.

She struggled, desperately trying to break away, but he was far too strong. She screamed, and his arms tightened across her body, one hand covering her mouth. She opened her mouth and sunk her teeth into his flesh as hard as she could. He cried out in pain, cursing, as she broke free.

She had barely gotten five feet away when he recaptured her. She turned, seeing the rage in his eyes.

Then, complete darkness engulfed her as she felt the blow across her face.

Jack Barringer surveyed the sparkling landscape around him through the window of his dark blue Corvette as he carefully sped along the road toward home . Despite the snowy landscape, the roads had been freshly plowed and were pretty clear.

The sky was sprinkled with stars, and the moon bathed the scenery with a picturesque glow. He turned up his radio. With the ground covered in a glittery white blanket, he could almost believe he really was in a winter wonderland. He rolled down his window for just a moment to feel the rush of the wind, deeply breathing in the cold, clear air. Ah, there was nothing like a Massachusetts winter.

It would be nice to be home for the holidays this year. Christmas was just a month away, and he had it planned to slow things down a bit and relax until the New Year. Business had been great lately. He could certainly afford to take some time off, and, besides, he needed the break.

He was among the best translators on the market, and the clientèle he served knew it. He was bilingual in six languages: Spanish, French, Italian, German, Russian, and Arabic. That's why he could do things on his terms. His father had spared no expense to ensure his son was afforded the very best education. He could still hear his cultured voice saying, "Trust me, son, this will all prove to be useful someday."

And, oh, how right he had been. Thanks to him, he had an extremely well-paying job and was allowed to travel the world at his ease. Just recently, he'd been asked if he'd ever considered giving speeches about how to achieve financial success. That would have better suited his father's expertise.

As the flurries upon his window became thicker, he clicked his windshield wipers on. If only he'd told his father how much he had appreciated everything. He was surprised to feel a sharp stab of pain at that thought. It'd been three years since his father's yacht had sunk, taking with it the only parent he'd ever known. At first, he'd been filled with helpless fury. Why his father who had been nothing but loving and kind to everyone? Why his father whose every intention had been to serve and glorify God?

He'd raged at the Almighty and pummeled him with unanswered questions until he'd finally realized that it was useless to be angry with him. After all, he was the Alpha and Omega, the beginning and the end. He had to know what he was doing. He must have a reason for all things. Jack ran a hand through his dark hair. He'd also learned that it did no good to dwell on the past either.

All memories put aside for now, he turned the next curve in happy spirits once more but then slowed as he spotted something lying on the ground on the left side of the road. He leaned forward and squinted through his window. It looked too large to be an animal—at least a domestic animal like a dog or a cat. He watched as part of the bundle jumped up and took off toward the shiny red Lexus he hadn't even noticed was there.

Warning bells began to go off in his head. What was this? He pushed his foot on the accelerator.

The door of the vehicle ahead slammed before the automobile took off down the road with a squeal.

Something wasn't right here. That man left with too much haste. Jack pulled his vehicle onto the side of the highway and stepped out.

The form upon the ground wiggled a bit as he started toward it. He heard a faint moan that sounded much like that of a woman. Wait a minute, a woman? His brows furrowed and his progress quickened. Alarm filled him as comprehension of what he had just witnessed dawned.

He knelt over the tiny body, oblivious to the wet snow seeping through his suit, and noted the red marks upon her face. Sympathy and anger imbued him. Sympathy for the poor victim. Anger at the heartless villain who would do such a thing. What man could possibly look himself in the mirror and not feel guilt over a crime such as this? How could a man ever physically hurt a woman and not feel shamed at his actions? He'd been raised to be a gentleman. Ingrained in him was the habit to treat all women with respect. He'd been taught early on never to strike a woman, even if angry. And that was one rule he'd always followed.

4

He squatted down and lightly touched her tiny wrist. She didn't move. She must have lost consciousness. He gently probed her joints. Nothing was broken at least. Although judging by the marks on her face, she would likely have bruises there and elsewhere.

She needed help, so of course he couldn't just leave her there. He put his arms under her and lifted her with ease, surprised at how light she was. Her long, golden hair fell away from her face and brushed his arms. She winced and cried out in pain. Her consciousness was returning. That was definitely a good sign.

Her lids shot open, revealing big blue eyes surrounded by thick lashes that cast shadows over her delicate cheeks. She screamed and struggled, her fists flying, but weakly. He barely blocked a swing to his mouth, capturing both her wrists in one hand, while still holding her with the other. "It's okay," he said soothingly. "I'm not going to hurt you.

I'm going to help you."

When she continued her vain attempt to escape, he turned her head towards him. "You're stuck out in the middle of nowhere. It's snowing, and if you don't find somewhere warm, you'll freeze to death. Trust me," he said gently. "What do you have to lose?" He wasn't sure if she understood what he was saying. She might have been in too much shock. Nevertheless, she stilled, and he carried her to his car on the side of the road.

Katrina's heart pounded in her chest as the stranger secured her in the passenger seat of the Corvette and closed the door. She watched as he passed in front of the car and got in. He was tall—very tall, at least six inches taller than she was and had dark hair and eyes. He carried himself with the ease of someone who was wealthy and sophisticated. She gulped. Just like Bryan. She shook at the mere thought of him.

Bryan was her father's manager. Her father, David Weems, was a successful lawyer, and Bryan worked for him. He was her father's most trusted friend and helped him with many of his cases. She could see them now, heads bent together busily conversing, occasionally laughing and patting each other on the back. She grimaced. Her father thought of Bryan as the son he'd never had. He depended on him. He trusted him—too much.

She shivered violently. She couldn't remember ever being this cold in her life, wearing only her black evening gown and no shoes. She'd lost those in her flight. She wished she'd have had enough sense to grab her fur coat before jumping out of the car, though at the time her only thought had been to flee.

As if sensing her thoughts and sympathizing, the engine roared to life, and heat hit her face. The stranger in the driver's seat removed his coat and then reached across the car toward her. She recoiled back, eyes wide, scooting as close to the passenger-side door as she could get, prepared to jump from this car too if need be.

The man, apparently, seeing her fear, simply placed his coat on the middle console. "To warm you faster," he nodded toward the coat gently.

"Thank you," she barely managed with a lump in her throat. She took the coat and hugged it around her shoulders as the car began to move onto the road. Suddenly, a new thought struck her. Who was this man and where was he taking her? Panic seized her. What if he were just like Bryan? He'd said he would help, but so had Bryan. What if she had escaped Bryan only to end up with someone worse?

Her hands gripped the edges of her seat tightly. "Where are you taking me?" she asked, her voice shaky.

He glanced at her. "To the hospital," he answered. "I checked your joints. Nothing's broken, but you should still be checked out by professionals."

"No!" she croaked out. He momentarily took his eyes off the road to glance over at her again. "I can't go to the hospital," she fairly shook. Bryan was smart and resourceful. If she checked into a hospital, he would surely find her.

The stranger pulled the car onto the side of the road, and she stared at his huge hands as he shifted the gear in the middle of the car into park. She stared at him warily as his muscular frame turned toward her. "What's your name?" he asked.

She paused. How did she know she could trust this man? Frantic questions ran through her mind, and she licked her lips nervously, her eyes darting out the window frantically. They were in the middle of nowhere. There was nowhere for her to run. Of course, there hadn't really been anywhere for her to run when she'd jumped out of Bryan's car either. She'd just acted on instinct then.

She glanced back at the driver. He was her only means of getting help right now. He was right. If he hadn't shown up, she would have probably become even more lost than she already was and frozen to death. Looks like it was either take a chance and trust him or become a frozen statuette. She would have to trust him.

Besides, if he had intentions of hurting her, he would have acted on them already, wouldn't he?

"Katrina," she answered hesitantly, pressing closer into the seat.

He noticed the defensive gesture, and his voice softened. "I'm Jack Barringer. And I'm not going to harm you. I'm just going to take you to a hospital where you'll be properly cared for."

"I'm not going to a hospital," she stated defiantly with a hint of panic to her voice. He raised his brows and studied her. "I'm not," she repeated firmly, uncomfortable under his scrutiny but adamant in her reiteration.

He didn't question her, just started the engine. "Where are you staying? With family, at a hotel?" His steady gaze rested on her.

Her stomach plunged as the gravity of her situation fully hit her. Here she was in the middle of nowhere sitting in a car with a complete stranger and nowhere to go. No purse, no credit cards, no identification—nothing. She almost laughed at the absurdity of it all. She didn't even have any shoes. Who would have ever thought that she, Katrina Weems, the Harvard graduate, would ever have been so stupid as to screw up this bad?

Her face paled as she thought of how angry Bryan was sure to be. She could only imagine what his wrath would be like if he found her. He was probably right now rummaging through her purse. He would know even more about her than he already assuredly did. He now had her social security number, her resumes and job applications, her money, and not to mention what else. She shuddered to think of him delving in her suitcase.

Oh, why had she been so naïve as to believe that he was only doing her father a favor by coming to pick her up at the airport? Why couldn't her father have just dropped his meeting and come to get her himself? Why did she agree to take an interview in Boston instead of flying straight home to Tennessee from California? The questions kept reverberating throughout her brain when she was jerked back to the present.

"Huh?" she asked, startled.

"I was asking if you had anywhere to stay," he repeated.

She shifted uncomfortably. "Um, no, not exactly."

He flicked his turn signal on and glanced at her curiously. "No problem then. We'll just find you a hotel to spend the night in, and we'll sort through everything tomorrow."

"It's not that easy," she said nervously.

"Why not?" He frowned.

"I don't have anyone, and all of my belongings—my purse, everything—are gone…with him," she explained uneasily.

He looked over at her and for the first time realized that she carried nothing but the clothes on her back. He let out a sigh of frustration. Yes, he pitied her situation, but he was definitely not feeling up to being this caliber of a rescuer. Having a big heart, he did try to help people in need. The world could be a cruel place, especially to women. This poor girl was proof of that. He felt his indignation rise again at the injustice of what he'd glimpsed. But he'd had small gestures in mind. He'd hoped to take her home to safety and be on his merry way.

So much for a relaxing vacation. Here he was stuck with a young woman who had nothing with her and was now totally dependent on him. *Why now, Lord?* Almost immediately, he realized what a jerk he was being and was chastised by his Heavenly Father. How selfish could he be? This wasn't her fault. He certainly couldn't leave her high and dry and scared as she was. God had obviously placed him there at that moment to help her, and he knew that's what he would have to do.

How was he going to do anything to help someone who didn't even have any proof of who she was, though?

She put her head in her hands, that long, golden hair falling on either side. She looked miserable, her fancy dress torn and dirty. He guessed she was a very attractive woman when not so unkempt as she was now. It was easy to imagine that a man would notice her. But what exactly had happened to put her in the state she was in now?

Compassion and remorse filled him at his selfishness. She had refused to go to the hospital. Was she afraid of being found by her attacker? What exactly had occurred by the time he arrived on the scene? She had nowhere to go. No friends or family in the area, no hotel reservation. Had she been staying with this man? Or was it something else? He hadn't pressed her for answers. She'd been through a trying ordeal.

No, she didn't want to be in this predicament any more than he did. It was worse on her part. She was the one who had been assaulted and left out in the cold with nothing.

"Hey," he steadied the wheel with one hand and reached out to touch her shoulder with the other. Mistake. She jumped at the contact, and he winced, mumbling an apology. She physically gathered herself together and raised her head, looking like a lost little girl. It went straight to his heart. "It's going to be okay. I'll pay for each of us a room. We'll sort through everything in the morning." He smiled. "I had planned to stay a night in Boston before returning home anyway."

She looked at him with skepticism and apprehension before slowly nodding her head. "Thank you," she weakly managed before looking back down as if she were ashamed.

CHAPTER 2

*B*ryan Garrison inserted the card in the slot to his condominium. When the button turned green, he clicked open the door and entered, glancing around the extravagant room he'd booked. His eyes darted from the table set with silverware adorned in fancily placed napkins to the lighted painting above the crackling fireplace. He glanced in the other two rooms: one, a bathroom with a Jacuzzi tub; the other, the bedroom. His expression soured. If all had transpired according to plan, Katrina would be on his arm right now, sweet and willing.

He jerked off his silk tie and threw it on the wine-colored bed. But no matter what he ever planned, Katrina always had plans of her own in mind. Anger filled him as he thought back on how she had thwarted his every attempt to ever date her. The constant rejection was trying. He'd thought she would come around eventually, especially with him being her father's most trusted friend.

He'd thought that was an ace in his hand he could surely count on.

He sat down on the bed. He remembered the first time he'd ever seen her...

He was twenty-four years old and fresh out of college with a degree in law. David Weems had just interviewed and hired him. They walked out of David's spacious and tastefully decorous office shaking hands and discoursing, and there she was.

This must be David's sixteen-year-old daughter (He'd remembered his new employer mentioning a sixteen-year-old daughter during their chit-chat after his successful interview.). She sat underneath the large fountain that graced David's expansive foyer. Her head was positioned in the center of the heart formed by the two glass swan heads meeting. She sat serenely, one slender leg crossed over the other, reading Gone with the Wind, was it? Anyhow, she was vibrant with youth, a delicately budding blossom, and a more beautiful sight he'd never seen. He swallowed.

As he and her father approached, she laid her book aside, and those deep ocean blue eyes looked straight into his. He felt his heart jump into his throat.

"Ah, Bryan, meet my daughter, Katrina," David introduced her with pride.

She stood, pushing that incredible blonde hair over her shoulder while extending a dainty hand. "Hi," she said with a sweet lilt to her voice, betraying her Tennessee origin, "pleased to meet you."

He noticed that the hand she extended was perfectly manicured, as was the rest of her. He took the proffered hand, noting its softness, and instead of shaking it, gallantly kissed it. "Hello, Katrina," he replied lowly, "I can assure you the pleasure is all mine."

He knew after that first day that he would do whatever it took to make her his. She was the most beautiful girl he'd ever seen. Hailing from Massachusetts, he'd expected all southern girls to be the same—tan, a little ditzy and uncultured but still fun. Katrina brought to his mind the image of a southern belle during the 1800s. Her fluid motion of grace, her sweet speech—he could just picture her in an extravagant gown with her hair piled high upon her head. Yes, she was perfect in every way—in body, intelligence, and nature.

Throughout that first year, when he would drop by to discuss business with David, he would try charming her. He would tease and cajole to make her laugh. He would entertain her with stories of his college days to see her smile. He would ask her opinions about various topics just to have an excuse to talk to her and be near her.

Yet, he never overstepped the boundaries. He never once tried to kiss or even hold her. She was young yet. She no doubt only thought of him as a good friend and her daddy's business associate.

She went away to college at seventeen—to Harvard, no less. Yet another way she was proving to be unique. How many students go straight from high school to Harvard's undergraduate program? He was proud to think of what a treasure he had—well, would soon have.

During her absence, he and David grew closer than before. Many times, he would saunter over to the Weems' mansion just to have a friendly chat with the man. He truly enjoyed David's company and found his conversations stimulating. He knew David thought of him as a son, and he returned the affection. All the more reason for him to believe that Katrina would accept him. He had her father's approval.

Then the day finally came for her arrival home. He and David were eagerly awaiting her at the airport. He'd taken extra care with his appearance that morning and looked smashing, if he did say so himself. He watched her every movement as she descended the plane, attired in designer shorts and a tank sporting the Harvard crest. She hadn't changed much. Her features were more defined perhaps, only adding to her attractiveness. But she was still the same Katrina, only now she was twenty-four and ready for a relationship...

He grimaced sardonically and poured himself a glass of the champagne he'd requested be included with the room. Yet, at his every request, she'd refused. Yes, she treated him with fondness but still with that childish friendship. She was always too busy or had other plans. The one time he'd convinced her to consent to a date was a month ago. And even then, she'd promptly slammed the door in his face when he'd kissed her after the date.

Not exactly how he'd imagined it, but she was worth waiting for. She needed more time to get used to the idea. Fine. He would back off for a while longer. He'd faithfully kept his distance. Then, the perfect opportunity had presented itself today.

He'd just entered David's office. "Bryan, I'm glad you're here. I was just going to call you," the man said in a rush, looking frazzled.

"What is it?" he asked, ready to help any way he could. "Is something wrong?"

He looked up from shuffling through his papers. "What? Oh, no, nothing's wrong—nothing drastic anyway—but I do have a slight dilemma. I was hoping you could help me out."

"Sure, what is it?"

"It's Katrina. You know she flew out to California for an interview with that big new corporation. Oh, what's the name?" he wracked his mind, frustrated. "Well, anyway, it doesn't matter. The thing is she's staying in Boston tonight because she's supposed to have another interview tomorrow morning up there." He glanced up at him to make sure he was following him so far.

"Yes, yes," Bryan motioned with his hand, "go on."

"I'm supposed to meet her at the airport in Boston and show her around, but at the last minute the Dupets called wanting to meet with me. They said it's extremely important, and you know as well as I do how much rests on this case. I tried to call Katrina to inform her that our plans have changed, but I can't get through because of the weather. I'd hate for her to get off the plane and be looking for me when I..."

Bryan couldn't believe his good fortune. He put up a hand and interrupted, "Say no more, David. I can fill in for you."

Relief washed over David's face. "Oh, thank you, Bryan. I knew I could count on you."

"I'm happy to help. It's no trouble at all, I assure you." Bryan had to restrain himself from doing a fist pump in the air.

"Just show her around the town, would you? You'll be recompensed for everything."

"Nonsense, sir. Think nothing of it."

"You're a good man," David replied in gratitude, clapping him on the shoulder...

It had been too good to be true. David had practically handed her to him on a silver platter. The two of them alone in the city. This was the opportune moment he'd been waiting for. Maybe he would take her to an opera, a grand theatrical appearance. Then again, the reservations were probably already filled. Perhaps just a nice dinner instead. He would finally break through to her. They would stroll through a park under the moon. She would tell him what a wonderful evening she'd had. And then...

He'd hurriedly packed and made reservations and was awaiting her at the airport by six o'clock sharp that night. She exited the plane, looking charmingly disheveled, and spotted him. He smiled to himself when he saw her rushing over to greet him. Was it only a few hours ago?

"Hey, Bryan," she greeted him, her surprise at finding him there evident. "What are you doing here? Why are you so dressed up? And where's Daddy?" She asked these questions in rapid succession, glancing over his shoulder, searching for her father, no doubt.

He reached for her hand and started walking. "He couldn't make it, so he asked me to fill in for him."

She frowned, obviously disappointed, her lips turning into a slight pout. He decided he wouldn't be offended at her disappointment. Of course she wanted to see her father, but just want until she saw what he had in store for her. "Why couldn't he come?"

"He had an emergency meeting at the last minute," he turned then and smiled down at her, "but luckily he found me and asked me to show you around Boston."

"Oh," she said, looking down. "Well, thank you, but I..."

"No buts," he interrupted cheerily. "I'm not taking no for an answer. I have the most wonderful reservations. I know you'll love them." He stopped outside the restrooms and handed her a bag.

"What's this?" she asked, puzzled, looking from the bags up to him.

"What you're to wear tonight. I guessed you didn't pack an evening gown, so I purchased you one before coming here." He mentally congratulated himself on his thoughtfulness.

"Oh, Bryan," she protested, shaking her head, "I can't accept this. There was no need for you to..."

"Just go get dressed," he ordered, pushing her toward the door. "We're to be there within the hour."

She finally relented. When she came out, he appraised her with approval. The dress fit her perfectly, as he knew it would. She looked magnificent, the black gown accentuating every curve. "You look lovely, my dear," he commented, hoping to flatter her.

They walked out to the new Lexus he'd purchased expressly for this trip, and then he drove them to the five-star restaurant he'd booked. They lingered over dinner, laughing. Everything had been going smoothly, until they got back in the car.

"Bryan, I've had a wonderful time," she offered as he drove them onto the interstate. "I haven't had this much fun with a friend since, well, college," she'd admitted.

"The night's still young," he responded, turning onto a smaller highway. Although it was almost midnight.

"I have an interview tomorrow and really need to rest." He could hear the frown in her voice. He'd always admired her dedication to her studies, but she needed to loosen up a bit.

"Oh, come on, Katrina. There's still time."

"Yeah, but..." she protested as he pulled onto the side of the deserted highway.

"What are we doing?" she asked disapprovingly.

"I thought we'd stop to look at the stars and talk," he answered while slipping an arm around her.

She frowned and pushed his arm away. Of course. He'd expected as much. She was always playing hard to get. He wasn't going to be deterred so easily, though. When he slipped his arm back around her the second time, she visibly stiffened. "Bryan, what are you doing?"

"Would you say we're good friends, Katrina? I mean, we've known each other for a long time, haven't we?"

Her eyes met his warily. "Yes, I've always considered you a good friend."

He smiled and pushed his advantage. "Well, then, you can trust me, can't you?" He posed this as a question, but it was really a statement. "I would never hurt you. You know that," he stroked her cheek gently before deeming it safe to lean over and cover her mouth with his.

She remained perfectly still for a moment, trembling. He couldn't tell if it was with fear or desire. He chose to believe it was desire, and if it wasn't, there was no matter. Her fear would leave her soon.

Or so he thought. When his kisses began to travel down the side of her neck, she resisted even more, pushing against him, but he tightened his arms around her. If he could only make her see how much he burned for her...

When she finally broke free, she put as much space as possible between them and regarded him as if he carried a disease. "I think you should just take me to a hotel," her discomfort was evident, but God, she looked beautiful with her face flushed, even if it was with anger.

Pride stinging, his own anger rose. "What's wrong, Katrina?" he asked with a bit of a bite to his voice. There was only so much rejection a man could take.

She flinched at his tone. "You know I don't feel that way about you, Bryan..." she trailed off.

His jaw clenched and he turned to stare straight ahead, unable to look at her as he asked, "What have I ever done to you, Katrina, that would cause you to regard me as if I have the plague?"

When he turned back to her, she was frowning, "Nothing, but, Bryan, you're like a big brother to me," her eyes begged him to understand.

Oh yes, he understood. He understood very well. She was rejecting him—yet again. "A big brother?" He shook his head in disbelief. How could she think of him that way? "I've got news for you, Katrina, I'm not your big brother," he replied curtly. And he planned to show her just how much of a big brother he was not.

She inched toward the door, and he responded by grabbing both of her shoulders, angry that she seemed to want to get away from him. "Katrina," he pleaded desperately, his eyes boring into hers, "I've loved you ever since I first laid eyes on you. I've waited all this time. I came out here today as a favor to your father. I think you owe me something." His eyes traveled over her face back down to her lips. He knew if she would just relax and let him love her, she'd like it and learn to love him back too.

"Let go of me!" she whimpered. She continued to struggle, but he was far too strong for her. "Please Bryan!" she pleaded.

Suddenly something inside of him snapped. Why was she acting this way? It wasn't supposed to be like this. She was ruining everything.

"No, you never were interested, were you?" his tone was icy. "You were always too good, weren't you?" He shook his head in disbelief, "My every thought has always been of you, and this is how you repay me? For my patience? My generosity? Do you know how many women would love to be with someone as

successful as me?" Granted, he hadn't remained celibate for her. He wasn't a priest, for God's sake, and a man had needs, but he'd always dreamed of her, imagined it was her many times. She just shook her head, which only served to anger him further.

He set his mouth in a grim line. "Well, I've waited long enough. We're going back to the room that I booked for us where we can discuss this further. Maybe you'll have come to your senses by then."

He saw disbelief fill her eyes and laughed harshly, the pain of her rejection causing him to unleash the monster within. "Don't look so shocked, Katrina. There's a price for everything. I didn't have to come here today. You should be thanking me for being so considerate."

And then one had thing led to another until she'd jumped out of the car and took off. He took another swig of champagne. He might still have had his way if that stupid man hadn't shown up when he did. His hand still stung from where she'd bit him. So did his ego. He'd bared his heart to her, and what did she do? The spoiled, ungrateful brat had spurned him—again. He slammed his fist against the bed.

Why did she have to be so stubborn and independent? He could offer her so much. Although he was considered wealthy, he wasn't nearly as wealthy as her father, but with time he could be. Couldn't she see what he had to offer her? She wouldn't even have to be getting interviewed for jobs unless she just wanted to. At that thought, he sat upright.

What was he going to tell David? The man would hate him if he found out he'd lost his daughter. He sat back against the bed. He would just tell him she wasn't at the airport. But then what if he wanted to call the police? He'd have to convince him that it would be best if he just searched for her. With David being a powerful business-man, the media would go crazy. Yes, David would take his advice. He hated the media.

He sat up straighter at his next thought. What if Katrina called and told David what happened? No, he assured himself, she wouldn't do that. But if she did, David would have his hide. Unless...he didn't believe her. Bryan was persuasive. If Katrina did happen to report his actions to David, he'd convince him that she'd misread the situation and overreacted. That it wasn't what it seemed. After all, how hard would it be for David to believe that his young, fanciful daughter who'd always had a penchant for dramas would overreact?

He sighed with frustration and clenched his fists. She'd no doubt be hiding from him now, but he'd find her. And this next time around, there'd be no more playing games. He'd convince her of how perfect they were for one another. One way or another.

CHAPTER 3

*K*atrina felt his arms tighten around her painfully. "Don't play coy with me, Katrina," he said. "I know you better than you do yourself. You may deny it now, but I know we're meant to be together. I've known it ever since I first laid eyes on you. For eight long years, I've waited for you to grow up and come home." His eyes burned into hers. "Don't you know I could have had any girl I wanted?" Yes, she did know. He was handsome, suave, and charismatic. "But I chose you. And what do you do? You spurn me!" She felt his hot breath on her face. His eyes were odd-looking as he asked her vehemently, "You think you're too good for me?

"No," she whispered, more frightened and confused than she could ever remember being in her entire life, tears streaming down her face, "it's not like that at all. I..."

"Oh, save it, Katrina," he spat. "I'm so sick of being fed your *I just want to be friends* line," he mimicked. His expression darkened. "Even when you were only sixteen, you were in my thoughts. I had to force my mind to other topics. Otherwise I'd go mad with wanting you." He gave a hoarse laugh. "And then *you went off to college. I felt I'd go crazy waiting for you to return." He looked down at her, a wild look in his eyes. "But now you're back and no longer a child."*

He pressed his mouth to hers ardently, his hands running up her back to the straps of her dress. She pushed him back and jumped out of the car. She had to get away from him. He wasn't acting like himself, like the Bryan she knew anyway. He was scaring her and wouldn't take 'no' for an answer, and she feared what he might do in his state.

She ran, but he caught her. She felt his hands running over her body. She kicked him, and he fell to the ground writhing in agony. She ran, for how long, she didn't know. Then she heard the engine of the car before it stopped again. A car door slamming. Oh, God, he was coming up on her.

She tried to run faster, but she tripped, and suddenly he was upon her.

"Where do you think you're going?"

Katrina bolted upright, hugging the thin sheets to her chest. Gasping, she looked around the hotel room. Only the chest of drawers with a TV atop it, a small round table with two chairs on either side of it, and the mirror that adorned the wall. Relief washed over her.

Of course, nobody was there.

She lay back down and snuggled into the covers but didn't close her eyes for fear the dream would continue where it had stopped. Funny how nightmares always picked up right where they had left off as if they were videos that had just been put on pause, and good dreams, try as you might to recapture them, seemed to be lost upon awakening. She trembled. The events from the night before haunted her. *Where do you think you're going?* His voice echoed in her head. Is that what he really thought? That she felt she was too good for him?

She'd never known that Bryan felt that way about her, though she must admit that after she returned home from college his attention hadn't gone unnoticed by her. But she'd thought it had only been due to the fact that she'd been gone for a few years. Sort of like old friends catching up on lost time. At least that was what she'd told herself. Sure, after she'd returned home from college, he'd asked her out on dates, but she'd never accepted—except that one time, as friends, or so she'd thought until he'd kissed her and she'd hurried into the house. They hadn't spoken of that moment since. She'd hoped it would just go away and things would go back to normal. He'd always been the charming type. It was easy for him to find a date. She'd thought it was no different from him asking out someone he'd just met. Apparently, she'd been wrong.

He had wanted her ever since she was sixteen? He had been twenty-four then—eight years older than she. Yes, he had flirted with her, but she never thought him serious. He'd been thinking of her for eight years? That was obsessive. She felt self-conscious to imagine what his thoughts had been.

Many women would have been flattered to have his attention fixed on them. He was extremely good-looking and wealthy. But she had never thought of him romantically. He was her father's best friend for goodness sakes. It wasn't that she thought she was too good for him. She just didn't feel that way about him. He was like family—or had been anyway, until recently.

Tears stung her eyes. She'd trusted him. She'd valued his friendship and then he…She quivered to think of what would have happened if Jack Barringer hadn't shown up when he had. She felt the humiliation rise up from within her. What must her rescuer think of her? To be found in such a state?

She moaned. And now what was she going to do? She had no way of providing for herself, seeing as how Bryan had her I.D. Should she go home to her father? She could convince Jack to buy her a plane ticket, and she'd pay him back. But wait…she couldn't get on a plane without I.D., and what would her father say when he found out what had happened?

She felt her heart tug. It would kill him. He would blame himself.

No, she couldn't go back just yet. Though what she was going to do, she didn't know. She rolled over and glanced at the clock. It was only six, but sleep had long since eluded her. She didn't know when her rescuer would get up, and she wished it didn't matter. Nevertheless, she threw back the covers and entered the bathroom.

Her breath jerked as she caught her reflection in the square mirror. An ugly bruise marred her face. Looking down at the rest of her body, she noticed other yellow, brown, and purple marks. She began to shake seeing the physical evidence of betrayal. To think she had trusted the man who did this to her! After helplessly staring at her once unscathed body, she stepped into the steaming hot shower.

An hour later, she stood before Jack's door, which was adjacent with hers. She raised her arm and softly knocked. A moment later, the door opened, and he towered before her, groggy-looking and wearing only a pair of shorts. His hair was disheveled, and her eyes lined up with a bare, well-toned chest. Cheeks flaming, she averted her gaze. "Hi, um, I'm sorry to wake you, but I woke up and didn't know what else to do," she rushed.

He nodded and rubbed a hand over his eyes. "I'll meet you downstairs in about twenty minutes." He turned and shut the door, and she stood in the hall uncertainly. Now what was she supposed to do? Turning back to her room, she flipped on the TV and settled down in a chair. A rerun of the *Golden Girls* played on the screen, but she wasn't really paying attention to it as she attempted to sort out her thoughts.

Twenty minutes later Jack stepped out of the elevator and made his way over to where Katrina's small form sat on a plush couch reading *Business Week*, a potted plant rising above her head. He remembered carrying that same small body in his arms to his car last night. Now he noticed her neatly groomed hair and clothes, so different from her bedraggled state the night before. He'd given her money last night to purchase clothing for today from the hotel's gift shop. She was wearing khaki pants and a pink sweater. As he got closer, he could faintly make out the bruise and cut on her face. At a glance, no one would ever have guessed what she'd been through. The wonders of makeup.

She laid the magazine aside as he approached.

"Good morning," he said. "You're looking better, considering the circumstances." She blushed and murmured a 'thank you.' He motioned her through the doorway to the hotel's restaurant. "We'll talk over breakfast if it's alright with you. I'm sure you're hungry. I know I am."

She proceeded ahead of him and sat at a table for two by a window decked with heavy green velvet drapes gathered at the sides and tied with gold tassels. A waiter was immediately upon them with menus. "What may I get you to drink? Sir? Miss?" Jack ordered a cup of coffee while Katrina settled for a glass of milk.

He perused his menu and looked up to see her staring out the window. He followed her gaze to the unrelenting snow. It must not have ceased since last night. "It's so beautiful," he heard her say.

"Yes, it is," he agreed. God's gift to the world.

"Have you never seen snow before?"

She turned and looked at him. "Yes, but I've only seen this much while I was in college. Back home in Tennessee, it only snows in January, if it snows at all, and it's usually no more than a couple of inches."

Ah, Tennessee. That would explain the southern accent he'd noticed. Though he found it only added a sweet note to her voice, unlike some whom it caused to sound simple.

"Your orders?" the waiter asked, hovering patiently.

Jack waited while Katrina ordered two pieces of French toast and then told the waiter, "I think I'll just have the same." They handed their menus over, and Jack noticed the perfectly white tips of her fingernails.

As the waiter hurried off, Jack turned back to Katrina. "Where did you go to college?" he asked.

"Harvard," she answered, running a hand through her hair. He raised his brows. A very prestigious school.

"Your family must have been proud," he commented.

"My father was," she stated. "He'd always hoped I would be accepted, and when the day finally came, I remember he was so happy. The first thing he did was tell Bryan—"she stopped short, a look of sorrow passing over her features.

"Is Bryan the man from last night?" he asked softly.

She turned her head away. He must have guessed correctly. "It's okay. You can tell me. In fact, you need to. Otherwise, I won't have any idea where we should go from here."

She slowly took a deep breath, sat up straighter, and placed one small hand over the other. After finally clutching her shaking hands together, she began slowly. "Yesterday when I got off the plane, he was there at the airport. I'd taken an interview with a rising new company in California and was going to stay overnight in Boston because I had another interview today." She frowned. "Which I've missed now. My father was supposed to meet me at the airport, and we were going to have a *night on the town* so to speak. "

"When I got off the plane and searched the crowd, I saw Bryan—not my father. He told me my father had been called to a meeting at the last minute and couldn't make it, so he was filling in for him." Flipping one strand of hair behind her shoulder, she continued. "I was disappointed but didn't think much of it. My father's a lawyer, so there've been plenty of times in the past when similar things have happened. Besides, Bryan is my father's best friend, and I considered him a friend also." Her face registered regret at her use of the past tense in describing her friendship with her father's business associate. "We had dinner, and then on the way to the hotel, he pulled over to *look at the stars*…or so he said." Her gaze dropped to her hands. "That's when he," her voice broke and she searched for words, "betrayed his friendship, and I jumped out of the car. When he caught me, he hit me."

Silence lingered between them for a moment. Then, Jack broke it with, "I'm sorry to have to ask you this, but did he harm you other than striking you?"

He watched her face color as the gist of what he was asking sank in. "No," she said, "thanks to you." He nodded. She hadn't been raped. That was a relief, at least.

"Do you have somewhere to go?" he asked. "Can I get you back to your father?"

Her eyes looked away from him, and she shook her head. He didn't know why she felt like she couldn't go back to her father, but he didn't press her. Maybe she had her reasons.

He leaned back as the waiter laid their plates before them. "Enjoy your meal." Jack nodded his thanks to the man.

Katrina watched Jack as he poured syrup across his bread and took a bite. "So you were being escorted by this man to your hotel, you had dinner, and then he assaulted you. You could file a police report on battery and assault."

Her face paled. "I can't go to the police," she stated.

Lord, why is it they think that staying silent will protect them? "Not reporting him to the authorities won't protect you. If anything, it'll make it worse. He'll think he can get away with it."

She laid her fork down. "It's not just that. It's…" she searched for a word, "complicated," she finished.

"How so?"

She frowned but instead of answering him, she said.

"I'm very thankful for your kindness. I don't know what would have happened to me if you hadn't shown up when you did, but, frankly, my dilemma is not your problem."

He leaned forward over the table and studied her. She had just told him all about what had happened and now she wanted to shut him out and say it wasn't his problem? He recognized her false bravado for what it was: a defense mechanism.

"I beg to differ," he told her. "It became my problem when I found you lying in the snow with nothing. It's even more my problem now that I know the cause for finding you there. Do you really think I can just walk away now knowing your situation? What if something happened to you? I would have to carry that guilt with me. No, thank you, I want my conscience to be clear."

She seemed to bristle a bit at his tone and retorted, "I can take care of myself. Really. You've done enough."

He stared at her. "Like you did last night? Like you're providing your food and clothing right now? How about your transportation? How do you plan on going anywhere without any money?"

Her face flamed in embarrassment as she said a bit sheepishly, "I'll pay you back everything I owe you and more. And as far as money goes, I can get a job."

"With no identification? Come on, do you really think an employer will hire somebody without a name?" He answered for her when she remained silent, "It's dubious at best."

He saw her determined veneer crumple as the reality of her circumstances once again hit her. "Oh, God, what am I going to do?" she murmured to herself.

He suddenly felt an urging and frowned. *Lord? She's a*

complete stranger. I want to help her, but don't you think that's a bit much to ask? Yet, it was unmistakable. He could almost feel the hand on his back, propelling him forward. He'd learned early on that it was best in the long run to obey—even if it did mean kissing all his tranquility goodbye. It was better not to take Jonah's path or he might end up in the belly of his own whale. He knew what he had to do, whether he wanted to or not.

"You could stay with me for a while."

Her head jerked up. She was clearly taken aback by his offer. "What?"

He shrugged. "I need a secretary anyway, and you could organize some things for me and get paid. You'd benefit. I'd benefit. It's a win-win situation." It was true, he grudgingly admitted to himself. He had been thinking of enlisting secretarial services.

Her brow furrowed. She was skeptical. "Why would you do that?"

"I told you. I need a secretary to manage my business and office. Seeing as how you're in need of employment and shelter, it seems the perfect solution."

Jack watched her consider his offer in silence. Let her think about it. She only had one option, didn't she? He could get her a plane ticket and send her home, but in light of the happenings involving plane hi-jackings throughout recent years, it was doubtful an unidentified person would be admitted on board.

She sighed. "I don't really have a choice, do I?"

He smiled at her reassuringly. "You're hired then."

Katrina stared out of the frost-covered window. The icy trees raced before her eyes, yet she didn't see them. What was she doing riding down the road with a man she scarcely—no, *didn't*—know and going to his home no less? She'd really lost it now.

Yet, what choice had she? Jack Barringer was exactly right. She wouldn't even be clothed properly if he hadn't given her the money to purchase clothing last night. The food in her belly was also due to his generosity.

As much as she hated to admit it, she was totally dependent on him now. And that thought scared her more than anything else. She was used to taking care of herself, doing things her way. True, she had led a very sheltered life, but she was in charge of it—most of the time.

She frowned. Maybe that wasn't entirely true, but she did decide what she would do and when, no matter that somebody was always there to escort her. Okay, so maybe she hadn't always been as independent as she'd thought. The time when she'd experienced the most freedom was at college, but even then, she was restricted, trying to maintain good grades. And maintain them she had, scoring in the top of her class.

So what she doing here? She should be making plans for a great and successful life like she'd always dreamed, not running away like a scared little girl. Was that what it was, running away? Or was she just trying to protect her father and herself? She could go home. She could tell her father everything. She could go back to her sheltered life believing everything was perfect. Nevertheless, even as she thought it, she knew she couldn't. She couldn't crush her father's heart by letting him know the truth about

Bryan. She couldn't go back to her seemingly flawless life, not now that she knew everything wasn't as it seemed. No, she couldn't go back—not just yet. Not until she sorted out her thoughts and decided what she was going to do.

Glancing over at Jack, she took in his finely chiseled features and tanned skin tone. Now that she really looked at him, she found his manner didn't really resemble Bryan at all, as she'd first thought. Besides, Bryan had blond hair, blue eyes, and a lighter coloring. He was also smaller. Jack's arm slowly turned the wheel, and she realized he was much more muscular than Bryan was. He was probably very strong. Certainly much stronger than Bryan, and he'd been strong, as he'd proven last night when he'd restrained her. Somehow, she didn't think that Jack would hurt her, though. Of course, she'd thought the same thing about Bryan, but Jack just had a caring air about him. That's what had brought her defenses down this morning and had caused her to tell him more than she'd wanted to.

She studied him once more. He wore slacks with a polo shirt and sweater, and his hair, worn longer, was carelessly tossed back in a way that gave him an appearance of danger and power yet still managed to look professional. He moved to switch on the radio, bringing her attention to his motions. She'd only vaguely noticed how he moved earlier, but now it hit her full force that he moved more fluently and elegantly than any other man she'd ever known. He moved with smooth motions, as if to a rhythm only he could hear.

He must have noticed her attention because he looked down at her and offered a smile of reassurance. Her breath caught, and she quickly turned back to the window. The man was far too perceptible. He was much too charitable also.

A nagging voice popped into her head: *There's a price for everything, Katrina.* This man was doing so much for her. What would he exact in payment?

She shook the unpleasant thoughts away. She was working for him. He needed her assistance as payment. She would accept his hospitality with thanks, and she would make certain that she never earned the wrath of his strength.

The curved turrets and arches stood out to greet him as Jack pulled into the driveway of his European-styled home. The dramatic exterior was boasted pale stones and numerous windows. Large plates of glass with arched tops graced the bottom floors and small rounded ones did likewise to the top floors. The quaint chimney and impeccable landscape lent an abandoned beauty to the place. Moreover, the mounting snow and English lamps gave it the glow of a romantic getaway. It was a getaway, yes, certainly secluded. But it hadn't held much romance.

He stole a look at Katrina. What did she think of it? By her nonchalant look, he guessed she was used to such finery. One had only to look at her to realize she came from money. The way she moved with an easy grace and spoke with flowing words. Not that it mattered anyway. She would be his employee for a short while, long enough to get her back on her feet. Then, he'd have to find some way to fix this mess with her identification and send her on her way.

Roy hurried down the steps to receive his luggage. "Hey! Jack, it's good to see you! You've been gone a long time on this last trip."

"Just taking care of business, but it sure does feel good to be home." He noted the surprised look on his butler's face as he looked into the car to find a female companion —actually any companion for that matter—with him. "It's a long story," he stated before the forty-year-old man could question him. "I'll explain later." Roy nodded and quickly toted the bags into the house.

Meanwhile, he opened Katrina's door. He offered her his hand, but she glanced at it warily before rising from the car on her own, not taking it. Jack retracted his hand, respecting his decision, half kicking himself for putting her in that situation. Of course she'd be wary of a man's touch now.

"Watch your step. The stones are slippery." Nevertheless, she still slid and collided with his chest, desperately grasping his arm. "It's okay. Steady there. I've got you." His hands firmly but gently gripped her arms to steady her.

She let out a breath, and it fogged in the freezing air. "Thank you. Once again, I'm in your debt." She smiled, and it caught him off guard. She hadn't spoken throughout the whole ride that day, and he hadn't been in any mood to coax conversation out of her, too busy sulking himself over how she'd put a crimp in his plans. He'd thoroughly contemplated all the ways his downtime had just went down the drain. So much for relaxation and solitude.

Ironically, a thought of the day he'd read in his planner

one morning had popped into his head: *We make plans, God laughs.* How true that was. He was a prime example of the situation. No matter how much he planned his life, if it was contrary to God's overall plan, he may as well forget it. The funny thing was you'd think he'd have learned by now to just take every day by faith, trusting that all would turn out as it was supposed to. He really tried, but being ordered to get involved in a situation like this made him wonder what God was all about. *Trust in the Lord with all thine heart; and lean not unto thine own understanding.* He suddenly felt chastised as he was reminded of his earlier thought that he would make the best of this situation, even if it was contrary to his own will.

"It's nothing," he replied and led her up the steps to open the tall oak door.

After they stepped inside the grand entry, he led her up the spiraling staircase to their right and showed her to a room located close to his own. It was centrally located and was one of his nicer guest rooms. "Here's your room. If you need anything, I'm right down the hall." He pointed. "Or you could ring the bell," he pointed to a little buzzer on the wall inside her room, "and either Roy or Elaine will assist you."

She nodded her head in understanding, looking weary from travel and probably worry too. With her silently standing in the doorway of what was to become her new quarters, patiently watching him, waiting for him to say more, he suddenly felt foolish. He couldn't exactly say why. He just felt at a loss for words and ran a hand through his hair. It had been quite some time since a guest had stayed in his home, yet still, he must be travel-weary himself to not be able to keep his thoughts together. "I can see you're tired. Do you like tea?"

She just nodded at him.

"Good. I'll have some brought to you." With that, he turned and strode briskly away, hearing her door close softly behind him.

Upon reaching his room, he called for Roy. When the man knocked on his door, he answered through it, "A cup of tea for our guest, Roy." Kneading his neck, he added, "One for me also. It's been a long day."

CHAPTER 4

The sun blared in Katrina's eyes and, rolling over, she propped her head up on her elbow and squinted at the red digital numbers. Ten o'clock? She never slept so late. She'd always been the early riser, getting up at five or six. She groaned and lay back down. She was tempted to stay in the bed's luxurious warmth all day, though.

Suddenly, she sat straight up. Looking around the room, the memories washed in on her. Was every morning going to be like this? Wake up and then suddenly realize nothing familiar is in sight?

Stepping out of bed, she made her way to the bathroom connected to her room. She found a set of brushes, a toothbrush, and other hygiene products arranged atop the sink. After brushing her hair, she grabbed the toothbrush and turned the facet. As the water gushed out, she took in her surroundings. He had provided her with a very nice room. The bedroom and bathroom were both decorated in a soft pink hue with white cast here and there to highlight it.

She turned the water off and made her way back through the main room to the closet. Opening it, she found the same sweater and pants she'd worn yesterday and hung up last night. The only piece of clothing that had been in the closet was the white robe, which she was still wearing.

Pulling the two articles out, she laid them out on the bed. Oh well. Normally, she would never wear the same outfit more than once a week, but these were special circumstances. There was no help for it. She would just have to make do. First, though, she would take a shower. Her stomach rumbled in protest. On second thought, maybe she'd search out breakfast first.

Opening the door, she peeked her head out. Where was the kitchen? This house was larger even than her father's and Bryan's put together.

When she saw no sign of anyone, she slowly slipped out of the door and thought. Of course, the kitchen was probably on the lower floor. Now what about the stairs? She'd been too tired last night to pay attention to where she was going. Were they to the left?

She started down the long, expansive hall. Peeking into the rooms she passed, she couldn't help but notice that the detail was exquisite. Her father and his circle of friends had been wealthy but not this much so. Why, this house must contain styles from every kind of architecture in existence. The doors even had delicate patterns engraved in them. Around every corner was more grandeur.

She came upon one room that housed shelves of

books: the library Entering it, she felt transported. She could remember when she was a child and her father would read to her while she sat on his lap in the chair by the fireplace in their own library. She ran her hands along the volumes, their scent wafting up to her nose. Some were large, dusty tomes while others were new and fresh from the press.

Pulling one out, she ran her hand along the smooth cover. It was a book of assorted poems. She flipped through the gilded pages. Of its own accord, it fell open to a page that read, *We Wear the Mask* by Paul Laurence Dunbar:

"We wear the mask that grins and lies,
It hides our cheeks and shades our eyes—
This debt we pay to human guile;

With torn and bleeding hearts we smile, And mouth with myriad subtleties. Why should the world be over-wise, In counting all our tears and sighs? Nay, let them only see us, while We wear the mask.

We smile, but, O great Christ, our cries To thee from tortured souls arise.

We sing, but oh the clay is vile
Beneath our feet, and long the mile;
But let the world dream otherwise,
We wear the mask!"

She felt a keen sense of empathy with the author. Wasn't that what she had done all her life? What everybody did? Wasn't that how the whole world was? False and full of pretendings? How many times had she smiled and pretended to be friends with people she couldn't stand? How many times had she dated men she could barely tolerate just to please her father?

Yes, she wore a mask every day of her life. And the sad part was, even if she wanted to, she couldn't remove it. To take off the mask was to make yourself vulnerable, and she'd recently learned that was something she couldn't afford to do.

Turning, she caught sight of a baby grand piano. Her breath caught. How had she not noticed it? It was the most beautiful feature of the room, sitting in front of a large window that reached from floor to ceiling. Red velvet drapes ornamented each side and framed the exquisite instrument perfectly.

Her father had always talked about how her mother had played the piano. That was what had inspired Katrina to learn to play, hoping she could have some small connection with the mother she'd never known long enough to remember. She'd died in childbirth along with Katrina's premature baby sister. Her father had always said she looked just like her mother when she played. She must have inherited her mother's talent for it. There was nothing she loved more than to run her fingers over the ivory keys.

Katrina walked over and softly pressed one key. Its high pitch resounded. She'd always had two ways to relax. One, she could read and escape to another world, or two, she could play piano. She preferred the latter because no matter how much read, the pages wouldn't come true. Though she enjoyed reading immensely, it was only temporary. But this…this was real.

Instinctively, she sat on the bench, and her fingers began to drift over the keys. Playing a baby grand was pure pleasure. It put her expensive keyboard to shame. She closed her eyes and could feel the stress leaving her as the notes to Beethoven's *Moonlight Sonata* washed over her. She gave in to the dreams, as she had time and again sitting like so at her own keyboard, all thoughts of food forgotten.

Jack folded the newspaper he'd been scanning and paused, craning his head slightly forward. Could that sound be what he thought it was? But surely not. The instrument hadn't been played since his father's death. Although his father had played, he himself lacked the will or ability, though he used to enjoy his father's performances. Elaine might just be playing another one of the classical CDs that she was suddenly consumed with. Laying down his cup of black coffee, he strode out of his office.

The sound was coming unmistakably from the library. Making his way down the hall, he slowed and crept to the edge of the dark mahogany door, carefully positioning himself over the soft rugs that covered the hardwood floor. Peeking in, he was surprised, then a bit annoyed, to see Katrina sitting serenely behind the baby grand. Where did she get off thinking she could just roam through his home? He started to barge in, but something in the scene held him back. Looking more closely at her small form upon the bench, his annoyance left him.

Her head was tilted back and her eyes closed. Her fingers drifted over the keys with skill and the soft notes to *Moonlight Sonata* filled the room. She was excellent, hitting every key perfectly, without flaw. This was the first time he'd seen such rapture in her expression. Of course, he hadn't known her long at all, and even for the one full day that he had, all that had been exposed to him was her desperation and need for help. Watching her sitting primly behind the piano, he began to wonder who she really was. What would she have been like if they'd met under different circumstances? Up until now, he'd viewed her as a disruption to his schedule. His curiosity stirred. Where had she learned to play like that?

She wore such a look of complete peace on her face that he hesitated to disturb her. Yet, he couldn't shake the feeling that he was a trespasser eavesdropping on something that was none of his business and felt the need to make his presence known.

He stepped out from the shadows of the door and made a soft "ahem". Her fingers faltered as she looked up, startled, and the music stopped. Jumping up, she hastily tried to explain, "I'm sorry. I was just going to find the kitchen when I stumbled upon this library. I didn't mean to snoop, but when I saw this baby grand, I couldn't help myself. I play the piano, but always on a keyboard and..." she trailed off, biting her lower lip.

He stifled his smile. She looked like a repentant schoolgirl who had been caught going ahead of the rest of the class. "So, you were sampling my piano, were you?" he asked. He walked over to stand next to her, though she took a step back as he approached.

"You're not mad, are you?" she asked hesitantly.

He couldn't stop the smile that spread the corners of his mouth. She truly looked distressed. "Mad is not the word I would choose to describe it," her eyes went wide, to which he hurried to reassure her, "I would say something more like pleased and astonished." He saw her visibly relax. What did she think he would have done if he'd been angry?

"Where did you learn to play like that?"

She looked back down at the piano, resting her hand lightly atop it. "I taught myself. My father used to tell me of how good my mother could play, which inspired me to test my abilities instrumentally. Turns out I inherited her musical talent."

He walked over to the piano and leaned his hip against the side. "You certainly do have a gift. Feel welcome to play it any time you wish."

She looked as if he had just given her the sunrise. Her eyes were shining. "Oh, thank you! You don't know how much this means to me!" She clasped her hands under her chin. She was certainly different this morning, much more exuberant than yesterday when she'd been quiet as a mouse.

He smiled. "It hasn't been used since my father died, and I suppose it's time it sees some action."

He watched her expression dim, her enthusiasm replaced by skepticism. Before he could question her, she masked it, and asked, "Could you please show me to the kitchen? I'm afraid I have no idea which way to go."

He studied her, looking for any hint of the caution he'd just detected in her face the moment before, and for the first time, realized that she was wearing the white robe she must have found in her guest room last night.

Catching his gaze, she looked down at herself, and cheeks flaming, pulled the smooth fabric closer around herself. She now noticed that he was fully dressed in black trousers and a long-sleeved white dress shirt that unbuttoned at the top to reveal a slight expanse of his chest. "I was going to eat first," she explained awkwardly.

He quickly turned his eyes away, choosing not to comment on her scantily clad state except to comment, "We'll have to purchase some clothes and other necessary items for you today."

He looked toward the door to avoid looking at her and making either one of them any more uncomfortable than they both undoubtedly already were. "The kitchen's this way," he stated and headed rapidly for it as if the flames of Hell were licking at his heels—Katrina trailing behind him.

Katrina obediently followed Jack down the long corridor. She could still feel the color in her cheeks. How could she have just walked thoughtlessly out of her room in her robe? She watched Jack's back as they quickly walked down the hall. What must he think to see her traipsing around his house wearing only a robe? He probably thought her everything bold and uncultured.

She felt a sense of confusion. She was making the worst impression possible on this man. She who had always been disdained for her perfect demeanor. She who had always had top marks in all her classes, winner of the essay contests, state business champion for years, her unwavering calm, her strong beliefs. She'd never let anybody penetrate her shell. Snobby Katrina, some of classmates had called her. Perfect, spoiled little rich girl. Though that couldn't be further from the truth. Quite the contrary. She wasn't snobby. She'd just been terribly shy growing up.

But she'd learned how to ignore it all and act like none of it fazed her. Even when the taunts had increased in magnitude and number, she hadn't let one trace of the hurt show.

Now, she was proving anything but flawless. Quite the opposite actually. Being found disheveled in the snow with nothing to her name and now waltzing around his corridors free as you please. What had happened to her?

"This way," he directed, leading her down the spiraling staircase she recognized from last night. The stairs were to the right of her room. She filed that.

She'd been going in the wrong direction.

They proceeded down the elegant stairway into the entrance hall. She now noticed features that she'd been too dazed to pay attention to when she'd first walked through the giant oak door. Like the magnificent chandelier suspended from the high ceiling, catching the sun's rays on its sparkling crystal glass and sending rainbow colors dancing throughout the room. And the large grandfather clock which was just now bonging eleven. However, she didn't have much time to observe her surroundings, for as soon as they stepped off the stairs, Jack turned and directed them down the main pathway.

She glanced on either side of her into the open doors. In one, she could see a wall made completely of glass, allowing the scenery into the soft yellow room. It was obviously designed to make the best of sunlight.

She guessed it to be the parlor or day room.

"This is my office," Jack said, gesturing toward a closed dark cherry door. "After you eat breakfast and get dressed, you can meet me here," he stated, as he glanced at her robed form again, gripping the doorknob hard. "The kitchen's at the very end of this hallway, a couple doors down," he nodded in the direction he was speaking of. "You can't miss it. Talk to Elaine, and she'll see to you." With that he spared her once last glance, averted his eyes, and then promptly closed the door. She immediately went to carry out his orders, relieved to be away from him after making such a fool of herself.

Upon entering the kitchen, she saw the woman whom she guessed to be Elaine bustling around, putting away miscellaneous items. She was slightly heavyset and looked to be in her late fifties. Yet, she was not an unattractive woman. She had soft, plump features that were pleasant.

"Excuse me?" Katrina asked tentatively as the woman placed the large metal pot inside the cabinet. At the sound of another human life form joining her, she turned and looked at Katrina with kind eyes, her shoulder-length brown curls bobbing.

Her eyes flickered with comprehension, and then she rushed over to Katrina, motioning her to a barstool. "Oh! You must be the guest he brought home with him! Just sit right there and I'll fix you up something to eat." She flitted here and there grabbing utensils and such. "I'm Elaine, by the way," she threw over her shoulder.

"I'm Katrina," Katrina replied simply as her eyes followed the animated woman across the room.

"Oh, what a beautiful name," Elaine praised. "Well, hon, what would you like?" She turned back to Katrina holding a teapot in one hand and a coffee pot in the other.

"Um," Katrina glanced from the teapot to the coffee pot and nodded toward the tea pot as she answered, "Tea."

Elaine placed the coffee pot back on the burner, grabbed a tea cup, and began to pour the dark brew that was obviously a breakfast tea.

"And to eat?" The maid as her as she set the cup before her.

"Oh," Katrina placed both hands around the tea cup to feel its warmth, though she didn't immediately pick it up, "just some fruit or toast, I guess."

Elaine stopped and looked her over disapprovingly. "And I'm sure that's why you're so skinny. Why, you have not one ounce of meat on your little bones." Shaking her head she decided, " No, I will not have it. While you're here, you'll eat more than fruit or toast. Just stay there, honey, and I'll fix you up a real breakfast."

Katrina started to protest, halfway offended, to say that she didn't eat only fruit or toast just to keep a figure like some women but that she really liked it. But as Elaine was pulling eggs and bacon out of the refrigerator, she thought better of it. The woman was like a mother hen, gushing with concern, and Katrina guessed that she would cluck loudly if her instructions were spurned.

When Elaine set the plate of toast, fruit, bacon, and eggs before her, Katrina's hunger awakened, though rarely ever did she partake in breakfasts such as this. And at least the woman had given her what she'd asked for, though she'd also tagged bacon and eggs along with it.

She glanced up at Elaine's plump face to see her beaming with pride. She was obviously very pleased with the meal she'd prepared. Katrina knew that she would never dare tell her that breakfast was her least favorite meal of the day and that she often skipped it.

When Elaine pulled out the barstool opposite her own

and plopped down onto it, Katrina was surprised but tried to hide it. At home, the staff had never sat down with them so casually. They had merely served the meal, then continued on to other tasks that needed doing. Katrina didn't know what to say to her other than 'thank you,' which Elaine waved off with a smile and a 'you're welcome, hon.'

But Elaine relieved her of having to start the conversation. Adjusting her weight on the stool she asked, "Where are you from, Katrina?"

"Tennessee."

Elaine nodded her head. "I knew you were from somewhere in the south the first time I heard you speak. I just wasn't sure exactly where. I happen to have relatives that live in the south—in Georgia, that is." Rolling her eyes she said, "And I swear I think they exaggerate their accents when I visit, especially my mischievous nephews. They find it amusing to see me trying to comprehend their slang." Katrina smiled accordingly.

"But your voice is so soft it almost seems to float," Elaine commented with a gentle smile. "It's soothing."

Before Katrina could reply, she jumped to another topic. "So Jack brought you back here with him. I almost couldn't believe what I was hearing when my husband, Roy, told me that the boss had brought home a beautiful young woman. Yet, as I can see, he was correct." She leaned over the table a bit more and said in a quieter voice, "In all the years I've worked here, and that's ever since he built this house, Jack's never brought home a young lady. You must be something special," she surmised.

Katrina stared down at her plate self-consciously. She couldn't let the woman believe that she and Jack were together like that, but she also didn't want to relive the humiliation of explaining her story to anybody else. She finally replied, "Jack and I aren't dating or even together in any way for that matter." Elaine gave her a knowing look and mumbled, "Umm-hmm." But, thankfully, she didn't pry any further.

Instead, she turned her attention back to Katrina's plate. Her disapproval was evident as she eyed the scarcely touched food. "When you're finished with that plate just leave it sitting there on the countertop, and I'll take care of it later, and if you need anything else, I'll be right over there taking care of these dishes," With that, she turned and bustled off to clean the kitchen.

Katrina stared down at her plate derisively. Her appetite had left her at her newfound knowledge. Jack had never brought a woman to his home before? He looked to be in his later twenties—maybe even early 30s— and was handsome and wealthy. Surely he could have any woman he wanted. She rubbed her hands over her eyes trying to make sense of it all. He had never had a woman live in his house before, but he was letting her? Was there some ulterior motive hidden behind his charity? Then again, how could there be? They were still practically strangers. He didn't know anything about her, and there were times when she'd sensed she was an annoyance to him, though he didn't say anything to indicate that was so.

Maybe he was sincerely trying to help her. He hadn't seemed cruel this morning. He'd even offered to let her use his piano any time she wished. At that, her mood brightened a bit. Playing the piano was one of her passions. Surely he wasn't too uncaring or miserly if he'd given his permission for her to use so precious an item.

She moved the food around on her plate, deep in thought. Did it even matter anyway? She had nowhere else to go. At least not until she worked for him long enough to earn a decent amount of money.

Pushing her untouched plate back, she stood up. Elaine wouldn't be happy when she saw the amount of food remaining on the plate. No doubt Katrina would be scolded thoroughly by the unrelenting woman, but she needed to get dressed and meet Jack in his office. She had dawdled long enough as it was.

CHAPTER 5

*J*ack startled at the knock on his door. He saw Katrina's head peep in looking like the blonde waif that she was. In going through his papers, he had forgotten all about his command that she meet him in here. His papers really were an unorganized mess. He realized now that he truly did need her help and was grateful that she was there to relieve him of the tedious task. Being gone these past two months, constantly working, his office had become even more cluttered than it had been, mainly due to the quantity of new faxes he had received and all of his unanswered mail. He'd requested that Roy and Elaine deliver his mail to his office, and now he despaired of ever sorting through the huge pile. In-person business he could handle. It was the paperwork he abhorred.

She entered the room, and he stood. "You told me to meet you in here," she said by way of explanation for her presence.

"Yes," he affirmed, walking around to the front of his

desk. "There are some matters we need to discuss." Taking in her appearance, he noted that she wore the same outfit she had yesterday. Of course. It was the only one he had purchased her as of yet. Though it was preferable to the flimsy robe she had been wearing earlier. Seeing her with only a robe on had invoked thoughts that he hadn't had in a long time. Thoughts that were treading dangerous ground. He'd take her out for necessities later. First, though, he wanted to establish her terms of employment.

"As I told you earlier, Katrina, I need a secretary."

Gesturing toward his muddled desk he added, "As I'm sure you can now see how badly." Reaching for his cup of tea, he took a drink. Even though he practiced the American habit of having a cup of coffee in the morning to start his day, he much preferred tea to the bitter taste of black coffee. It was a habit he had acquired from his time in England.

"But I need to know your last name." He realized she'd been through something traumatizing, but he did at least need to know the last name of the person who would be staying in his home and working for him.

She looked at him warily but supplied it anyway, "Weems."

He nodded and continued. "I'll supply your room and board and give you a decent wage. All you'll need to do is bring order to this mess." He smiled sheepishly. "And send replies and memos to my clients."

He watched her small frame as she looked around his magnanimous office. She was extremely tiny. She couldn't possibly be more than five foot three. She had a delicate structure that made her look like the petite porcelain dolls he had seen in gift stores all across the world. He glanced over at the doll that graced the dark round table set up in front of a window draped in wine-colored curtains—it had been his mother's most prized possession, his father had told him. If Katrina only sprouted curls and wings, she would be a life-size replica of the carved angel.

She interrupted his thoughts with, "What do you do?"

He stared at her dumbly and then realized she was asking about his career and he answered, "I'm a translator."

Raising her brows, she tested him. *"Buenos días. ¿Cómo te llamas?"*

He also said good morning in Spanish, though it was really almost noon, and then smartly answered his name. *"Me llamo Señor Jack Barringer. ¿Y tú?"* he asked, raising his own brows.

She raised her chin and tested him further. *"Soy Katrina Weems. ¿Cómo estás?"*

Hiding his amusement, he replied, *"Encantado, Katrina y estoy bastante bien, gracias. Hace buen tiempo, ¿no?"* Nice to meet you, Katrina, and I'm pretty well, thanks. The weather is nice, isn't it?

She laughed, "Okay, I see you really know your stuff. What other languages do you know?"

This time he did smile. She was an enigma, really. So far she'd been reserved, but today she seemed almost friendly. But then, he was only going on day two of knowing her, and the night leading up to their meeting had been clouded by misfortune. Perhaps her real character was starting to show.

Waving his hand to the wall that sported his accomplishments, he stated, "I'm certified in six different languages."

Her eyes widened as she took in the frames hanging above his massive desk. Then, she turned those eyes on him. "How did you learn so many?" she asked incredulously. "It would have taken years to study all these languages at a university."

"My father hired a tutor to teach me every day after school. I guess that was my extracurricular activity." His gaze fixed beyond her, staring at nothing. "Although I didn't appreciate it at the time, I'm very thankful for it now."

A sense of nostalgia overcame him, but he pushed it off. This was not the time to reminisce childhood days. He had too many other things to attend to. Again he looked at Katrina. Like getting her clothes.

He leaned back against his desk and crossed his arms over his chest casually. "What do you say to a day of shopping?"

She quickly jerked her head up, obviously surprised, her hair rippling with the movement. Had he been so sulky yesterday that she thought him a jerk? That one ungrudging act of goodness was hard to believe of him? He felt bad for his negative thoughts all over again. "Don't you want me to begin working?" she asked hesitantly. "I haven't earned any money yet."

He shrugged. "I can pay you your first two weeks salary early. I'll take you out to purchase clothes and whatever else you need. You'll begin work tomorrow. There's no rush."

She looked down at herself and frowned. "You're right. I can't wear the same outfit all the time."

He took out his wallet. Counting out two thousand dollars, he handed them to her and closed the rest of the bills back up. She took them with a modest 'thank you' and put them in her pocket without counting them.

"When did you want to go?" she asked.

He looked at her eager face. A typical woman, brightened at the prospect of shopping. While he wasn't overly fond of shopping himself, if this was the one comfort he could offer her to make her feel more at home and to help her forget about her attacker, he'd gladly do it. "How about now?"

Pulling the seat belt out, Katrina firmly clicked it in place. Jack started the engine, and she found herself once again staring up at him. She had expected him to be stern and miserly. Though now she wondered why. He didn't appear unpleasant, harboring dark brown hair that almost looked black and deep chocolate-colored eyes that had looked at her that morning with such kindness. Maybe she was so quick to assume he would be callous because every other wealthy man she'd known had always been pompous and conceited.

Yet, Jack Barringer was anything but those things. He was taking her shopping and had paid her two weeks in advance. Still, she wasn't sure what to make of him.

"A penny for your thoughts," his deep voice said, after sitting several minutes in silence. She must have been deeply absorbed in her musings.

"What?" she asked, puzzled.

He briefly glanced over at her, then directed his attention back to the road. "You're from Tennessee, and you've never heard that saying?"

"No."

"It means I'm curious to know what you're thinking."

"Why?" she asked, perhaps a bit too defensively.

He shrugged. "I don't know. Maybe it was the pinched, deeply thoughtful look you had on your face." He adjusted his hands on the wheel. "Like you couldn't figure something out." She was silent.

He sighed. "You're not a very good traveling companion, are you?"

She blanched at the insinuation. "I noticed you didn't have much to say yesterday either," she pointed out.

He didn't speak for a long moment. Then he conceded with, "I see your point."

Immediately she felt regret. When had she become so touchy? She who had always been even tempered. Well, not always. But she had withstood insult after insult in high school without one comment. Why was she now being so edgy? And to a man who had done nothing to her.

"I was trying to figure you out," she offered.

He raised his brows. That obviously was not what he had expected her to be thinking of. Why did she tell him that anyway? What was it about him that made her tell more than she wanted?

"What do you mean?"

"There are certain kinds of people," she explained. "Before you know what to expect from a person, you must first figure out what category they fall into."

"Meaning?" he asked as they pulled into the parking lot of an overcrowded mall. She rarely ever shopped at large malls, preferring the smaller one-of-a-kind stores her father always took her to on vacations.

"Take that woman for example," she said pointing through the glass to a tall, thin brunette who was heavily painted with makeup and whose hair was stiff from hairspray. She walked with one hand on her hip and her nose high in the air. "First, you can easily determine that she's vain and probably thrives on attention. She's the kind of person you would shower with compliments, even if they were false ones. And," she raised a finger as if to emphasize her point, "you would never tell her anything you feared having repeated."

He turned the keys, and the buzz of the car died. He stared at her, and she squirmed under his penetrating gaze. "You really think you can just judge people by appearances?" he asked disbelievingly.

"Not all people, but some are thoroughly predictable," she explained. "I've known enough to know. Some are caring, but most aren't. Even the ones who hide behind a righteous façade. They sometimes take longer to place. But ninety percent of the time, deep down, they're all the same. They don't care about anyone but themselves. Even the ones you think you can trust..." she trailed off.

"What about me?" he asked softly. "What slot do I fall into?"

She looked into his eyes, staring compassionately into hers. She had made a fool of herself. Again. She'd revealed too much. Again. And now he pitied her—again. She felt the embarrassment well up within her. How many times would she subject herself to humiliation before this man? She'd always hated for people to feel sorry for her and had held contempt for those who coveted pity. Several unpleasant faces conjured in her mind. She could see them now making more of everything than there really was, trying to get attention.

Well, she'd already confessed this much. May as well answer his question truthfully. "I honestly don't know. You fit no mold I know." She turned and pulled the door handle, stepping out onto the hard asphalt.

Jack also stepped out of the vehicle, and they made their way toward the sprawling building. When she'd first assessed the hapless brunette, he'd felt a bit of irritation at her haughty attitude. Did she realize how she came across? As uppity? Snobby? Though he had to admit that what she'd said was probably true. Still, it was the principle of the matter. But when she'd went on to say all that about how the majority of people were all the same, all uncaring, he'd sensed her despair.

In those few words were vague reflections of her life.

She seemed like she came from a happy, rich family. Perhaps that was not the case? Perhaps she hadn't come from an untainted childhood? Something must have happened for her to have such a negative outlook on the world.

A red car zoomed in front of them, music blaring from its windows. As the shiny wheels rushed past, Katrina jumped back and bumped his chest just as he reached out an arm to jerk her back. He steadied her and looked to the driver of the Pontiac, who had turned his head and yelled some catcall at Katrina. He couldn't make out all that was said but could guess its meaning. He glanced down at Katrina. Her face was an unreadable mask.

"Are you okay?" he asked, holding open the mall's door.

She nodded once and entered ahead of him. Following closely behind her, he couldn't help but feel like he was her bodyguard. He saw the attention she attracted. The double glances many gave her. And why not? She was beautiful. Yes, he admitted it. Just like the men he saw giving her hungry stares, he couldn't help being attracted to her, and he would be a hypocrite to pretend otherwise. He frowned. At least he had better control over his feelings, though. At least he didn't stare at her as though he hadn't seen a woman in years.

He walked up beside her: partly to establish ownership, partly to try to read her face. Did she notice the stir she caused? No, of course not. She was used to turning men's heads. She'd probably had to reject would-be suitors every day. Although judging by the plight he'd found her in, one hadn't set too well with the rejection.

They walked past store after store. Couldn't she just pick one? Then he glanced into the ones they were passing and realized why she hadn't chosen to enter those. They were crowded with scantily clad teens and employees who had brightly colored hair and pierced noses and eyebrows. That was not her scene at all, he could tell.

Finally, she was turning into a doorway. Of course, she would choose a store that bespoke elegance. It was clean and neatly arranged. He looked up and his eyes caught the sign. *Vanity.* Humorously, he recalled her conclusion about the brunette. She had judged her to be vain and now she was walking through the doors of a place called, of all things, "vanity." Did she notice the irony?

She turned to the left and made her way to the petite section. She stopped by a display table that held many soft sweaters and corresponding scarves. He looked up and was taken aback to see the tall brunette Katrina had evaluated in the parking lot giving him a million-dollar smile, though what she was doing in the petite section, he didn't know. She certainly wasn't petite, standing somewhere around five foot eight. When the woman sauntered off, he looked down at Katrina. She raised her brows with a self-satisfied smile. So, she wasn't as oblivious as she seemed. Had she led them to this store on purpose just to prove her point? He found a smile and simply raised his own brows back at her in concession. The sneaky imp.

Maybe proving her point had played a part, but it seemed she really wanted to shop there, too, if what she voiced next was any indication. "You don't have to stay with me if you don't want. We could meet up somewhere later if you want to go elsewhere." She picked up a white sweater and a matching pink and white plaid scarf.

He fought his amusement. As if he needed her permission, anyway. "It was a nice suggestion, but I'm in need of nothing and don't feel like browsing. If you don't mind, I'll just follow and wait on you." That was true, but the main reason he felt pressured to stay was for her safety. What good would it have done for him to rescue her from one dangerous man just lose her to another?

"Fine," she shrugged. "Suit yourself," and went back to her shopping. She paused a moment in consideration and then offered, "I'll try not to take too long," to which he just nodded.

For the next few hours, he watched as she modeled

clothes in several stores—well, he knew she wasn't really modeling them for him, per say. She simply had to step out of the dressing room to view herself at all angles in the three-way mirrors to assess the fit of the items she tried on. He could tell by her frown and critical assessment of herself that she was probably used to more custom-made stuff.

Nevertheless, she put some clothing back, decided some were keepers, and lingered indecisively over others. So much for not taking too long.

The employees rushed to do her every bidding, hoping to make a big sale. One woman talked her into trying on a dark blue evening gown. As Katrina was ushered into a fitting room, he checked his watch. Almost six o'clock. They'd have to be leaving soon, whether Katrina was ready or not.

He hadn't wanted to rush her. He knew that she was probably welcoming the distraction to take her mind off of everything. He knew from experience that a lot of women lost themselves in shopping as a therapeutic practice.

From inside the fitting room, he heard the employee's Spanish accent. "Let's see what your handsome man thinks of it."

Followed by this remark were Katrina's muffled protests, but the dark-complexioned woman shepherded her out nevertheless.

Jack felt his throat tighten as she stepped out of the dressing room. She was lovely, enchanting. The thin, spaghetti straps revealed her creamy shoulders, not tan like he would expect coming from the south, but ivory white. The rest of the dark fabric flowed down and settled around her ankles. Her hair fell over her shoulders as she looked down. He realized he was staring.

"She is gorgeous, no?" the woman asked proudly, taking in his expression.

"Yes, she is," he admitted and met Katrina's eyes. She instantly looked down and blushed.

"Purchase it, and then we need to go," he said, he said gently.

The woman steered her back into the fitting room, praising her with compliments. "He loved it. His face lit up when he saw you. Just beautiful." He frowned. So he did notice Katrina's beauty, but he certainly didn't need that employee pointing it out to her. He didn't want her thinking he was like all the other guys she'd ever been around, and he certainly didn't want her to feel even more uncomfortable around him than she already did.

The sooner they left the better.

CHAPTER 6

atrina rolled back the bed covers, slid underneath them, and switched the bedside lamp off. Her feet ached from walking around the mall all day, and her body was still sore in several places where Bryan's fists had connected. Consequently, once Jack had bid her good night, she'd closed the door to her room and dropped her shopping bags on the floor, her only thoughts being of rest.

Now she lay curled up on her side staring out the glass doors of the balcony connected to her room. She had left the gauzy white curtains open, but the doors themselves were closed, seeing as how winter's chill prevented them staying open. Not that she would have left them open anyway.

Nighttime could be scary. Many nights at home she would pull the curtains together just to keep out the penetrating darkness filled with leering shapes and shadows. But nights like this that were softly lit with moonlight weren't frightening. They were almost magical. That's why she'd left the curtains pulled back tonight. So she could see the magic.

She watched the snow fall and land on the rail of the balcony. Watched it lay there and glisten under the moon's rays. Yes, magical. She remembered when she was a child, and even a teen, how she used to lay in bed at night and fantasize. She would dream even before sleep overcame her. How happy those times had been. She had seen so many different futures for herself.

Yet, never had she imagined finding herself in this predicament. At the mercy of a stranger. Too scared to go home or talk to her father. What had become of her? What *would* become of her?

Was she going about this all wrong? Maybe she should call her father. He would be crushed, though. He would blame himself. That is, if he even believed her. She never would have entertained the notion that one day her own father would believe someone else over her, but Bryan could be very persuasive, and her father was already very emotionally attached to him. There were times she thought her father loved Bryan more than he did her.

Too bad the magic of the night couldn't fix her problems any more as it so often had when she was young. As a child, when problems assailed her, she could just dream, enter her own little world, and everything would be okay. Now she was in the real world, and, unfortunately, that wouldn't work anymore.

She didn't know if staying with Jack was the right thing to do or not. She only knew that thoughts of telling her father or going home filled her with terror and shame, whereas thoughts of staying safely hidden in Jack's sleepy, dreamlike, almost castle-like house calmed her somewhat.

And, strangely enough, she suddenly felt that staying there *was* the right thing to do.

An incredible peace that she couldn't explain settled over her. It was as if some unseen force or presence was suddenly with her, assuring her that everything would be okay. She must be losing her mind. Nevertheless, she burrowed deeper into her covers, deciding that she would no longer worry about it. Whether she was going crazy or imaging things she didn't know or care, but she was finally letting go. Whether it actually was right or not, she was going to do what felt right. She was going to stay here with Jack—as long as he would have her—until she felt impressed upon to do otherwise.

After tossing and turning restlessly for almost an hour, Jack threw back his covers, pulled on a pair of sweatpants and an undershirt and made his way down the stairs to the far back of his house on the west side where his gym was located. He passed the indoor pool, tennis court, and the game room before finally reaching his small yet top-of-the-line home gym.

Like most men, he prided himself on his workout toys. He owned several different machines, from a treadmill to a pressing bench. He'd amassed them over the years, and he found it nice to have a variety to choose from.

He wasn't really in the mood for an intense workout tonight. He'd just come here to think since he couldn't sleep. Therefore, he settled on the treadmill. Turning the knob to a moderate speed to start off with, he began to walk—and examine his current predicament.

He didn't know if having Katrina stay with him was wise or not. He knew nothing at all about the woman, other than what little he'd witnessed. He had no reason to believe anything she said, but then again, he also had no reason not to. He didn't know why these thoughts were coming to him. Honestly, up until now, it had never crossed his mind that she had lied to him about anything. Still, he'd need to make sure he ordered a background check on her just to make sure she was who she said she was. You never knew. There were a lot of crazies out there, and while he seriously doubted Katrina was one, he'd feel better if he followed all the proper channels. Plus, he was just curious to learn more about her.

He flipped the knob up higher, bumping his speed up several notches. He was deeply troubled. What was he supposed to do? Was he to take charge and decide when to find her home and send her back? Should he let Katrina decide when she was ready to go home? How long should he allow her to stay? How long would she even want to stay? This had to be the most complicated situation he'd ever gotten himself into.

Well, actually, he hadn't gotten himself into anything. He'd been pushed into it. He checked himself as he remembered exactly Who had chosen him for this dilemma. It must be okay for Katrina to be here for a time if He had ordained it. Jack also reminded himself that he was not in charge. When the time for Katrina to leave was right, it would be so. He took that to mean that he was to do nothing at the moment. Feeling a bit better, he turned off the treadmill and silently prayed for forgiveness for worrying. He knew that worrying was a sin and not acceptable. It was like telling God that he didn't trust him to take care of everything in his life, and Jack certainly didn't want to do that.

Once finished, he made his way to the shower, which was to the left of the weight bench at the back of the gym.

After showering, he went to his office, fired up his laptop, and got to work ordering a fast-track background check. He was willing to pay the extra fee to get immediate results and satiate his curiosity.

He clicked open the results in eager anticipation as soon as he got the notification they were ready.

Katrina Weems. Twenty-four. Five-foot-three-inches. Blonde hair. Blue eyes. Harvard. Tennessee. Father: David Weems of Weems & Associates Law Firm.

Jack's shoulders visibly relaxed. So, she checked out. Everything was exactly as she'd said.

Jack pulled up another tab and typed the name of her father's law firm into the search bar. He frowned as he scrolled down the page and saw the name "Bryan Garrison." Bryan…that had been the name of the man she'd said had hurt her.

Jack clicked on the photo gallery and saw a picture of an older man who must have been Katrina's father— though she looked nothing like him (Katrina must have taken after her mother)—standing next to a handsome man maybe a little older than Jack.

Jack felt his blood begin to boil just looking at the man. Suave and debonair-looking, he looked exactly like the cocky kind of prick who would think he was entitled to any woman. Of course, Jack was probably biased too, based on how he'd found Katrina.

After reading more about her father's practice, Jack finally closed the lid to his laptop. He bowed his head and said a silent prayer, asking God for wisdom and strength in navigating the situation he found himself in.

Ten minutes later, refreshed in both body and soul, he started back to his room, hoping for a good night's sleep. On the way, he made a small detour to his guest's room to make sure she was alright. Briefly peeking his head in the door, he was pleased to find her sleeping soundly. That accomplished, he quietly shut the door and made his way back to his own bed.

"Oh Roy," Elaine breathed, "how awful!" That poor, poor girl. Her husband had just told her everything that Jack had confided to him about why Katrina was there. She'd thought it strange for Jack to bring a young lady home. He never had before, but she hadn't thought it impossible. She should have known the young woman was in trouble and not some girlfriend of her employer's. "How long will she be staying here?"

Roy just shrugged, looking out the window. He and his wife lived in one of the bedrooms on the east side of Jack's home. Jack had graciously allowed them a room in his house rather than causing them to buy a home they would scarcely ever be in and requiring them to drive back and forth to his house every day. Elaine especially appreciated this gesture. When the majority of their day was spent tending to this house, they certainly didn't need another one to tend to at night too.

"It is a pitiable situation," Roy commented, crawling into bed beside her. "But we know Jack is a good man and will do everything within his power to help her."

Elaine thought back to that morning when she'd met Katrina in the kitchen. She'd been shocked to find herself so talkative around the young woman. She was, as a rule, a very shy and reserved person until she got to know the other person well, but the truth was that she'd felt immediately at ease and comfortable around Jack's guest. She recalled the sense of fragility surrounding the girl. Funny she hadn't noticed that until now that she knew the girl's experience. Perhaps the young woman's hurt is what had opened her up to her so early.

Whatever the case, she'd felt warmly toward Katrina earlier, but she did so even more now. "I wish there was something we could do," Elaine said, snuggling up against her husband.

He slipped an arm around her shoulder and lightly kissed the top of her head. "There is, honey. We can pray."

Katrina sat behind Jack's massive oak desk and popped a Weather's Original into her mouth. During this past week, she'd become accustomed to doing so while organizing and filing his documents. She'd learned that he always kept a bowl full of the creamy, buttery, hard toffees sitting on his desk, and now she allowed herself the pleasure of savoring one. She looked around the office. She had definitely earned it.

It was Friday and throughout the preceding days, she'd sorted faxes by sender and then dates, earliest to latest. She spotted a wayward fax sitting amidst a pile of envelopes. She must have missed that one. Picking it up, she walked over to the humongous filing cabinet, found the slot for Malcolm Moore, and slid the paper in between the correct dates.

She looked back at the menacing piles of envelopes. She had spent one week sorting through the cyber mail. Now she'd spend the next doing likewise with the good old-fashioned kind.

She walked back over to the desk and rummaged through the pile. After about ten minutes, her head started to ache, so she pushed back from the desk and stood. Jack had told her she could take as many breaks as she liked, but she made sure not to abuse the privilege. Though it didn't really matter. Ever since he'd taken her shopping on Monday, he'd been scarce, hardly dropping in every now and then to see how everything was coming along.

She glanced at the clock on his desk. Twelve thirty, it read. She normally ate lunch around this time, but she wasn't hungry today. Probably due to the fact that she had skipped breakfast also. She had found that whereas if most people skipped breakfast, they would be ravenous at lunch, she was just the opposite. If she skipped the first meal of the day, she wouldn't be hungry for the next. Likewise, if she ate breakfast, then she would want lunch also. Her body was just weird like that, she guessed.

Turning, she walked out of the room. As she came upon the room with the wall of windows, her footsteps slowed. Throughout this past week, she'd explored all of the house and grounds, from the laundry room to the small gym and tennis court. Yet, she'd never entered this room. She peeked into it. She'd been curious ever since she first saw this room. She glanced behind her. Nobody was around, and Jack hadn't forbidden her from entering any rooms. With one last look behind her, she walked decisively into the room.

The pale yellow walls enhanced the sunlight. Everything in the room seemed to play toward making the most of the light and nature. Walking past the cream-colored settee, she made her way over to the rounded wall of glass. She gazed upon the unbroken setting. The bare trees with icy ornaments, the unmarred snow, the sun smiling down upon it all.

A bird flitted to the window, and she held her breath as it came closer, then realizing it could not pass through the solid barrier, flew away. How different it was from home. When they did get snow, there would be signs of animal life everywhere: deer, bird, rabbit, and raccoon tracks would be scattered all over the landscape. Yet, she couldn't say which she liked best. She'd always loved nature, in both its neat, manicured state and its wild, natural one.

She recalled a plenary session she'd attended one night in college. The speaker had been contrasting classicism and romanticism. Being a nature-lover herself, she'd always favored romanticism over the logic and reasoning of classicism. She'd always been one who yearned to experience the wildness and freedom of nature, perhaps because she was seldom permitted to do so.

She frowned. Her life had been so sheltered, she rarely ever had moments alone to just roam the earth and do as she pleased. And the few moments she had stolen, she'd savored. She could still remember how wonderful it had felt to lay in the grass with her hair unkempt and feel the breeze wash across her face. To hear the chirps of the birds, watch the squirrels scurry up trees, feel the rippling of the pond, see the beauty of the dogwoods. When she was alone, surrounded by nature, that was when she could truly be herself. She didn't have to put on a mask or play a part. She was simply Katrina.

She sighed as she turned away from the glass. She could remember her first day of school. Her father trying to reason with her. *Come on, honey. You'll love it. Just think, you'll get to be around all kinds of other little boys and girls. You'll have so much fun.* She'd pouted and answered, *But Daddy, I want to stay here outside with the kittens.* He'd only laughed and called her his cute little princess.

Yet, he was right in some ways. She did love school. She had a passion for learning, and it came easy for her. But she liked the academic aspect—not the social. She had an eager mind and could remember the other kids laughing at her and calling her the "bookworm" for reading all the time. Little had she known when she'd gone to school that liking reading was actually a very uncool thing. She would have been all alone at recess if not for Saffron.

She felt a pang for her childhood friend. They'd almost been sisters when growing up. She was the one and only true friend Katrina had ever had. They'd stood through all the taunts together all throughout school: in elementary, the "bookworms;" in junior high, the "teachers' pets;" in high school, the "snobs." For as long as she could remember it had been Saffron and Katrina, the untouchables. When their other classmates had baited them, daring them to go back on their morals, they had stood firm. As long as they had each other, they could conquer anything.

Katrina sat down on the edge of the plump settee and shook her head. No, as much as she loved the grassy plains where she grew up, she'd never fit in there. Nor had Saffron. Perhaps that's what had joined them so. Just like Katrina, Saffron had felt smothered and trapped in that small town. She smiled. She could remember when they were just freshmen in high school, discussing their hopes for a better future. Katrina dreaming of attending Harvard and adventurous Saffron ready to tackle life in England. She could still hear Saffron's hopeful voice, *Do you ever feel like you're in a waiting room? Waiting for college, when your life will truly begin?*

She'd summed it up perfectly right there. And when a new gibe was invented to throw at them, Saffron was always there to remind her, *We're going to do it, Katrina. We'll show this whole town that we're not just a couple of dreamers. We're going to get out.* That was the hope that had gotten them through the days. And they'd succeeded, just like Saffron had always said they would. They'd made their dreams a reality.

She looked around her. Yes, she had gone to Harvard, but what now? She was lodging with a stranger, hiding from a "friend." Maybe dreams really were for suckers.

She sighed. She'd had a long enough break. Better get back to work now. She stood and walked across the room and out the door—and smacked into something solid. She felt hands upon her shoulders, steadying her, and looked up into a pair of startlingly green eyes. She jumped back with a gasp.

The muscled, black-haired man appraised her and gave a low whistle. "Well, hello. And who are you?" Before Katrina could answer, Jack strode up.

"Eric!" Jack exclaimed with surprise. "What are you doing here?"

Katrina looked between the two men in confusion. The tanned man waved his arm. "I heard from your man, Roy, that you were back and thought I'd pay a visit." She relaxed. They must be friends, she assumed, by the informal way they spoke to one another.

The men hooked hands and pulled in toward one another in what was supposed to be the manly version of a hug. The one Jack had called Eric turned his attention back to Katrina. "I was just about to make acquaintance with this beauty when you showed up. Shame on you, Jack, for never telling me you had a woman."

Katrina could feel the flush crawling up her neck. Jack glanced at her, "I don't. Katrina is my secretary," he explained.

The man turned to her with renewed interest and stepped in front of Jack to block him from her line of sight. "Well, hello there, then. I'm Eric Sharpe. And in that case, I hope you'll join me for dinner one night."

Flustered, Katrina searched for an answer. She'd just met the guy, if you could even call her bumping into him "meeting." "Well, I don't know—"

Jack cut her off with, "Why don't you take the rest of the day off, Katrina, while Eric and I catch up on some things?"

She nodded and hurried off, thankful for the escape. She hadn't known Jack would be having guests. While she was glad for the break from her tedious work, she didn't know what she would do with the rest of her day.

She glanced out of a nearby window at the sparkling landscape outside before deciding she'd go out and bask in the glorious day. Her footsteps quickened with the thought. Maybe she'd even talk Elaine into picnicking with her. It was amazing how quickly she and the woman had become friends, especially since she'd never been one to make friends very quickly. She smiled and silently thanked Jack for his offer that she take the rest of the day off. Hopefully today would shape up to a be a wonderful day.

CHAPTER 7

*J*ack led Eric into his parlor. Although they'd been best friends since their freshman year of college when they'd been paired together as roommates, they were as different as two men could be. He glanced over at his friend. Heavily muscled, dark-headed, green-eyed, tan. Top it all off with charismatic and fun, and he was many a woman's dream.

He frowned at that thought. Eric had always been a ladies' man, and he'd recognized the look his friend had been giving Katrina in the hall earlier. Good thing he'd stumbled upon them when he did, or Eric would have been mercilessly pursuing her. For some reason, that thought nagged.

Jack had been busy all week doing miscellaneous things, trying to get caught up with his work. Having been preoccupied with accepting some offers and declining others, he'd only seen Katrina when he dropped by his office to check on her, which hadn't been often.

He felt a guilty pang. He knew from experience how

boring it could get sitting in that office day after day. Though there were times when he'd heard her music from the piano drifting down the hall. He looked up at his friend standing before the wall made of glass. Finding him in the hall had certainly been a surprise.

"It's amazing," Eric commented from the other side of the room. "You almost feel as if you're outside yourself."

"That was the idea," Jack responded, walking over to sit on the settee.

Eric turned and joined him. "You always were the one with all the bright ideas. I never could find the time to create them, though."

"Perhaps that's because you were always the one leading the parties. If ever a fun event occurred on that campus, you can bet you had a part in it."

Eric laughed. "So you're right."

"What are you doing now?"

He shrugged. "I was selling beachfront properties."

Jack knew Eric had earned a vast amount of money in the real estate industry. He'd always been persuasive, a perfect salesman. "But now?"

"I'm taking some time off to roam and do as I please. I didn't know where I wanted to go first, but then you suddenly popped in my head. It's Christmas season, and you live up here in the snowy North. It gets rather tiresome spending the holidays alone year after year, so I thought I'd enjoy a white Christmas with you this year."

Eric was orphaned when he was three and didn't have much family to speak of, seeing as how he'd been raised by his stern aunt and uncle who never did sit well with his wild nature and had only taken him in out of a sense of duty. As far as he knew, Eric hadn't seen them since he'd shot off for college. Jack guessed there was no love lost between Eric and his relatives.

Jack smiled and shook his head. "You haven't changed a bit, Eric." It was true. He was still the same wild, California beach boy he'd known when they went to college together in New York.

"Well, you know my motto: live it up while you can." He stared pointedly at Jack. "Which reminds me. Where did you get that gem?" Jack knew he was speaking of Katrina.

"Eric…"

"You certainly have changed. I don't ever remember you even inviting a girl up to the dorm, much less living with one. You must be bit bad, huh?"

"Eric," he said, frustrated, "we're not involved in any way like that. She was in trouble, so I brought her back here. She really is only my secretary."

Eric leaned back on the couch and draped an arm over the top of it. "What kind of trouble?"

Jack shook his head. "I don't even know the whole story. I came upon her as she was being attacked. The man jumped in the car and shot off. She was left with nothing."

Eric shook his head. "Oh, man, that's awful. It's a good thing you showed up when you did."

"Yeah," Jack agreed, "But then it was like what was I supposed to do with her?"

"Take her to the police?" Eric supplied.

"She wouldn't go. Besides, she has no I.D. now," Jack answered.

"Why didn't you take her home or wherever she was staying?"

"There was nowhere. Apparently she's from Tennessee and stranded here. She has a father, but for some reason she's scared to go back to him. I'm working on figuring out what to do with her."

"Have you talked to her about it?"

Jack shook his head. "We talked briefly and decided she could stay here and work for me. But since then, she hasn't brought it up again, and I don't want to push her."

Eric made a low 'humph.' "So she'll be here for a while then?"

Jack rubbed the back of his neck. "That's the way it looks."

"Well, that explains it."

Jack glanced over at Eric. "Explains what?"

"That wary, doe-eyed look she gave me when I asked her to dinner sometime."

Jack raised a brow and stated sarcastically, "Of course, that must be it. I mean, it's unbelievable to think that even one woman alive may be immune to your charms."

Eric jested back. "It would hurt my ego too much to believe otherwise."

They both laughed. "Hey," Eric suddenly brightened, "I have an idea."

"God help us," Jack answered dryly.

Eric ignored him. "What do you say we find your doe-eyed guest and go out and have some fun?"

"Eric…" Jack began. He didn't want to overwhelm Katrina with Eric's huge personality.

"I saw a fair on my way in," Eric interrupted him. "Today's Friday so they'll be open extra late. And don't even start to argue. If I know you, you've kept her cooped up this whole time, probably bored to death. Besides, it's time you had some fun too."

Eric raised a brow at his friend as he added," Unless you've loosened up, that is. Which I doubt."

Jack had heard about the winter fair. Usually fairs weren't held in the winter due to the cold, but this one was supposed to be some sort of holiday event, guaranteed to bring out the crowds and the money. He started to protest it was too cold, Katrina may not want to go, etcetera. He sighed instead and watched Eric jump up to go carry out his plan. Once Eric got something in his head, he was undaunted. They'd all be going to this fair tonight, whether they wanted to or not.

Jack stood. Maybe it would do them all good.

Katrina looked up as Jack's visitor strode toward their spot on the patio. When she'd presented her idea of picnicking to Elaine, the maid had laughed and pointed out that the blankets would be wet from the snow. Katrina hadn't thought of that. She'd only thought of how much she'd wanted to be outside. Nevertheless, Elaine had compromised and fixed their lunch on the patio table.

Now Katrina watched as Eric got closer, followed by Jack.

"Elaine," Eric smiled, taking a chair, "you're still as beautiful as ever."

Elaine's rolling laugh boomed out. "Still the charmer, aren't you, Eric? Well, in case you've forgotten, I'm married. You'd have better luck with this one." She jerked her head toward Katrina, and Eric's eyes shifted to hers.

Katrina shot a scathing look at Elaine. She liked Elaine and counted her a friend, but the woman blurted out whatever popped into her head.

Jack came up behind Eric. "Elaine, what are you two doing out here in this freezing cold?" Though Katrina and Elaine were bundled up like eskimos, their cheeks and noses were pink from the cold.

Rolling her eyes, Elaine said, "This one came waltzing into my kitchen and announced that she wanted us to take a picnic. After reminding her that we would be soaking wet from sitting on the snow, she agreed to just eat on the patio."

Katrina shot her a look of annoyance for making her idea sound childish and silly. "I was merely thinking of what a beautiful day it was and how we should be outside to enjoy it," she retorted.

Elaine stood to clear their plates and commented to the two men, "She's got a lot of fire, boys. I'd watch out if I were you." Katrina's face flushed, and she wanted to stomp her foot and say *Hello, I'm still here!* She hated it when people talked about her like she wasn't even there, even if they were just kidding around. What was Elaine thinking even saying something like that? Katrina's face flushed crimson as she crossed her arms and stared daggers at Elaine, who sauntered off into the kitchen. It was one thing to make her sound silly, but then to talk about her as if she were a child. She looked up and saw the grins on both men's faces.

"What?" she snapped a bit more harshly than she'd intended.

Jack sat down in the chair beside her. "Elaine's just teasing."

"Yeah, Elaine really likes you if she feels familiar enough to tease. It took me months to acquire that status," Eric commented seriously. Taking her hand, he went on, "But we didn't come here to discuss the virtuous traits of Elaine." Katrina fought the urge to yank her hand away from this stranger's. He was Jack's friend, and she wouldn't be rude.

Eric smiled crookedly before going on, "Of which I am sure there are many. We came fair lady"— and at this he raised her hand and gallantly kissed it—"to whisk you away from this melancholy and to a carnival."

Katrina looked up to see Jack frowning. When he caught her eyes, he quickly masked it. "What this bone-head is trying to say is that he wants all of us to go to a fair he saw on the way up here."

Katrina looked down at her hand still trapped in Eric's and tried to wiggle it free, but he covered it with his other hand as well. "If I know Jack, and I do, you haven't had an ounce of fun here. He's probably been tied up in his errands and paid you no mind. Am I right?"

Yes, he was right, but that hadn't bothered her. She'd needed the time alone, time to just think—or not. Time to just exist and be away from all the pressure of her previous life. She looked up at Jack studying her.

He answered for her. "True, I've been busy, but I had planned on taking her somewhere today if she wanted to go out." Katrina looked up at him, surprised at that.

Jack smiled down at her apologetically. "I was just coming to find you when Eric showed up. I'm sorry that I may have slacked in my hosting duties, but, as Eric said, I was caught up in my work."

She caught Eric watching her. "Well… I've never been to a fair before."

Eric interrupted, "Never been to a fair before?" His voice was incredulous. "Then you must come," he insisted.

She looked between the two sincere faces and was torn with trepidation, all anger at sparring with Elaine forgotten. Part of her wanted to stay here in Jack's mansion where she felt safe. But then, there was that trusting part of her that wanted to go out and have some fun. She distrusted most people, but she felt safe with Jack. Why was that? Was it because his was the first kind face she had seen after her plight, like a baby duckling assuming the first face it sees to be its mother? And his friend didn't seem menacing either—quite the contrary. He was very friendly. She looked down at her hand still wedged in between his two large ones—maybe overly so. A thought struck her. Hadn't she thought the same about Bryan? She shook at the thought. She couldn't take any chances. "No, I think I'll just stay here," she decided, pulling her hand out of Eric's.

CHAPTER 8

*T*wo hours later Jack sat in the driver's seat of his four-wheel drive truck with Katrina in the middle of Eric and him. After she'd declined their invitation, Eric had used every trick in the book to change her mind. He'd mercilessly presented her with reasons why she had to go until she'd finally agreed to accompany them—probably too exasperated to argue with him anymore. Jack shook his head and fought to suppress a smile. The man should be a lawyer. With his persuasive nature and good looks, he could make the guiltiest client seem like an innocent, newborn baby.

Jack looked down at Katrina pressed snugly between them. She was buttoned up in the imitation fur coat she'd bought on sale at the mall complete with matching gloves —both of which she would need going to a fair in December. Luckily, there was no wind-chill tonight, but some rides would still be torture to ride. Her blonde hair slid loosely over the deep brown, knee-length coat. She'd been sitting sullenly, pouting throughout the whole drive, probably steaming over being bested—or better yet bullied—by Eric's persistence. Yet as Eric kept trying to draw her into conversation by pointing out various scenery highlights and landmarks, he saw her resistance crumbling. Ah, well, Eric had that effect on people.

Jack turned his attention back to the road. He'd been negligent of Katrina this first week. When he and Eric had walked out to find her and Elaine picnicking on the patio, he'd been shocked. Elaine usually didn't form familiarity so fast, but there she'd been acting like Katrina was a long lost friend. And Katrina had been relaxed and at ease. How much had he missed getting to know her, to help her, this week? You could learn a lot about a person in one week. He could have taken more time to check on her and talk to her, but he hadn't thought of her much. After the shopping spree on Monday, he'd been so busy that he had sometimes forgotten she was even there. Well, not entirely. Ever since he'd first found her on the side of the road, she'd been in the back of his mind. If he was being honest with himself, it was more like he'd purposefully kept himself busy to keep his mind off of her. He looked at her now chatting with Eric. He was painfully aware of her presence, especially now that Eric had shown up.

He pulled the black truck into the snow-dusted parking lot of the fairgrounds. Throughout the hour-long drive, the snow had become less dense the further south they went. Still, for just in case more came and made the roads difficult, he had his four-wheel drive. That was the only reason he even owned the vehicle. If not for the weather conditions that had required him to purchase the truck, he would always use his Vette.

He parked, his tires scooping aside the snow to reveal

the black asphalt beneath. He stepped out of the truck, his shoes crunching on the snow, and reached up to give Katrina a hand only to notice with annoyance that Eric was doing likewise on the other side. She looked between them, and Eric surprised him with, "Go ahead. I'll go get the tickets."

Katrina placed her small hand in his and he helped her out, careful that she didn't slip. Eric usually never surrendered a woman to him willingly, preferring to command all the attention himself. While Jack had always been the mysterious, intelligent, brooding type, Eric was one who demanded attention in every situation. Jack felt a rush of triumph, then realized that Eric had said he was 'going to get the tickets.' By that, he knew that Eric was buying his own ticket and Katrina's, establishing his ownership for the night.

When he and Katrina approached the window where Eric stood, Eric engaged her in conversation while detracting her hand from Jack's and placing it securely in his own. Smooth. Very smooth. Eric began leading her into the bright lights and tents, giving her smitten schoolboy eyes, while Jack stood at the window and paid for his admission. If Eric thought he was going to make him the third wheel of this little escapade… His anger boiled as he slapped his money down on the booth.

As Katrina and Eric walked side by side into the bright, festive lights, she looked down, surprised to see her hand once again on Eric's arm and covered with his own hand. When he'd first taken her hand from Jack's arm and placed it on his, she'd pulled it back, but he must have so distracted her with their conversation that he was able to once again capture it. She started to pull it free once more but thought better of it. People did this all the time. It was a friendly, casual gesture that she'd become accustomed to in college since her high school social experience had been limited. Why then was she so skeptical now?

Because of Bryan. Well, Eric and Jack weren't Bryan, she reminded herself. She had nothing to fear with them. Jack had been nice to her so far, and Eric had been proving himself all day. She looked around at the bustle of people, the game stands, the rides that Saffron and she had always wanted to ride together but had never been able to because Katrina's father thought carnivals were dangerous. Better stick to the balls thrown at home where scoundrels disguised as gentlemen came into their home and drank their sherry and eyed his daughter where he could see them. She forced her thoughts to turn at that thought. That wasn't fair. It wasn't her father's fault about what had happened. Anybody could have a lapse of judgment. Hadn't she herself trusted Bryan?

She turned her attention back to her surroundings. This was her first fair, and she wanted to enjoy it. She was now glad that Eric had weaseled her into coming. She didn't need to hide. Bryan wouldn't control her life. She was safe staying at Jack's mansion. Speaking of Jack…She stopped walking suddenly and looked around.

"What is it?" Eric asked, stopping with her.

"Where's Jack?" she asked.

"Oh," he shrugged, "he'll catch up." He started walking again with her in tow.

She looked back over her shoulder and saw Jack

emerge from behind a stand with bags of multicolored cotton candy hanging from the roof. She gripped Eric's arm and pointed. "There he is."

Eric reluctantly halted, and they waited while Jack strode up to them. "What took you so long?" Katrina asked when Jack came and stood before them. A man with a handful of balloons for sale passed beside Jack, and he bent his head to avoid being smacked with one. To answer her question, he briefly glanced at Eric and just shrugged. "Come on," Jack said, leading her over to the man with the balloons.

He bought a yellow one and handed it to her. A scene flashed to her mind. The sun was shining brightly. The wind tugged at the large balloon that had *Happy Birthday* printed across it in flowing red letters, and she gripped the ribbon tightly with both hands. An orange speckled butterfly flitted before her eyes, and she momentarily let go of the balloon to chase after it. She looked up and saw the bright spot of color floating up into the sky, far out of her reach. *Daddy, I lost my balloon.* Her father's voice strong and reassuring. *It's okay, pumpkin. Look.* He pointed up to it in the sky. *It's dancing in the sky because it's happy to be free. If you kept it in the house forever, it would eventually lose all its air and die.*

She now knew that even if she did let them go, they would still lose their helium and deflate, but still, she always let them soar up into the sky rather than keep them tethered to the ground. Perhaps it was because she yearned to be as free as a balloon. Free to dance in the sky, if only for a little while.

She clutched the balloon and followed Eric over to a stand where he threw a ball, knocking over glass bottles one after another. He won an airbrushed hat, which he placed on her head with a flourish. She caught her reflection in a mirror and laughed at how ridiculously silly the hat looked with her coat and gloves.

"What do you think?" she asked as she tilted her head to the side. "Good enough for Vogue?"

Eric and Jack both chuckled. Then Eric grabbed her arm and pointed to a ride swirling lop-sided in the air. "What do you say?" he asked with a glint of mischief in his eyes.

She eyed the tilted ride warily. "Do you think it's safe?"

"Of course it is," he scoffed. "I've ridden it dozens of times."

"I don't know…" she eyed the ride dubiously.

"Well if you're too afraid of a little thrill…" he commented teasingly.

She stopped and looked fiercely up at Eric. "I am not afraid." She didn't want either of them thinking she was a victim or a scared little girl.

He gave her a look that said 'prove it.' With a frustrated sigh, she freed her balloon to the air and handed her hat over to Jack, who'd been silent throughout the whole ordeal.

She followed Eric over to the short line. She looked up at the contraption. *The Orbiter.* She watched as the next load of people was admitted. The gate closed with Eric and her first for the next round. The pairs scrambled to get seats, and once they were safely buckled in, with a low buzzing noise, the seats rose off the ground and began to spin.

Ever so slowly, it began to tilt and spin faster. She gulped as it tilted almost straight up into the air. Why had she said she would do this? She caught Eric grinning down at her. Looking back over the crowd of people, she spotted Jack leaning against a post. She didn't have to do this. She could join Jack right now. Eric could still ride. She'd seen several people riding alone.

"Eric..."

"Yes?" His taunting tone did not go unnoticed by her. She saw the challenge in his eyes. He didn't think she would go through with it—had probably been waiting for her to chicken out all along.

He put his hands in his pockets. "Was there something you wanted to tell me?"

At that moment, the gate swung open to admit them to the now empty seats. She raised her head.

"No. It's our turn."

She saw the amusement in his eyes, and his quickly suppressed smile as he grabbed her hand and found them a seat. Fine, let him laugh. She was doing it, wasn't she?

She slid into the sparkly blue seat first. Then Eric sat down next to her, reaching over to grab the buckle to the right of them. Since the seat was one flat platform, the one buckle was supposed to fit across both bodies. Eric snapped it securely into place to the left of him.

There was barely two inches of space between them, and as an attendant came by to check their buckle, he tightened it even more, leaving no room at all. The metal bar lowered over them, and slowly they began to spin.

Eric leaned over to her. "It would be awful if this thing broke, huh?"

She glared at him.

He laughed. "Just kidding."

They picked up velocity. This wasn't so bad, she

thought—until they started tilting. At the first tilt, she was thrown against Eric, and he instinctively wrapped his arm around her. She was grateful that he was on the outside edge of the seat rather than she.

She could feel the cold wind whipping at her hair and skin and clung to Eric, despite her better judgment. Eric threw up his hands and screamed along with others, entreating her to do so too.

"Are you crazy!" she yelled.

He just laughed again and put his arm back around her. After minutes—or hours—of torture, they suddenly righted and slowed.

She stood with shaky legs and ran her hands through the hair that had fallen over her face. Eric loped his arm around her as they descended the stairs; she discreetly shrugged it free.

"How was it?" Jack asked when she stood before him.

"Let's just say my legs feel like jelly."

Eric grinned wryly. "From the ride or me? Hopefully the latter."

She didn't dignify that with a response.

He put his arm around her shoulders once more.

"Come on, Kat, lighten up."

Jack rescued her by pointing. "This way."

He led them to the bumper cars. Turning to Katrina, he said, "This is the real way to begin your first fair. Everybody loves the bumper cars."

As the long line formed behind them, she guessed that was probably true. They'd gotten there just in time to beat the rush of people.

Jack grinned. "It gives you the chance to take out your road rage without worrying about bent fenders or nicks."

She laughed. Eric looked sullen but turned to a middle-aged couple behind him when addressed. He and Jack obviously knew them, for soon Jack was drawn into the conversation too. She watched the little cars attached to poles jerk across the floor as they were bumped. Then the head of the person in the unfortunate car would turn, spot the assailant, and take off seeking revenge. *Road rage indeed.*

She watched as one of the operators maneuvered a car along, practically standing in the car. That couldn't be safe, but maybe the employees were trusted enough to be allowed to ride the cars however they chose.

Suddenly, Katrina was startled by a commotion just in front of her and looked down. The little girl ahead of her who had brown pigtails started wailing loudly, demanding to be taken to the "potty." Her parents tried to reason with her. They had waited in line so long. Their turn was next and she'd get to drive her own car. Couldn't she wait? No, she couldn't, so the family excused and apologized their way down the line with the little girl's siblings venting their angry words at her.

That left her at the front of the line. The other operator sat behind the gate, blatantly watching her. Feeling self-conscious, she resumed her watch of the bumper cars but still felt his gaze. Out of the corner of her eye, she saw his bald head and the tattoos on his arms exposed by a sleeveless shirt. How could anybody not wear a coat in this chill?

"Having a good time?" the operator eyed her in a candid way that unsettled her.

She turned, but Jack and Eric were still chatting with the couple. She looked at the operator and now realized that he did have a coat, but it was shrugged halfway off as he slouched in the high chair.

"Yes," she answered stiffly and started to turn again.

"Smile a little," he said, offering her his own. He gave her the creeps.

She tensely flashed him a smile, then turned to Jack who was solemnly watching her. He flashed a glance at the operator and gave her a quizzical look. She was relieved to see the gate swing open. They all found themselves a car, and Eric pointed to her, marking her his target. She attempted a laugh, but it was forced. She couldn't shake the feeling that the operator's eyes had never left her. She looked at Jack, but his attention was focused on the tattooed operator, who was now, his coat buttoned up, standing in a car. The two operators must have switched positions.

Katrina turned back to the wheel as the cars started to come alive. She'd barely taken off when she felt a bump from behind. She turned, expecting to see Eric or Jack but instead saw the operator. He gave her a toothy grin and took off to bump a red car with a couple in it. She warily watched him out of the corner of her eye. He didn't bump her again and seemed to be preoccupied with attacking others, so she allowed herself to relax somewhat. She was just being paranoid after the fiasco with Bryan.

She noticed Jack watching her and gave him a reassuring smile. He must have noticed the whole exchange. Eric gave her a sound bump from the side, and she turned to him and laughed at his playful vengeance. She turned her car toward his, determined to let the pall that the operator had brought onto her go. Then she felt a hard bump from behind and turned. Her smile faded as she saw the operator grinning down at her once again.

Any merriment she'd mustered faded. It seemed as if the operator's green car was circling hers. She looked up to where the other operator controlled the machines. Why didn't it stop? The other rounds hadn't lasted this long.

She saw the operator's green car coming straight toward her and she turned, but he followed her. As she turned, she saw that Eric, too, had now caught on to what was happening, and she saw both Jack and Eric's bumper cars head straight for the one following her. Jack got to him first and rammed his car into the operator's, pushing the offending car against the wall.

"Hey, man, what's your problem?" the operator yelled at Jack. Jack didn't say anything, his mouth set in a grim line. Katrina was thankful for the diversion.

Thankfully, a few moments later, the ride stopped. She got out of her car and made her way over to the exit gate with Jack and Eric on her heels, the operator still steaming since he hadn't gotten another chance to approach her.

"Are you okay?" Jack asked her as they filed out of the gate. She nodded but didn't say anything, clearly not wanting to talk about it.

Eric came up on her other side, "Hey, don't worry about that, guy, Katrina. There's a lot of creeps out there. Besides, you were safe with us. We weren't going to let anything happen to you."

"I know," she said, surprised by how much she really did know it. "So what's next?" she asked, determined to prove she was fine and enjoy the rest of the evening. She couldn't let one insensitive jerk ruin her night.

"That's the spirit," Eric beamed while Jack continued to gaze at her with concern.

Over the next hour, Eric led her to various booths where he played games and won prize after prize. He coaxed her into riding a few more rides that only accommodated two people. Jack assured them he didn't mind sitting out, but she noticed a few tense moments between Jack and Eric.

When her cheeks felt so wind-chapped that they stung and her feet ached, they finally climbed back into Jack's truck. She was exhausted, and the heat blowing on her face and feet felt like heaven as she buckled up. She laid her head back on the seat and drifted off to sleep between the two men who were now the closet people she had to calling friends.

CHAPTER 9

*J*ack forked an egg into his mouth. Eric may have thought her wary at first, but last night must have broken the ice. It was as if there was some strange bond connecting them. They spoke with the familiarity of old pals. Katrina certainly hadn't been this forthcoming after knowing him for only one day.

Eric and Katrina sat at the long table with him in the breakfast room chatting away. He had bought the large table because it looked great in the room, though he rarely ever needed to seat so many people. He'd only had occasion to fully use it twice, and both those times he'd been negotiating a deal between businesses. Jack zoned back in on their conversation.

"What's the plan for today?" Eric asked.

"Organize more files," Katrina answered taking a sip of orange juice.

Eric laid down his fork. "Jack…"

Jack held up his hand. "I know, Eric." He turned to

Katrina. "You don't work Saturdays or Sundays. I thought you knew that."

"You forgot to tell me." She took a bite of flaky biscuit, then dabbed at her mouth. "Now I don't know what I'm going to do all day."

That was Eric's cue. "Weekends were made for fun. What do you say to a day in Boston?"

"I think I want to just relax today, Eric," she said, glancing out the window.

Jack followed her gaze. He didn't blame her. It was a gorgeous day. There was still snow on the ground, but it was beginning to diminish, thanks to the unrelenting sun. Today would be the perfect day to take it easy and enjoy God's creation. He looked at Katrina. Was that how she felt? Did she appreciate nature's beauty and recognize it as God's handiwork, or was she one who just appreciated nature? So far, there'd been no indication that she followed faith, but there hadn't been any that she didn't either.

"What about you, Jack?"

"What about me?"

Eric rolled his eyes. "You going to Boston with me?"

"Not this time Eric."

Eric shook his head. "You two are going to make me go to Boston seeking thrills all alone. Sheez…" Eric splayed his hands, "I guess I'll be going then. I would've headed out sooner if I'd have known that."

He stopped at the door and looked back at Katrina longingly. "Sure you don't want to go? I hear it's a woman's prerogative to change her mind." She restated her 'no.'

Eric looked hopefully at Jack, and he shook his head.

Eric sighed and walked away singing Eric Carmen's *All by Myself*.

Katrina waved him off. Even for all his talk of going alone, Jack knew Eric would be fine. By at least halfway through the day, he'd have a dozen female companions if he wanted them. And no doubt he would.

"Thank you for not making me work weekends." Katrina's blue eyes looked up into his.

He noticed the blue stretch pants and corresponding tee and jacket she wore. If her hair were only in a high ponytail, she would be the perfect picture of a high school cheerleader.

"Did you really think I would expect you to work seven days a week?"

She shrugged.

He leaned back in his chair. "I'm not a complete miser."

"I know." Her eyes smiled, and it warmed his insides like a cappuccino.

He started to speak, but Elaine swooped down to clear their plates. It was just as well. He was eager to enjoy his first real day off. Because of his errands his first week home, his vacation had never truly begun. As Katrina engaged Elaine in conversation, he left the table, heading for his library. He'd start his day by reading scripture.

Ever since Katrina had looked out of the window of Jack's breakfast room that morning, she'd known exactly what she was going to do with her day. She waved goodbye to Elaine, rushed to Jack's office, and peeked her head in the door. As soon as she'd determined the coast was clear, she pushed the door open and headed to Jack's desk.

The drawer slid open smoothly. She pulled a spiral notebook from the supplies. She knew Jack wouldn't mind. Besides, she'd pay him back the next time they went to the store. She rummaged atop his desk in search of a pen. *Eureka.* She lifted the pen triumphantly. She was all set now.

She exited a pair of French doors next to the kitchen and stepped out into a screened area. It was tiled with cobblestones. There was a white, delicately curved table sitting over to the side and several cushioned lawn chairs scattered upon the stones. A hanging lamp was suspended over the table in the corner. There was even a small heater set up, which led Katrina to conclude that Jack must come out here at night sometimes.

She continued on through the screened door and marveled at the beauty around her. There were dry patches of earth peeking through the snow, but even those were white with frost. Reaching the gazebo that was as expertly designed as everything else she'd encountered in Jack's world, she ran her hands along the smooth surface. The stone of the gazebo was of the same pale pink hue as the stones of the house. It was hard to imagine Jack choosing such a shade. He was such a…man. But then it wasn't. Somehow, it seemed to fit. He seemed to surround himself with extravagance and beauty. In his home could be found beautiful candelabras and ornate statues and architecture. Jack Barringer had a confidence about him. An almost unnerving self-assurance. It was that same trait that made her feel safe and frightened at once.

He was cultured, suave, handsome, and a little too knowing. He was also generous. Far too generous. Like letting her play his piano. He'd said that his deceased father was the last one who'd played it. Why let her touch something that was obviously so special?

She felt her suspicions creep in. Nobody was that nice.

She shook her head as if to clear it of her paranoid thoughts. What was she thinking? The man had been nothing but nice to her. He'd taken her into his home and been hospitable, and here she was doubting him. He hadn't bitten once. Hadn't even barked. Yes, at the beginning, before they ever reached his home, he'd seemed moody. For the next week, he'd been busy. But the times that they had communicated, he'd been cordial and caring. And his friend had proven likewise. Where was last night's peace when she'd ridden home contently between the two of them?

She looked around at Mother Nature's landscape. Here. Here was peace. In this shining brilliance. She would recapture her calm. She looked around her. At the colorful sun, its brightness fading the farther the rays spread from the burning center. The fluffy, cottony clouds amid the swirl of yellow and blue. When she was little, she used to imagine the birds sleeping on the clouds, and always wondered if they were softer than normal pillows. She suspected they were.

She shifted her gaze back down to the ground. The bare, naked trees shimmering with unabashed pride. Some full, leafy evergreens contrasting starkly with the former unembellished trees. Yet, they all played their part. They each added to the overall finished product.

She breathed the crisp, cold air deeply into her lungs.

It was a refreshing change from the humid air in Tennessee—sometimes even in winter. She heard a soft rustling and turned to see a squirrel scurry past an unadorned rosebush and up into the haven of a tree.

She placed the notebook and pen on the bench and went over to the empty rosebush. She fingered the bush thoughtfully. The slender branches rose up from the ground and twined around the small white fence provided to support them. Their tops were covered with snow and frost, but their green color peaked through the underside. Sharp, spiky thorns broke through the snow, revealed in the absence of blossoms. She studied the plant and wondered what color its buds would be. With a start, she was reminded of the first real poem she'd ever written — the first meaningful one anyways.

Planting the Rose. She closed her eyes and spoke softly:
"There is a garden in my soul
An orchard filled with many flowers
Petals blooming to and fro
Oh what to grow, what to grow!
Tulips, daisies, marigolds
Blossoms budding all around
How these flowers should I mold?
Especially the beautiful rose.
Of course, there's always the radiant red
Enigmatic, dazzling, and bewitching
Bold and brazen, without a care
A caress to the eyes, an irresistible snare.
Then there's the white
Pure and true
Gentle, angelic, and divine
Its silver halo entrances the mind.

Finally, the charming pink
A happier medium you could not meet
Lovely and innocent with a sweet blush
Its enchanting beauty turns the heart to mush.
Choose the rose carefully, do not rush!"

She sighed. That had been the product of a confused sixteen-year-old who hadn't known which path to take when she came to the roads that diverged in a wood. What rose had she turned out to be? She mused. It was difficult to say. She didn't fall into any one category. Maybe she wasn't a rose. Maybe she was just a regular old flower. Not everyone in the world could be a rose.

She jumped at a hand on her shoulder. Spinning, she saw Jack step back, arms up in surrender. Heart pounding, she glared at him. "Don't sneak up on me like that!"

Readjusting a glove, he replied, "I didn't sneak. You were so wrapped up in your prayer that you didn't hear me."

A rush of embarrassment filled her. How much of her poem had he heard? He probably thought her senile, talking to herself like that. Then she realized he'd said *prayer*. He'd thought she was praying?

She shook her head and protested, "No, I don't do that." There. Let him know she was talking to herself and think her crazy. At least she wouldn't mislead him.

She didn't know what she'd expected his response to be, but it certainly wasn't a penetrating look and a 'why not?'

She shrugged, "I just don't." She took in his slightly tousled hair, so deep a brown it could almost be called black and his hands thrust in his pockets in typical a *bad boy* stance. "I hope you don't mind me saying so, but you don't exactly look like the bible-hugging sort yourself."

"Yeah?" he asked, shifting his stance. "What sort do I look like?"

"I don't know." She went on with, "And even if I did, it wouldn't be proper to say."

"Ah," he said knowingly, "so you do have an opinion. You just don't want to tell me. It must be bad."

When she didn't respond, he urged, "Come on, Katrina. You can tell me. You won't hurt my feelings too much."

She raised an eyebrow. "You don't have to make fun."

"Make fun?" he said with exaggerated incredulity. "If I was going to make fun, I would have asked you what you were saying to yourself a few moments ago since you weren't praying, but being the gentleman that I am, I bit my tongue—in spite of my overwhelming curiosity." He said this last bit with humor in his eyes and a slight smile.

Katrina raised her chin. "On second thought, I've changed my mind. I know exactly what you remind me of."

"Oh?" he raised a brow and his smile spread, which only served to irritate her more.

"Yes." She looked up at him fully. "A pirate."

Hands on his hips, he threw his head back and laughed. Indignation coursed through her, and she couldn't help but think she'd chosen exactly the right noun to describe him.

"A pirate, huh?" He bent down to pick up a long, thin stick. He made as if to pull it from his hip and cut a few swings in the air. Stick still poised in the air, he asked, "Good enough to be Captain Jack Sparrow?"

Seeing that his teasing was gone, her annoyance evaporated. "Not quite." She cocked her head and studied him. He did rather resemble the unruly pirate. Not so much in physical characteristics as in his overall manner. She remembered a comment she had overheard after seeing *Pirates of the Caribbean: The Curse of the Black Pearl*. A lanky old man had been walking out of the theater with his wife and had remarked that Johnny Depp's character, Jack Sparrow, was now his favorite Disney character. A nonconformist with a heart, he'd called him. She looked at Jack and thought the same. He had a confidence about him that suggested he knew what he was about and hang what the world may think. Yet, at the same time, he was compassionate and really cared about things.

"What?" Jack asked skeptically.

Katrina shrugged. "I was just thinking you're not as roguish as he, but your take on life seems kind of the same."

"Is that a good thing?"

"I think so. I always liked him."

Jack tossed the stick aside and walked over to the gazebo and sat. He patted the spot next to him, and she joined him on the bench. Spotting the spiral notebook, he picked it up.

"I borrowed it from your office." She picked up the pen that was rolling off the bench. "I didn't think you'd mind. I was using it to write."

He flipped the blank pages. "You didn't get very far."

"Well, I was going to, but then you came." She bit her lip. Oh, that sounded like a complaint.

He looked up at her, a strand of hair falling in his eyes. "Do you want me to leave?"

She shook her head. "The mood's gone anyways."

Jack leaned back on the gazebo and rested his arm on the top bench behind them. "Just how many talents do you possess?"

She sat up straight to avoid leaning against his arm.

"What do you mean?"

"You're a musician and a writer. Can you also paint?"

"No, I don't paint. Music and words are as far as my artistic abilities go. The most I can draw are stick people."

He chuckled. Then a thoughtful look came over his face. "What do you write about?" he asked.

Way too personal of a question. She never shared her writing with anyone. It was the part of her that was most vulnerable. One time she'd caught Bryan reading her poetry. She'd felt so exposed and had been furious with him.

When she didn't answer, Jack prompted,

"Emotions, life, love, nature, God?"

"God?" She repeated. "What would I write about God?"

"Of his love, his unending mercy, his divine creations…"

"I'm not very religious," Katrina said slowly.

"Good," Jack answered, which startled her. She looked up at him questioningly. "I'm not very religious either," he explained. "I'm more spiritual, as in I have a relationship with God. God wants us to love and glorify him—not to get tied up in a religious hierarchy."

His unwavering gaze was pinned on her. She shook her head, "You speak of such a loving and merciful God, but if God's so loving and merciful, then why am I here? Why are bad things allowed to happened?"

"God has a purpose for all things, Katrina," Jack answered softly, "even if we don't always understand them at the time."

Katrina just shook her head again and fell silent.

Jack leaned over and took her hand. His eyes earnestly beseeching hers, he gently said, "Katrina, what's happened to you isn't God's fault. Sometimes men come between God's will, but God works all things to the good of those who love him."

She looked up into his eyes. This man who was becoming less and less a stranger. "But what if you don't love God? What if you don't know God?"

"He loves you anyway," Jack answered simply as if it were a basic truth.

"Why do you care so much? You know," she looked down as she asked him softly, "about helping me?"

He squeezed her hand. "Because I was charged with your care. Katrina, God led me to you that day to help you, and that's what I'm going to do. I know I've been negligent this first week and I'm sorry. I've been busy."

"No," Choosing to ignore his former statement about God, Katrina protested the latter, "you've been nothing but kind. You've provided me with food, clothing, shelter, and work."

"Nevertheless, I've left you alone in that stuffy office and proved myself to be a horrible host. I've been selfish. I'd like for us to start over. Forgive me?"

"There's nothing to forgive," she protested.

"Do you or not?" he pressed playfully.

She rolled her eyes with a smile. "Fine. Yes, I forgive you."

"Good." He stuck out his hand. "Friends?"

She gripped his hand. "Friends."

He smiled. "Now what do you say we go get some lunch?"

She smiled back and stood.

When they were halfway through the kitchen door, Katrina suddenly stopped. Jack turned to her questionably.

"Elaine went out to get groceries today. I forgot until now," she said.

Jack took her hand and pulled her into the kitchen.

"So?"

"So?" She tugged her hand free of his and looked up at him.

"So, what does that have to do with anything?"

"Elaine's the cook. And she's not here." Katrina looked endearing flustered as comprehension dawned on him. Had the girl never cooked a meal in her entire life? He'd definitely pegged her right when he had determined her wealthy.

"We can fix our own lunch," Jack replied.

Katrina stared at him as he went about the kitchen opening cabinets. "You mean you're going to cook?"

Jack glanced over his shoulder at her standing in the middle of the kitchen, hands on hips. "No, we're going to cook." He laid a loaf of bread and a package of cheese slices on the counter. "I'll admit Elaine's meals are better than mine, but I can prepare something for myself in her absence." He held up the bread and cheese. "You ever made a grilled cheese sandwich?"

She shook her head.

"What did you eat at college?"

"I always dined out," she answered simply. Of course. She went to Harvard, didn't she? No doubt it had more than regular cafeteria food. Probably five-star restaurants. He turned a skillet onto medium heat and dropped a dab of butter into it.

He cocked his head. "Well, come here. This is your first lesson in cooking. How to make a grilled cheese sandwich. It's simple." He picked up the top piece of his bread and watched with amusement as she did the same, paying rapt attention. He opened two pieces of slice cheese, placed them on the bread, and then replaced the top piece of bread onto he first with the cheese nestled in between the two slices. Katrina followed suit.

She looked up. "Now what?"

"Now, we grill them." He took the two sandwiches and placed them in the skillet that was already heated with melted butter. Katrina came up beside him, watching, but she didn't say anything. He let the sandwiches sizzle for about a minute.

"Would you hand me that spatula, please?" He pointed to the big black spatula that was hanging from a hook, along with other kitchen tools, directly in front of Katrina. She reached over, then handed it to him.

He slid it under one sandwich and flipped it. As he proceeded to do the same to the other one, Katrina intercepted the spatula from him and flipped her own. He cocked his head and studied her, mentally listing independent as one of her characteristics.

"Are they done now?"

He looked down at the lightly browned pieces of bread. "Yes, I believe they are."

She fumbled with the spatula a bit, but finally scooped the two sandwiches onto the plates and set them on the bar. Jack poured them each a glass of milk, then sat next to Katrina.

She lifted the sandwich to her mouth, but stopped mid-bite when he bowed his head. "Father, we thank you for this meal and all of your blessings. Please lead and guide us according to your will. Amen."

Jack lifted his head.

"Do you always do that?" Katrina asked.

He took a bite of his sandwich and answered her without looking up. "Yes, I pray before meals, for God is the one who provides them for me."

What did she have against faith? Her comments in the garden had alarmed him, and he wanted to know what had caused her to have such an outlook on God, but he knew better than to be pushy where spiritual matters were concerned.

He scrutinized her. She looked as if she would say more, but at that moment, Elaine came noisily into the kitchen, arms laden with brown paper bags, Roy behind her likewise.

Elaine dropped the bags on the counter and sent a disapproving glance their way. Jack mentally rolled his eyes. Oh no, they were in for it now.

She stalked over to them. "What is this?" She asked, looking between the two of them.

Jack sat back in his chair. "Why, Elaine this is lunch."

"This is not a lunch," she countered, hands splayed toward their plates of grilled cheese.

While Elaine continued to rant and rave about Jack's poor food choices, how he still ate like a ten-year-old boy if left to his own choices, Roy deposited more bags on the counter, and then came up behind his wife, moving his hands together as if to say "blah, blah, blah." Katrina let out a little giggle that was music to Jack's ears. Elaine, catching the direction of Katrina's gaze, turned and caught Roy red-handed in his mocking shenanigans. Jack grinned as Elaine turned her sharp tongue on her repentant-looking husband.

Poor guy. He wouldn't want to be in Roy's shoes right now for all the money in the world.

When Katrina had eaten the last bite of her *pitiful excuse for a lunch* as Elaine had put it, he motioned to her with his head, and they slipped out onto the enclosed porch.

"Did you have any plans for the day?" he asked her.

She shook her head.

"I didn't either. In that case, would you like to join me for a walk?"

She looked a bit surprised but answered, "Sure."

He noticed her bare hands. "Do you have gloves?"

"Yes."

"You might want to put them on then."

Once she'd dutifully pulled the gloves out of her coat pockets and put them on her hands, he held his black-gloved hand out to her. She hesitated a moment, then placed her much smaller, brown-gloved hand in his. Her hesitance reminded him of the circumstances that had probably caused it. Anger boiled inside him again as he recalled her limp form on the snow.

They walked around the grounds in a comfortable

silence for several minutes, each lost in their own thoughts, until Katrina broke the silence.

"Jack?"

"Hmm?" He asked absentmindedly, still deep in thought. Then, sensing Katrina's nervousness, he stopped and gave her his full attention. "What?"

She was wringing her hands together and turned away from him. He gently took her shoulders and turned her toward him. "Katrina?" What was she so tense about?

She wouldn't meet his eyes, so he nudged her chin up, forcing her to do so. "Katrina, what is it?"

"I was just wondering when I should, I mean, well, how long I can stay," she looked down as she finished.

That's what she was worried about? He turned her head back to his until their eyes met. "Katrina, you can stay as long as you need to. I've been thinking about this for some time now, and I remembered you briefly mentioned your father. I trust he's who you live with?"

"Yes," she answered, eyes filled with apprehension, "now that I'm not at college anymore. I've never had a place of my own yet."

"I don't know why you fear calling him and having him come get you, but it's your decision. The way I see it when you're ready and the time is right for you to leave, you'll call your father. I know what you've been through has probably left you confused and searching. And I think that maybe you're trying to sort out other parts of your life as well. You're welcome to stay here as long as you need to. I'm not going to kick you out. Understand?"

"Yes," she whispered. It still stung him to think that she had believed he'd kick her out. But then, she didn't know him. He looked down at her. Her arms were wrapped tightly around herself, and she was staring off into the distance. He took her hand once again and began pointing out different species of plants—the ones that were in bloom, that is—and marveled at her eagerness to learn and her inquisitive mind. Perhaps, since it seemed she was staying for a while, he would have the chance to remedy the fact that she didn't know him.

David Weems held the phone up to his ear. "Any word?"

"Not yet, sir, but I'm on it."

"I know I call often to check, but it's just that I'm worried. It's been a whole week and no sign of her where-abouts." He couldn't keep the discouragement out of his voice.

"I know, David. I'm worried too. I'd give anything to find her."

David heard the concern in Bryan's voice. Yes, he guessed he would. Bryan cared for his daughter. He'd known that for some time now and had encouraged it. He couldn't think of a man he trusted more. He considered Bryan his son, his protégé. "I know you would. Just call if you find anything."

"Of course, sir," he answered solemnly.

David placed the receiver on the hook. If anybody could locate Katrina, it was Bryan's team of expert inves-tigators. When he'd first heard that Katrina was missing, his first instinct had been to call everybody he knew, get the police involved. However, Bryan had been right that the media would have gone crazy.

They'd have had a field day with that one, and it would

most likely have accomplished nothing. Bryan had connections. His private eyes were highly trained and discreet. Yes, surely they would find his daughter.

Yet, he couldn't stop the worry any more than he could stop the sun from rising. His daughter, whom he had taken care of all her life, was somewhere out there beyond his reach. What if she was hurt? Lost? Afraid? What if she were…? He couldn't even allow that thought. Yet, what if she were? What was he going to do? He'd tried to protect her, yet the time when she'd needed him the most, he hadn't been there for her. His mind kept swirling with questions of *what if.* What if he'd now lost her? He'd already lost her mother. He didn't think he could bear losing her too. She was all he had left of the woman he loved. Not to mention she was the precious child he's raised since infancy. He lowered his graying head, and a tear slid down his roughened cheek.

CHAPTER 10

*K*atrina's hands, already balled together in her lap, clenched tighter as the lean preacher proceeded to the stand in silence. Whatever had possessed her to agree to come here? Was it because of Elaine's disapproval at the thought of her not attending? Was it because of the pressure that all in the house were going—even Eric? Or was it because of the silent plea that had been in Jack's eyes that morning at breakfast when he had asked her if she were attending the service or not? She supposed it was mixture of all, but what had most prompted her to dress for church for the first time in years was the prospect of disappointing Jack.

She and Jack, it seemed, had reached a peace and understanding yesterday. She had gone to bed last night not worrying about how soon she should leave and what a burden she must be to everyone. Last night was the first time since Jack found her that she hadn't had a nightmare. And so, this morning, in the wake of her newfound friendship with Jack, she simply couldn't bring herself to refuse his request. It seemed that religion—or rather, spirituality, as he'd called it—was important to him. Yet, why it should matter to him whether she went to church too or not, she couldn't fathom.

She and her father used to attend church up until her preteens. It was a small, and Katrina always thought, uncivilized church, which housed members prone to exaggeration and quick judgment. She shuddered at the memories. Cold, condemning stares from the men. Silent nods of disapproval from the women. These were all she ever got out of church. Yet, what she failed to understand was what she had done to deserve such. She was a good child. She didn't tell lies. She prayed every night. Then one day she learned that it wasn't so much what she'd done as what she was.

A young girl of eleven, she'd been walking past her father's office one day when she'd heard heated voices coming through the door.

Curious because her father never raised his voice, she stopped outside the door and listened.

"You're asking us to leave?" her father asked incredulously.

"Well, David, the church feels that you and your daughter," Katrina peeked through the crack in the unclosed door and saw the plump pastor squirming and wringing his hat in his hands under her father's angry gaze, *"are a hindrance to the members."*

Her father seemed genuinely confused. "A hindrance? Please, preacher, tell me upon what that conclusion is based. My daughter and I are active in all the church activities, and have I not made several generous donations toward the upkeep of the church? I thought we were accepted by all the members. I received no hostility from anyone. In fact, I have been treated with the warmest of welcomes, as has Katrina."

Katrina couldn't help thinking that wasn't true. She'd never felt welcome there.

The pastor began pulling on his ear with his meaty fingers. "Uh, yes, they wouldn't say anything to you directly, but I have heard it said that you make them feel inadequate." He held up a hand and rushed on before her father could comment. "Your worldliness unsettles many of the members, David. Your fine clothes, your grand house, and even your large donations, although greatly appreciated, seem to suggest to some that you're better than they, and therefore, causes tension in the church. It's the same situation with your daughter. It is my duty, David, to keep peace in the church. The deacons and I have all met, and we've agreed that we must, regrettably, ask you to leave. I'm sorry David."

And with that the preacher had taken his leave and also any desire of Katrina's to attend any church. She then knew the cause for all the looks she received from the adults when her father wasn't looking. She then knew that all the other children who she'd thought were her friends were not. She then knew that church was really a false place that people went to so they could think they were good and righteous as they pointed fingers at those who were different.

"Let us pray." Katrina's head snapped up at the softly spoken phrase. Where was the booming, authoritative voice? The one that spoke only of sins and their punishment? Why was this preacher praying so softly and thanking God for blessings and talking...as if he were talking to a real person?

She glanced around the congregation and realized that she was the only one whose head wasn't bowed. As she quickly lowered her head, she caught Eric peaking at her.

He gave her a quick wink and smile before her eyelids shut.

She no sooner dutifully assumed the proper praying pose than the preacher said, "Amen." She lifted her head and stilled herself for the loud, rumbling storm that was sure to come. Instead, it was as if the sun had appeared and welcomed Spring. She was filled with amazement at the pastor's sermon. His message didn't fill her with terror but wonder. He spoke of a love so great as Katrina had never known. *For God so loved the world that he gave his only begotten son to die upon the cross.* But it also left her floundering in a morass of doubt. What kind of father would have his son die on a cross? And how could she know that this church wasn't like the last? Yes, it seemed different, but how could one recognize truth once tricked?

Her mind had been so busy and confused that she'd missed the last of what the preacher had said. The choir sang one last hymn, and then they were dismissed. Katrina stood, turned, and found two pairs of eyes on her. Jack looked puzzled and inquisitive, while Eric merely appeared amused.

Before Katrina could surmise what their expressions meant, she felt her hand grasped solidly and warmly. She turned and found herself face to face with the preacher's gray eyes. He was telling her that his name was Mr. Firmin.

"Nice to meet you. I'm Katrina Weems." She tried to still her pounding heart for fear that Mr. Firmin, Jack, or Eric might see her tension.

Mr. Firmin smiled at her kindly. "And are you new in town, Ms. Weems?"

"I, uh," Katrina stuttered, searching for an answer. She couldn't tell him the real reason why she was in Massachusetts.

Thankfully, Jack came to her rescue. "She's visiting. Aren't you Katrina?" He looked at her.

"Oh, yes, I'm just visiting." She thanked Jack with a grateful look.

Mr. Firmin smiled kindly at her again, and she saw no malice or judgement in his eyes. "Well, we'd be happy to have you join us for services any time, Ms. Weems." With that and one last handshake, he was off to greet others.

Katrina then felt Eric's hand surround hers. He leaned down and said in her ear, "Let's get you out of here before you're swamped. Everybody will want to meet you since you're new."

She and Eric left Jack conversing with a young couple, stopping every few steps to answer the polite inquiries about Katrina. Finally, they reached their destination. As they stepped out into the cold, Katrina looked up at Eric's six-foot-two frame. "Thanks for expertly maneuvering me out of there. I never would have escaped all on my own."

Eric's green eyes twinkled and he bowed to her, paying no heed to the people around them. "It was my pleasure, madam," he joked.

"Stop it Eric!" she exclaimed, cheeks flaming.

He just laughed. "What's wrong, Katrina?"

"You know what these people will think if they seeing you acting like that toward me," she hissed.

He arched a brow, clearly enjoying himself. "Oh, really? No, I don't think I do know. Tell me, what will they think?"

She glared at him. "They'll think we're…involved."

He took her hand once more, all teasing gone from his emerald green eyes. "And would that be a bad thing?"

Before she could answer, Jack came strolling up to them. Katrina was glad to turn away from Eric, while Eric, on the other hand, turned toward Jack with obvious annoyance.

"There you two are. I've been looking all over for you. Come on. Mr. Firmin and his wife are eating dinner with us. Elaine and Roy just left to go prepare it." He began walking toward the vehicle. "We should go too. The pastor and his wife will be over after they stop by their house and change." Jack popped in the truck, and Katrina and Eric did the same. This time Katrina and Eric were both feeling the same emotion: dread.

Eric moodily forked a potato. He glanced up and saw Elaine's hurt look. To reassure her, he smiled and popped a bite into his mouth. That apparently appeased her because she turned once again to Mrs. Firmin. Truly, Elaine's cooking was mouth-watering, as always. He just didn't have the appetite.

He looked at Katrina where she sat directly across from him. So close and yet so far away. She looked as lovely in a pink sweater and khakis as she had that morning wrapped up in a white sweater, a billowing blue skirt, and a matching scarf. She was so different from the women he was normally interested in. A rare jewel. Sweet, innocent, adorable, lovely, beautiful.

He'd never considered becoming serious with a

woman. He'd always been resigned to having the life of a loner. Yet ever since he'd met this little nightingale who seemed to have found her way into Jack's nest, his every thought had been consumed with her. That morning he hadn't heard a word Pastor Firmin had said. Of course, he never really heard a word the pastor said on those rare occasions when he attended church, but that wasn't the point. He'd sat studying Katrina the whole time. The only reason he'd attended anyway was because she was going. He never went to church. It wasn't really his thing.

He knew these feelings were sudden. He'd known her but a few short days. Yet, something in him would not let him ignore her. At first, he'd only mildly noticed that she was a pretty package, but then something happened. Her lost and lonely eyes had looked straight into his. It was as if he'd been living his whole life in a meaningless daze until her big blue eyes had snapped him wide awake. Those crystalline depths seemed to mirror his own soul. He'd never thought of one woman constantly, but Saturday night when gorgeous women surrounded him, he'd found that Katrina was the only woman on his mind. Part of what drew him to her was her hurt. He knew pain and loneliness. He knew what she felt, and that made him want to take her, protect her, shield her.

It was the strangest thing that had ever happened to him. He felt connected to her somehow. Her voice, her face, and her movements all seemed like something out of a familiar dream. He couldn't explain it. Is this what was meant by love at first sight?

He knew the events that had brought her to Jack's house had left their mark. But maybe he could help her, show her that all men weren't mindless beasts—that is if Jack would stop interfering.

It seemed that every time he got Katrina to himself, Jack would pop up and ruin everything. He liked his old college buddy. That's why he'd come to see him, but he could be as frustrating as a bad toothache sometimes. Like inviting the pastor and his wife over for dinner. Eric had wanted to convince Katrina to have dinner with him, but Jack had shot those plans down.

"What do you think, Eric?" Eric jerked his head up to find Mrs. Firmin waiting for his answer. To what he didn't know.

"Pardon?" he asked.

She smiled. She was a bit on the hefty side, unlike her husband, and had short brown hair and eyes. "I was asking your opinion on Katrina playing the piano at our annual Christmas talent show. You know we have one for the adults and children. Both are the weekend of Christmas. It's just a fun way for everybody to get together and celebrate the holidays." She gingerly placed a bite of chicken into her mouth.

He looked at Katrina. Talking to Mrs. Firmin, he replied, "I think it's a wonderful idea. I've heard Katrina play. She's very good. She can play anything. Beethoven, Mozart, Tchaikovsky, you name it." Katrina blushed at his praise. Was there ever a sight more beautiful?

"Really?" Mrs. Firmin fairly squealed with delight. "Then I insist you must perform. I simply will not take no for an answer."

"Yes, you must," her husband agreed.

"Well," Katrina looked unsure, her eyes flitting around

the table between Jack, Eric, Elaine, and Roy, "I don't know."

Jack jumped in with, "You'll do fine, Katrina. You're great, and you know it."

She lingered indecisively a moment more over her decision.

"Please, Katrina," Eric added with a mischievous smile, "you don't want to cheat the audience, now, do you? Don't make me beg."

She laughed at that, a musical sound. "Okay, okay. I'll do it."

Mrs. Firmin and Elaine burst into excited chatter as Mr. Firmin, Jack, and Roy began talking of performances past. Eric's eyes locked with Katrina's and he couldn't help but add, "You'll be the star of the show," to which she bestowed upon him a radiant smile and sparkling eyes— to his satisfaction.

Katrina wrapped her arms around herself and stared up into a moonlit sky from underneath the gazebo. The dinner had not gone bad at all as she had thought it would. The pastor and his wife had been as kind to her as if they'd been acquainted with her all their lives. Now she truly believed that they were different from any other Christians she'd ever known. She was really beginning to enjoy it here with Jack and Eric. And to think she would get to do a piano recital!

She'd always dreamed of performing, but the kids at school had always made fun of her when she played the piano that was in the music room. Was there anything she hadn't been made fun of for? She sighed. The past was the past. She would not allow herself to become melancholy thinking about it. She was in the present, and it was wonderful. She was accepted for who she was and praised for her abilities. She'd never known such happiness. Even thoughts of Bryan couldn't sadden her. She was safe now.

But for how long? And what about her father? No, she would not think about it. He would be fine, and she could stay here until she was ready to go back.

Until she got a grasp on things.

Suddenly, she felt hands on her shoulders and spun around to find green eyes peering down at her. She relaxed. "Eric," she said with a hand on her chest, "you scared me! I didn't even hear you approach." What was it with Jack and Eric both creeping up on her? Or, was it just that she was that oblivious to her surroundings when she was deep in thought? Is that how Bryan was able to trick her? Was she really that much in her own world?

She stepped back and lifted her head to look up at Eric. "How did you know where I was? Or were you just coming out for some fresh air too?"

"I was in the hall when I saw you slip out. I wondered what you were doing." He sat down on the bench and pulled her down beside him.

"I was just thinking." She felt his arm go around her, pulling her closer to him. Since she was cold, she didn't protest.

"About what?" he asked.

She shrugged. "Just about how different things are here from back home."

"Are you homesick?"

She turned to him. "No. Things are different in a good way."

He looked surprised. "Really? How so?"

"Well, I'm accepted for who I am. I feel free—for once." She searched for more words and then settled with, "I don't know, Eric. It's kind of hard to explain."

"Come on," he said lightly, "I can't imagine anyone disliking you."

"Well, you didn't go to my school," she said seriously.

"That bad?"

She shrugged. "I had one friend. Saffron. We kind of stuck together." She couldn't keep the old feeling of rejection out of her voice.

"Katrina?" She lifted her head. His expression was sober now. "I haven't known you long, but I do know that I certainly don't hate you. I like you. Very much." He smiled, and she felt on the brink of tears at his kindness. "Even if you are afraid of the fast, flying fair rides," he cracked a grin, obviously trying to lighten up the mood, and for once she was grateful for his teasing.

He stared down at her for several moments, his expression unreadable, before she felt his hand brush the hair back from her face, and she saw his green eyes searching hers. He wrapped his arms around her and pulled her closer until there was no space left between their bodies. She tensed, noticing how small and insignificant her tiny frame was against his large and powerful one. Her heart was pounding, and she tightly shut her eyes. Then he kissed her very gently, one hand on the small of her back and the other lightly caressing her throat. When she began to shake uncontrollably, he pulled back from her, stroking her hair back from her face, the moonlight shining upon his thick black hair.

Trying to sort through her thoughts, she licked her lips. "Eric…" her voice came out breathy and shaky.

"Sshh…" he quieted her with a finger to her lips. "Don't be afraid. I'm not going to hurt you. Just relax." Her trembling began to subside. "There. See."

His eyes were compassionate and she calmed. "It's okay," he reassured her again.

"Now," he smiled gently, "perhaps we should try that again." She couldn't tell if his eyes were teasing or not.

She put up her hands for in case he was serious. "Please don't."

A flash of disappointment passed over his face before he quickly masked it. "You have nothing to fear with me, Katrina. I would never do anything you didn't want me to."

They sat there for a few minutes eluded in silence, Katrina nervously fidgeting.

With a sigh, Eric stood and offered Katrina his hand. "Shall we go in? It's getting late." And more casually, "And cold too. Brrr."

She gratefully let him lead her into the house to her room, where hopefully she could come to terms with what had just happened.

CHAPTER 11

*K*atrina wandered throughout the halls aimlessly, still pondering the happenings of last night. She was beginning to have doubts about the church again. She was wondering why she'd agreed to perform in their talent show, and she hadn't a clue as to how she felt about Eric's kiss.

Last night, while trying to go to sleep, she'd thought back on when she'd been outside with Eric. She had to admit that she'd felt a comfort in Eric's arms, his strength, even his kiss. As she'd come to trust and be unafraid of Jack, so had she done the same with Eric. Actually, she'd loosened up around Eric a lot sooner than she had Jack. Maybe it was because Eric had come in after she'd already had a week to wind down and recover from that awful night with Bryan.

She somehow knew deep down that neither Jack nor Eric would ever harm her. Of that, she was certain. She liked Eric's company, sometimes even felt more comfortable around him than Jack whom she had known longer, but she didn't know if she wanted the kind of relationship with him that he obviously wanted with her.

Oh, it was all so confusing! Her whole life it seemed was one big muddle. She was living in Massachusetts with a man who had rescued her freezing in the snow from a trusted friend who'd turned out to be a downright scoundrel, and now she'd agreed to go to church, perform in a church function, and was finding herself presented with decisions she didn't want to make.

"Ugh!" she moaned, pulling at her hair as she stalked into the room with the wall of windows and flopped down onto the cream couch. How long she lay there she didn't know, but when she opened her eyes and sat up, she saw Jack look at her and then busily go to a sketchpad. Her cheeks flushed when she realized he'd probably seen her stalk in and flop ungracefully onto his couch.

Her curiosity got the better of her, though, when he didn't speak to her and busily worked on whatever he was working on. She walked up behind him where he sat at an easel that was positioned at an angle with the wall of windows. "How long have you been in here?" she asked.

He answered her without looking from his work. "Long enough to see you come in distressed and fall on the couch."

"You could have made your presence known," she added with a touch of irritation.

"I didn't want to disturb you," again he answered without taking his eyes off the easel.

Katrina peeked over his shoulder. "What are you drawing anyway?" Her breath caught when she saw the image. It was the beginnings of the way she had been just a moment before—eyes closed, sprawled out on the cream settee, hand over her forehead. "It's me!"

At this he finally turned to her, "Yes, well, it's not very good, but..." He ran his hand distractedly through his hair.

"Not good! Jack, how can you say that! It's wonderful! It looks exactly like me and how I felt." She bent to better study it, and Jack turned back towards it also.

"Do you really think so?" He asked, his head cocked, considering.

"Absolutely," she answered with a bob of her bent head, which sent her hair brushing against his arm. Straightening, she placed her hands on her hips and looked at him with raised brows, "You never told me you were an artist."

He ducked his head to study his work again. "You never asked."

"But that day on the gazebo. The subject came up. You could have mentioned it then."

He chuckled. "Katrina, I honestly didn't think about it. Besides, I think you had more worrisome topics on your mind that day, as I remember, which you also seem to have today." He gave her a knowing look, and she shifted her gaze. "What is it, Katrina?"

She shrugged. "I don't want to talk about it. Well, it's nothing really anyway."

Jack sat in front of his easel one foot propped on one knee, when he suddenly smacked his thighs, stood, and said, "I've got it!"

Katrina looked at him as if he had just sprouted horns, to which Jack only smiled. What was wrong with him? "You've got what?" she asked warily.

"Come on. I've something that will cheer you up in no time." He took her hand and started pulling her toward the door.

She pulled against his hand. "Wait! Where are we going?" When he didn't stop and pulled her out into the hall, she tried again. "Wait! Stop! Jack, will you just listen to me for a minute!" She finally jerked her hand from his and stood peering up at him.

He let out an exasperated breath. "Do you want to ruin the surprise?"

Her brows furrowed. "Surprise? I don't think I like surprises."

"Well, you'll like this one, so come on." His fingers grasped hers once again.

"Jack, I don't…"

He turned to her and grasped her shoulders. "Gosh, are you always this stubborn, Katrina? Will you just trust me?"

Will you just trust me? His eyes seemed to pierce hers with their intensity. Would she? Could she? She mutely nodded her head.

"Thank you," he breathed and continued on with her in tow.

He led her out of the kitchen, through the screened-in terrace, across the now clear ground (for the snow had melted), past the gardens, and to a huge stable and corral. He turned to her with a boyish grin plastered across his face.

She was obviously supposed to be impressed, but she didn't know why they were there. "Well? What do you think?" Jack asked.

By the look on his face, he had expected her to jump

up and down in glee. "What am I supposed to think?" she asked slowly and cautiously.

His face fell. "Don't you like horses?"

"Horses?" she repeated dubiously.

"Yes, why do you think I brought you to my stable?" He looked at her skeptical expression. "Don't tell me you've never ridden a horse before!"

She shook her head, "I don't know the first thing about horses."

"Wow," he replied, shaking his head. He'd pegged her for an equestrian and been way off the mark.

He eased his hands into his pockets in a casual gesture. "No matter. I could teach you."

"No," she shook her head again. Of course. She should have known. What extremely rich man dressed in designer labels didn't ride pristine horses and talk about it at the country club? Moreover, did he really think she was going to hop astride some fearsome and magnanimous beast?

"I'm an expert, Katrina. I've been riding since I was five. You'd be safe with me as a teacher." He leaned against the doorway of the stable. "But, of course, if you're afraid we can forget the whole idea, though it is a lot of fun."

What? First Eric insinuated she was a coward and now Jack? No way. She hadn't let Eric think her a 'fraidy cat, and she certainly wasn't about to let Jack either. She shrugged and acted indifferent. "I guess it wouldn't hurt to try."

"I know exactly which horse I'll teach you to ride." Jack's smile spread slowly, and she saw the victory in his eyes. The cunning man knew what he'd done and was proud of it. She fought an insane urge to kick him.

They entered the stable. It smelled of animal, leather, and the outdoors and contained a high ceiling and long rows of stalls that housed horses of all colors.

Brown, black, mixed colors, all big and terrifying, though she would never admit that to Jack.

He glanced over his shoulder at her. "Almost there." After passing at least ten stalls, Katrina couldn't help but wonder why he had so many horses and asked him.

He tossed over his shoulder. "I breed them for sale. Some I keep, and some I train for competitions."

"But how do you find time what with flying all over the world as a bilingual consultant?"

"That's why I have Roy. He manages the outdoor tasks, which include care of the horses, and Elaine manages the indoor ones. However, you're right. I don't have much time to work with my horses. They haven't been in competition since my father died."

Although the stable was infinitely warmer than outside, Katrina shivered and pulled her fur coat tighter. "Was your father a horseman?"

They reached the end of the stable, and Jack turned to her. "The best. He loved horses. Training them, grooming them." He glanced at the walls, the beams in the ceiling, "I guess I'm just carrying on his tradition. He cared so much about horses. Riding was his passion, along with music."

She knew how that was. When she played piano, did she not feel somehow connected to her mother? Did she not imagine that somehow her mother could see her, hear her playing, and be proud?

"How did he die?" Katrina asked softly.

Jack hesitated, shifted, and then his eyes met hers. "Three years ago, he went out on his yacht. It was summer. It would have been he and my mother's anniversary. She died shortly after having me. I guess since it was their anniversary, memories of her flooded him and he began missing her. I suppose that was why he felt the need to be on the water."

He glanced at her and elaborated. "They met at sea."

His eyes then moved from hers to stare blankly over her head at nothing. "I remember he called me and asked if I wanted to join him. I usually went with him when he requested it, but I'd been with a client that day. I was sure he'd be fine. He and I used to go out on the yacht for a week at a time when I was a child."

He paused for a moment and then went on, "That night I got the phone call. A storm had risen. The captain lost control. My father died at sea. I went into a numb stupor. My father was all I had left. I'd never really known my mother."

He swallowed before continuing. "At first I didn't believe it, but when it was proven true I couldn't help but think if I'd only have canceled my meeting and gone with him maybe he'd be alive today."

Katrina ached for him. "Don't say that. It wasn't your fault at all. You couldn't have done anything to change fate."

He looked down at her, a great sadness in his eyes. Confident Jack, who had the whole world and his life figured out, who rescued her from her problems and whom she'd thought didn't have any of his own. "It's true, Jack. There's nothing you could have done to change what happened."

"Yes. What God has preordained no man can change."

"You know I never really knew my mother either,"

Katrina offered as a gesture of empathy. "She died giving birth to me."

Jack looked down at her in understanding. "I guess that's a pain we have in common then."

Katrina nodded sadly.

Jack turned and pointed to the two stalls on his left and on his right, changing the subject.

"This is where the two white horses are kept. On the left is my mount, Caesar, and on the right is the horse you'll be using, Rose."

She took his cue and followed the new subject line. "Why do you keep the white horses back here? It seems like discrimination."

He smiled. "I can assure you they're not discriminated against. Quite the opposite actually. They're pampered and given the best stalls."

Katrina looked at their stalls again and then at all the others, comparing them. The white horses' stalls were considerably larger than the others' stalls.

"You've made your point," she admitted.

Strolling over to the stall on the right, Katrina peeked in at Rose and jumped back when the large white head loomed before her. Jack chuckled, and Rose gave a soft neigh. "She already likes you. She's begging you to pet her. Go on. Just give her a gentle pat."

Katrina looked up at the white horse. Rose was beautiful. She had a shiny white mane and a light pink spot on her forehead. Beautiful or not, though, Katrina wasn't sure she wanted to touch the large animal.

"Here," Jack moved up behind her and guided her hand toward the horse's outstretched head, Katrina's heart pounding at both Jack's touch and fear of the horse.

His hand covering hers, he moved their hands in a slow stroke across Rose's neck. "You don't want to startle her. You have to be very slow and gentle. Let her get acquainted with you," Jack advised.

Katrina's tension began to dissolve, and she moved her hand away from Jack's. She could still feel the warmth of Jack's gloved hand over hers as she stroked the horse on her own.

"Did you name her Rose because of the pink spot on her forehead?"

Jack looked down at her, impressed, "Yes. Quite observant of you to pick up on that."

Katrina gasped as Rose's head moved in and nuzzled her. She stroked Rose's face in return before pulling back.

Jack had a strange expression on his face when she turned to him. "What?" she asked as he studied her.

"Nothing," he replied. "Come on. Time for your first riding lesson." He walked over to Caesar's stall and began saddling the horse.

"But," she protested, "I thought you said I was to ride Rose."

He kneed the air out of the Caesar's belly while glancing over at her. "That's right, but first we're going to ride together so I can teach you a few things." Finished saddling the horse, he stood and fully faced her. "Is that okay?"

She nodded, "Sure," while warily eyeing the other white horse, Caesar, who was much, much bigger than Rose.

Once he'd led the horse outside the stable, Jack motioned her over. "Get acquainted with Caesar as you did with Rose. A horse dislikes nothing more than a person it doesn't know climbing atop its back."

Caesar was a bit more suspicious of Katrina than Rose had been, but after a few strokes, if his affectionate nuzzle was any indication, she'd won him over too. With Caesar's head still pressed against hers, she smiled triumphantly at Jack who was leaning against the wall patiently waiting while she and the horse got to know each other.

He pushed himself from the wall and strode toward her, placed his hands on her waist, and lifted her up onto the huge horse's back. The horse neighed loudly and stomped one foot. *Oh no,* Katrina thought, as she grasped the saddle tightly with both hands.

With one hand securely tightened around Katrina's waist, Jack soothed Caesar with the other. When the horse was under control, Jack jumped up behind Katrina and took the reins, his arms encircling her small body.

This might not have been a good idea. The way she'd bonded with the horse, her face pressed against its muzzle, had went straight to his heart, and the feel of her body pressed against his didn't do anything to his already wayward thoughts.

He saw the evidence of her tension in her tight grip, so he reached down and deftly pried her hands from the saddle. "First rule of riding. You have to relax. If the horse senses your tension, it'll make him nervous and could result in disaster."

He peered over her shoulder into her petrified face.

"It's okay. Just relax. Lean on me." He pulled her against him and felt her loosen up.

It was necessary. The fact that it felt good to hold her like this had absolutely nothing to do with it. After a moment, she moved away from him a bit but retained her ease. Taking a deep breath, she announced, "Okay, I'm ready."

"Okay, first, I want you to just ride. Get the feel of a horse. Watch what I do. Learn how to handle him." He slapped the reins and they were off to a slow trot, and he felt her immediately tense again.

Caesar's ears pricked up, sensing her tension. Jack had to put her at ease. "Katrina, what do you want to do with your life?"

She appeared a bit startled at his sudden question, but answered, "I majored in business in college and interned with Ernst and Young. I'd hoped to work as an auditor for them, even had an interview, but now I just don't know." Her face took on a lost look.

"Wow, working for one of the Big Four. That must have been exciting."

She nodded.

He started to ask her about her father but caught himself just in time. He didn't want her to begin thinking of leaving. He selfishly wanted her to spend Christmas here with him. Ever since his father had died, his Christmases had been spent alone. The last time he'd enjoyed another person's company so much was when his father had been alive. He knew that he couldn't expect her to stay forever. She would want to go home eventually, but he didn't want to see her go yet. When he'd first brought her home with him, he couldn't wait to see her packing, and now he dreaded it.

He could feel her tension resurfacing again in the silence and came up with another distraction. "Let's play a little game. You tell me your greatest wish, what you want more than anything in the world, and I'll tell you mine."

She thought for several minutes before responding, "I don't know what I want." Her brows were knit in deep thought. "I guess I want to know what I want. I want to know my own heart."

"A very good wish," he noted. "Now mine. I want to get a tattoo, pierce my eyebrow, buy a Harley, and live life on the edge." He tightened his mouth to keep a straight face.

Katrina stared tilted her head to stare up at him for a moment, astonished, and then burst out laughing. He grinned and then laughed with her. Caesar turned his head toward them as if to see what was so funny. "Oh, Jack, I could never picture you like that."

He smiled. "Okay. I'll be serious. My greatest wish is to live a happy life in Scotland with a wonderful family."

She nodded knowingly. "The isles are beautiful. At least what I've seen of them. I've been to England and Wales but not Scotland."

"Really? When were you in England and Wales?"

"During my third year in college. I studied abroad." She turned toward him. "But what's Scotland like?"

He looked down at her head turned toward him. "It's the most beautiful place in the world, and trust me I would know. I've seen the world. Scotland is like no other place. Mountains, rolling hills, emerald green as far as the eye can see dotted by sparkles of sapphire blue, the lochs. It's full of nature and beautiful little villages."

"Sounds wonderful."

"It is."

A moment of silence.

"Hey Jack?"

"Yeah?"

"What's all this stuff for?" She pointed at the bridle and bits.

He laughed and then taught her what everything was and its use. As he moved the horse into a canter, leading him through the gardens, their conversation flowed to other subjects. Likes and dislikes. Memories. Katrina described to him Tennessee in summertime and he to her Scotland in springtime. By the time they returned to the stable with Katrina guiding the horse, he felt as if he'd known her since childhood.

He jumped off Caesar's back and lifted Katrina down in front of him but didn't take his hands from her waist. Her eyes, a deep ocean blue that he could drown in, looked up and locked with his. "This was a good attempt at getting my mind off my problems," she said.

"Did it work?" he asked deeply, pulling her closer to him, his eyes searching hers.

She tried to look away, but he held her gaze.

"Yes," she whispered.

"Good." His mouth curved into a smile, and then, on impulse, he leaned down and kissed her, slowly, afraid she would push away from him, and although he felt her hesitance, she did not. She tasted of the strawberry ChapStick he'd seen her put on numerous times before, and he deepened the kiss. He couldn't have stopped if he'd wanted to. He sank his fingers into her glorious mass of blonde hair as he angled her head upward. He could feel her heart racing against his chest, and he knew that she could feel his where her hand covered it. Her arms slipped around his neck, and his own tightened around her possessively in triumph, glad that she hadn't pushed him away.

He watched her eyes flutter open as he pulled back from her, breathing heavily. Her lips rivaled the red of any rose, and he saw the innocence in her eyes. He cupped her face in his hands, tenderly stroking his thumbs across her cheeks, her silken hair falling over her shoulders to brush the backs of his hands. Her big blue eyes were wide and questioning and he couldn't help it—he kissed her again.

CHAPTER 12

*E*ric watched from inside the frosted gardens as Jack leaned down and kissed Katrina outside the stables. His mouth parted and his eyes closed in pain as he noticed that she didn't push Jack away but wrapped her arms about his neck. He turned his face away from the sight, hurt coursing through him.

When he turned back, Jack was caressing her face, and as he kissed her again, jealousy welled up in Eric. His hands clenched as he watched Jack caress the very cheek that he'd caressed, hold the very body that he'd held, kiss the very lips that he'd kissed. *Katrina*.

When they finally pulled apart again, Eric strolled out of the garden toward them casually as if he knew nothing of what he'd just seen. "Hey," he greeted them as if he were surprised to run into them. "Where have you two been?"

Katrina looked uncomfortable and moved away from Jack while he answered, "I've been teaching Katrina to ride."

"Is that so?" Eric glanced at Katrina's flushed cheeks.

Even if he hadn't seen Jack kiss her right before his very eyes, he'd have known something was up by Katrina's face. It was an open book. "Did it prove successful?"

He watched Jack look at Katrina. "I'd say it proved very successful," he replied, to which Katrina's cheeks turned a shade redder.

He fiercely wanted to punch Jack for his arrogance, but instead told him what he'd come to tell him in the first place, "Jack, some guy called for you. I told him you were on break and weren't taking any calls, but he said he was a friend. I think his name was Malcolm Moore."

He saw recognition pass across Jack's face. Touching Katrina's elbow, Jacked asked, "Same time tomorrow?"

She nodded, and then Jack was headed to the house—where he belonged.

A moment of silence stretched between them before Katrina asked, "So what have you been doing all day, Eric?"

He looked down into her sweet, innocent face. He wasn't angry with Katrina. She wasn't to blame. Jack was. "Actually, I've been looking for you."

"Me?" She blinked. "Why?"

"I thought we could go on a picnic."

She looked down at the soggy ground. Though it wasn't covered in snow as it had been a few days ago, it was still wet. "I was thinking of eating in the sunroom," he supplemented.

"I don't know, Eric."

He bowed and did his best butler impression. "I've sodas, crackers, cheese, fruit, and every other imaginable snack food prepared for your disposal, madam."

She smiled. "Stop, Eric."

He went one further as he led her up onto the gazebo out of the soggy ground. "Do you want me to take a knee?" He bent before her on the gazebo where his pants wouldn't get wet, took her hand, and very seriously asked, "Would you do me the honor of embarking on a picnic in the sunroom with me?"

She burst into girlish giggles, to which he grinned, and answered him with, "Why not?"

"Not exactly what a guy hopes to hear when he proposes," Katrina slapped at his arm playfully, "but why not indeed," he added as he held out his arm to her.

Katrina watched Eric's bent head as he spread out their picnic in the sunroom. When he'd stumbled upon her and Jack right after Jack's kiss outside the stable, she'd suddenly felt very guilty. Though why she didn't know. It wasn't as if Eric—or anybody else for that matter—had a claim on her. Also, it wasn't as if she'd kissed Jack. He'd kissed her.

She'd been a bit frightened at Jack's kiss, just as she'd been with Eric's. Both kisses had confused her. It had been so long since a man had shown her attention—with respect—as Jack and Eric were doing. In fact, had one ever? She inwardly groaned. It was becoming apparent that both Jack and Eric wanted a relationship with her. But what did she want? Did she even know?

She liked Eric, and she liked Jack. She felt that they'd been the two to pull her out of the deep depression she would have undoubtedly sank into after what had happened with Bryan. Unlike other battered women—

thankfully that's all it was and she hadn't been raped—she hadn't stopped living, which she'd been very tempted to do. And all because of Jack and Eric.

When Jack first discovered her scared in the snow, did she not distrust him? Did she not the next morning tell him that her problems were none of his business? But he wouldn't hear it. He'd doggedly rescued her, and for that she would always be grateful to him.

And hadn't she been suspicious of anyone outside Jack, Elaine, and Roy? Hadn't she been afraid of even going out in public? But Eric had changed that. He'd made her go out and have fun. He'd made her trust him.

He'd made her not fear the world.

She'd accepted both of them as friends, but was she ready to date either one of them? And if so, which one? They were so alike in some ways and yet so different in others. They were both sophisticated and handsome, but Jack tended to be more serious, while Eric tended to be more impulsive. Oh, how could she ever choose between the two?

Eric snapped his fingers in front of her face.

"Earth to Katrina. Is anybody in there?"

She shook her head. "Sorry, Eric. I guess I was just daydreaming."

"Of me, I hope." He winked at her.

She looked down at the selection of food spread before them on a classic red and white checkered tablecloth. He hadn't exaggerated. Every snack food imaginable was represented. She glimpsed a basket thrown aside and smiled.

"What?" Eric asked around a mouthful of crackers.

She nodded at the basket. "You even brought everything out in a quaint little basket."

"Yeah," he swallowed, "and I felt like Little Miss Riding Hood, too."

Katrina spread cheese on a biscuit and then took a small bite. "I feel sorry for the big bad wolf. He doesn't know who he's messing with."

Eric grinned and barred his teeth at her.

Katrina closed her eyes. "Mmmm. This is good, Eric."

"It's not the best, but it's pretty good." He sank his teeth into an apple.

"Tastes like heaven to me. I skipped breakfast."

Eric raised his brows. "Does Elaine know?"

She shrugged. "I suspect she does. I've skipped breakfast two or three times before while I've been here, and she's scolded me like I was a child and not a grown woman capable of taking care of herself."

"And are you?" His eyes sparkled mischievously.

She savored a juicy green grape. "Am I what?"

"Capable of taking care of yourself."

She tossed her head. "Of course I am!" What kind of a question was that?

"Can you cook?"

She pointed a finger at him. "That is unfair, Eric Sharpe and you know it! You know I can't cook."

"So then, you can't completely take care of yourself?"

"Well….no," she ground out. "But I will learn." To that, Eric let out a booming laugh.

"It's not funny!" she objected

"I'm sorry, Katrina," he was holding his sides, "but I just can't see you being domestic and sweating, dirtying your perfect finger nails."

Katrina looked down at her manicured nails, frowning. "You don't think so?"

He continued to grin, to which she impulsively volunteered, "Then I'll prove you wrong. I'll make dinner tomorrow night, and it'll be the most splendid meal you've ever eaten."

Eric's green eyes turned blue. She noticed that they tended to do so when he was serious. "I'm sure I will enjoy every bite of it just knowing that your hands prepared it." He bent his head, and she felt his lips lightly brush her hand.

The next thing she knew, she felt his arms around her and saw his face looming closer and closer to hers. She stuck her hands up just in time to stop his advance.

A wounded look crossed his face. "I'm sorry, Eric. I can't." She couldn't let him kiss her, him or Jack, until she'd sorted out her feelings. It'd be better for her to keep her distance from both of them.

Eric's arms dropped, and a strand of hair fell in his eyes. She thought she saw his jaw clench, but she must have been mistaken, for his face was calm and normal when she looked at him again. "I do want to kiss you Katrina, but as I told you once before, I would never do anything you didn't want me to."

She nodded, relief filling her. "Thank you, Eric."

He shrugged, and then stood, pulling her to her feet also. "What do you say to a game of tennis?"

He caught her off guard with his sudden question, rendering her speechless for a moment. Once she regained her thoughts, she countered back with, "How did you know I played tennis?"

He squeezed her arm. "Only a woman who plays tennis has arms like that."

She flexed her arms, thankful that he'd lightened the mood again and that he hadn't been offended by her refusal of the kiss. "You're on."

"Great." Eric led her past Jack's many amazing facilities, including the game room where Katrina had once seen him and Jack playing air hockey, to his indoor tennis court.

"Wow, I don't think I've ever seen an indoor tennis court in a home before," Katrina commented, looking around the court as the door slammed noisily shut behind them.

Eric shrugged while gathering rackets and balls. "Jack must have wanted to make sure he could play regardless of the weather."

"His house is really amazing. It has just about everything you could think of that you might want," Katrina commented while taking the proffered tennis racket.

"Yeah, he overlooked nothing when designing his home. I like to tease him about this place being more like a condo than a home."

They both laughed at that. Not in a mocking way but in the way of friendly banter.

"You used to sell condos, didn't you?" Katrina asked, securing her hair in a scrunchie that had been snapped around her wrist.

"Yeah." He offered the small, yellow ball to her. "Do you want to serve first?"

She shook her head. "No, you go. I'm not very good at serving."

He did as she requested, and as they hit the ball back

and forth across the net, they kept a steady stream of conversation going too. They talked mostly of their pasts, Eric of his jobs and sights he'd seen, Katrina of her college days and travels.

Finally, Katrina swung too early, missing the hit, and the ball bounced to the ground. They both leaned over with their hands on their knees, panting. They looked up and smiled to see each other in the same position. "You're more competition than I thought you'd be," Eric admitted.

She stuck her nose in the air, as he'd probably known she would and turned to pick up the ball and attempt to serve it. The first time she missed it completely. The second time turned out much the same. On her third try, she hit it, but the wretched ball didn't go over the net. Her face flamed at Eric's snicker. She'd never been good at serving.

She retrieved the ball from the ground once more while Eric made his way over to her side of the net.

"Here," he commanded reaching for the ball.

"I told you I couldn't serve well," Katrina said in her defense, thinking Eric was going to take the ball back to his side and serve it himself.

Instead, he laid his own racket down and stood close behind her, positioning one of his hands on hers holding her racket. With his other hand, he held the ball and led her through the movements, teaching her how to hit it, his arm and chest pressed fully against her. "You want to make sure you get it high enough," he was saying in her ear as he demonstrated.

She tried not to stare at his large hand engulfing hers and concentrated on learning what he was trying to teach her. After guiding her through the steps three times, he left her to try it on her own. She finally mastered the serve, and they played vigorously for another hour until they were both weary. Katrina was rather proud of herself. She had almost won.

"Malcolm? Hey, I heard you'd called." Jack sat down in his office.

The fifty-year-old man's voice came across the receiver. "Yes, I called not too long ago. How are you doing?"

"Oh, fine. How about you? Are you and your wife doing okay?"

"Oh, you know her. She's just as bossy as ever, and the push-over that I am, I do everything she says, as usual." Jack smiled. He'd never known another married couple that loved each other more than Malcolm and his wife, Sophie—well except for Roy and Elaine. If he got married, that's how he wanted it to be. Katrina's face flashed to mind, but he pushed it back.

"That's good. Did you need anything in particular, Malcolm?" Malcolm had been a missionary, and he and Jack had met when he'd needed a translator to accompany him and his wife to Arabia for a year. Somewhere along the way, he and Malcolm's relationship had gone from professional to friends. Malcolm had even been the one who'd helped him come to terms with his father's death.

"Nothing in the order of business. I just felt that I needed to call you. I don't know why exactly. Suddenly I just thought of you." He paused and then went on, "Has there been anything on your mind lately?"

Again Katrina's face flashed to mind. Jack leaned back in his chair. "Actually, there has. I have a guest who's been staying with me. I found her lying on the side of road. She was assaulted, and I think she'd have been raped if I hadn't gotten there when I did." He could hardly say the words. "She was left with nothing. I came upon the scene just in time and brought her home with me."

"You brought her home with you?" Malcolm asked, though his voice betrayed no judgement.

Jack ran a hand through his hair. "I know it sounds crazy, but I also know that I was supposed to bring her here with me. It was an unmistakable feeling. You know what I'm talking about?"

"Yeah, I've had that feeling before too."

A pause.

"So what are you doing with her?"

"She's working as my secretary until she goes home to her father."

"When will that be?"

"I don't know. She's so….I can't explain it. Confused, searching. She doesn't know what she wants out of life. She's like a child. I think she's afraid to go home. The man who did this to her was her father's best friend and business associate."

A low whistle rang on the other end of the line before Malcolm reminded him, "Yeah, but she's got to go home sometime, Jack. Christmas is this Saturday. Her father is probably sick with worry."

"I know. I know. I just…"

"What?"

"I don't want her to go yet."

"Do you have feelings for her?"

Jack picked up a pen off his desk and clicked it several times. "I've come to care for her," he admitted carefully. "There's just something about her that makes you want to protect her. I admit, at first, I didn't want her here, and I know she didn't want to be here. She just didn't know what else to do. I was grudgingly allowing her to stay. Yet, now that I've come to know her and she's come to trust me, I don't know if I ever want her to leave."

He paused before continuing. "However, I don't know if she feels the same way, especially after everything that's happened to her. To make matters worse, Eric is spending Christmas here and I think that he really likes her. The other night when he went out, he didn't stay out nearly as late as he normally does. He said he *wasn't in the mood.* Eric is never not in the mood to party." He tossed the pen back down onto his desk.

"Does she share your faith?"

"What?" Jack's brow furrowed at the question.

"You know what the scripture says about an unequally yoked relationship, Jack. They never work," Malcolm said gently.

Jack pictured Katrina beside him at church Sunday. She'd looked like a trapped bird. Her discomfort had been palpable. And that day he'd stumbled upon her in the gardens, she'd told him she didn't pray—ever.

He swallowed. "I don't think she does."

"You have a problem then, Jack, because…."

Jack interrupted him. "I know that she doesn't share my faith now, but I believe that in time she would. I don't see why God would have sent her here, knowing I would care for her, and then take her away from me. I've been praying that I would have a family one day and that God would send me a woman to love, and it seems that it might finally have happened."

"Yes, Jack, but what if she is there for some other purpose? What if she is meant to be with Eric? What if you're mistaken about all this? What if she agrees to marry you and then doesn't come to share your faith? What then?" His old friend's voice was gentle but insistent.

Jack glanced down at the time, not wanting to hear the very questions that had been running through his head all day voiced aloud. "I've got to go, Malcolm. I'll talk to you later."

"Jack, I know you don't want to hear what I'm telling you, but I'm only trying to help. I think of you as a son, and I don't want to see you get in trouble."

Jack's resentment ebbed. "I know you're only trying to help. I'll talk to you later. Tell Sophie 'hi' for me."

"I will. Take care, Jack. I'll be praying for you."

"Thanks" Jack clicked the phone off and, leaning his elbows on the desk, put his hands together under his chin, deep in thought.

CHAPTER 13

*B*ryan sat in his Lexus, tapping his fingers on the steering wheel. It'd been longer than a week and no sign of her yet. Where could she possibly be? He'd checked all the hospitals, expecting that man to have dropped her off at one after finding her. He'd seen no sign of her on the streets either. What if she was still with that man?

What was going on? If she was still with him, was she involved with him? His blood boiled at the thought. He was dying of curiosity. He had to find out where she was. Soon.

His blood ran cold at his next thought. What if she was dead? Was he a murderer? Well, technically speaking he wouldn't be, but he would have contributed to her death.

He hadn't wanted to hurt her. She'd forced him to. If she'd have just listened to reason, none of this would have happened. All he'd wanted was to have her be his. They could have been happy together. They were friends.

They'd known each other a long time. They'd had a great basis for a relationship.

And what about David? Ever since his daughter had gone missing, she was all he'd thought about. The man had gotten to where he called Bryan several times a day. He wasn't the same man Bryan had once known. He'd changed. And it was all Bryan's fault.

He shook off the thought. He had to find Katrina. Yet, even when he did, how could he convince her not to tell her father? How would he convince her how perfect they were for one another?

He shook his head. He'd worry about that when the time came. He brushed back his hair and straightened his tie, resolved to continue his search.

"Are you throwing your Christmas Eve party this year, Jack?" It was the third time that day Eric had asked him that, and like the other times, Jack prepared to tell him with great exasperation that he didn't know.

"You host a Christmas party?" Katrina chimed in inquisitively.

"I used to. I haven't since my father died." They were all sitting out on the patio. They'd just finished one of Elaine's wonderful breakfasts and were sipping coffee outside in the sunroom.

Eric tried again. "Aren't you going to begin the tradition again?"

"I don't know." He propped one foot up on his knee. "Why are you so interested?"

He shrugged. "I just thought it would be a good idea.

Jack pondered it a moment. "I suppose I could."

"I definitely think so," Eric winked at him, and Jack scowled. Of course, Eric was never averse to a party.

"Don't you agree, Katrina?" Eric turned to her for support. *Ah, perhaps there was the real reason*, Jack thought. A dance with a certain blue-eyed nymph. The thought didn't settle well, and his scowl deepened.

Katrina spooned some sugar into her coffee. "I don't know. I've never been to a Christmas party before."

Eric's jaw dropped as he stared at her and shook his head. "Katrina, you have been sheltered from many of the finer things of life back in Tennessee. I'm beginning to think you grew up way out in the boonies." Katrina laughed at Eric's candid comment.

Jack considered the idea. It had been three years since his father's death. He'd stopped having the party due to his grief. "I suppose it's time to begin celebrating again," he mused thoughtfully.

He knew that everyone had always enjoyed themselves at the Barringers' annual Christmas Eve bash. In fact, several people at church had asked him if he would be holding a Christmas party this year since he was home. Ever since his father had died, the holidays had been hard, so he'd always managed to make sure he was away on business so he'd have an excuse not to mingle.

He looked at Roy and Elaine to get their opinion, and they both said, almost in unison, "I think it's a good idea."

"Everybody always enjoys it," Roy stated.

"Oh, it will be so much fun," Elaine added. "I'll, of course, do the decorations and book the band. It's about time this house sees some gaiety again."

"Is it a formal party?" Katrina wanted to know.

"Yes," Elaine answered for Jack and started talking of times past. The annual Christmas Eve party had been Jack's father's tradition. When Jack had become an adult and built his own house, they'd started having it at his place instead of his father's.

After they'd all thoroughly discussed how wonderful the party was going to be, Eric stretched and announced, "Well, I'm off to hit the gym." Jack's small gym had never been used so much as when Eric had come. Every day, without fail, Eric lifted weights and ran on the treadmill.

As Eric got up, so did everybody else, all headed to perform their duties: Elaine and Roy, their household tasks; Katrina, her office organizing; Jack, business.

The clouds hung low in the sky, threatening. It was a day shadowed by a gloomy, wintry pallor. Even with all the excitement of the party a few days away, the sky looked anything but gay.

Refreshed from a shower after his morning exercise, Eric headed toward Jack's office where he knew Katrina would be busy at work. Humming a tune she'd played that had drifted down the halls to his room last night, he turned the corner and stopped dead in his tracks, his humming coming to an abrupt halt. He stood eye to eye with Jack, each of them in front of the door to the office where Katrina was supposed to be working.

Silence strained between them for a moment, during which the two studied each other carefully, and then Eric asked, "What are you doing here?"

Jack straightened. "I thought I'd check in on Katrina in

my office." The slight inflection Jack had put on *his* office hadn't gone unnoticed by Eric. "What are you doing here?" Jack asked him warily.

Eric lifted himself up to his full height also which, he noted smugly, was slightly more than Jack's was. "The same."

They stared suspiciously at one another a moment longer, until Eric made the first move by turning and opening the door. He stepped inside the room to find it empty and behind him heard Jack exclaim, "Katrina! What do you think you're doing?"

Chagrined that his attempt to be the first to see her hadn't succeeded, Eric stepped out of the office and saw Katrina striding toward them, hair flying out behind her, with a small bundle in her arms.

As she drew closer, Eric watched the furry bundle move, and Jack pointed, asking, "What's that?"

"It's a kitten," she answered, looking lovingly down at the Siamese-colored ball of fluff. "I was taking a walk through the gardens when I found it huddled under a bush, meowing pitifully. Something must have happened to its mother."

"Katrina..." Jack began in a tone of exasperation that let Eric know Jack didn't want an animal in his house.

Before he could tell her she couldn't have the cat inside, Katrina turned wide eyes up at Jack, and Eric suppressed a smile. "It's all alone. It would freeze outside. That's why it has to stay here." Katrina patted its head and received a loud purr in response. The kitten arched its head up into her hand.

"Katrina..." Jack began again. He looked to Eric for help but Eric took a step back and shook his head. He wasn't going to help Jack break it to her. *Not getting any help from me, buddy*, Eric thought.

Katrina wasn't paying any attention to either of them. She was busy crooning at the little fur ball. Jack ran a hand helplessly through his hair.

"I'm sorry, Katrina, but I don't have animals in the house." Jack glanced over at Eric again, but Eric simply pursed his lips together. He wasn't getting involved in this. If Jack wanted to shoot himself in the foot with Katrina, that was on him.

Katrina's lips turned into a slight pout as she pleaded, "Please, Jack. I'll keep her in my room. She won't be any trouble."

Eric stepped in to help—but not Jack—since it seemed Katrina had already become very attached to the little fur ball. "Aw, come on, Jack. What's it going to hurt? Besides, it's cute." *As was its master*, he thought silently.

Jack shot daggers at him. Katrina stepped closer to Jack and held the kitten up for him to see. "Please." Eric watched as Jack looked into the kitten's blue eyes, then closed his own and ground out, "Alright."

"Oh, thank you, Jack!" Katrina gushed, eyes shining.

"But you are completely responsible for it," he added sternly, sounding much like parent who'd allowed a child to have her first pet.

She nodded solemnly. "Yes."

With that, Jack walked away, and Eric heard him muttering about what a fool he was. Well, what man wouldn't grant Katrina's every wish when her eyes were pleading to him? Eric knew from the get-go that Katrina hadn't even needed his help in securing her kitty a place in Jack's home. He'd only offered his assistance to score some brownie points with her.

Katrina turned to him with a smile. "Thanks for your help, Eric."

He shrugged. "So, does she have a name?" He reached down to stroke the kitten. It was so tiny it could fit in the palm of his hand.

"I haven't thought about it yet" She was quiet for a moment, studying the animal in her arms. Finally, she decided, "I think I'll call her Fluffy."

"Fluffy?" he asked with amusement. "Kind of childish, don't you think?"

"What do you think?" she asked the kitten, holding it up to look at her. The little cat rubbed its head against her, purring loudly. "She likes it," Katrina patted the kitten's head again.

"Clearly I'm outnumbered," he replied dryly.

"Yes, you are." She stroked Fluffy once more before telling him, "I need to talk to you."

Eric grinned. "Always a pleasure, my lady. I live to serve." He walked into Jack's office and plopped down on the sofa.

Katrina followed suit, sitting down on the sofa next to him. "I need to ask you a favor."

He propped his elbow up on the back of the couch. "What is it?" If she only knew he'd give her anything.

She hesitated, during which time Eric watched Fluffy move about on her lap, searching for a more comfortable position. "Can you take me into town?"

"Why, Katrina, are you asking me out?" he teased her.

She blushed. "I just need to get a few things—like some things for Fluffy, for one—and I don't want to ask Jack because he's already done so much for me, and he's always so busy."

Yes, Jack had given her so much, most recently a kitten, and he'd given her nothing.

"No problem. Of course, I can take you." He'd love every minute of it.

"Thank you," she smiled up at him.

"But only on one condition," he added.

He saw her smile falter.

"You agree to go out with me tomorrow," he rushed to add, seeking to quell her alarm. What had she thought he'd demand?

She paused, and then slowly nodded. "Tomorrow it is then."

Eric smiled. He'd definitely gotten the better end of the bargain.

Katrina watched as Eric turned the key to his black Mustang. They backed out of the driveway and headed toward the shopping strip about thirty miles from Jack's house.

"Where all are you wanting to go?" Eric asked her.

"Just one place," Katrina named off a store she knew carried pet supplies but that also carried a few other items she wanted to pick up. It was true. She hadn't lied to Eric. She did need to get some things for Fluffy, but the main reason why she'd wanted to go out was because she wanted to get a Christmas present for Jack and Eric.

Something to show her appreciation for their friendship.

She already knew what she was going to get both of them. Call her old-fashioned, but she was going to make them each a scarf . She might not be well-versed in domesticity, and she might not be able to cook, but she'd learned how to knit as a hobby when she discovered how much she loved scarves and wanted to make a few unique ones for herself. Giving gifts that you had spent time making seemed to say so much more than simply buying a store-bought one, and she wanted to show them both how much they meant to her. All she needed was the materials. She was thinking a black one for Eric and a brown one for Jack.

When they got to the store, Eric put the car in park and started to get out to escort her inside.

"Oh," she began, "Eric, you really don't have to get out. I'll just be a minute. I'll run straight in and straight out."

Eric frowned. "I don't know if I feel right about sending you in alone, Katrina."

She scoffed. "I'm a big girl, Eric. I can take care of myself."

Eric still looked dubious, so she took a deep breath and played her ace card. She'd already thought of what she'd say if needed to get him to let her go in alone. "Look, um, it's just I need to get some..." she paused for dramatic effect and looked down as if she were embarrassed, which she certainly would have been if the situation were really the case, "personal items."

She peeked back up at Eric who was still frowning and tapping his fingers on the steering wheel, but she saw the moment when what she alluded to registered because for the first time, she saw *him* look uncomfortable.

"Okay, yeah. I'll wait for you out here. But if you're

gone too long, I don't care what you're buying," he looked at her seriously. "I'll come in looking for you," he warned.

"I appreciate it," she said, and she truly did. She knew he was just trying to protect her. "I promise I won't be long."

She glanced down at the time before opening the car door and jumping out into the cold. She'd have to hurry. She still had a riding lesson with Jack and a cooking lesson with Elaine.

She felt a prick of conscience at having deceived Eric, but it was a white lie for good, right, if she'd told it so she could buy them something for Christmas? Nevertheless, she really did pick up some feminine products to ease her conscience. There, now she hadn't lied to him.

CHAPTER 14

*J*ack glanced down at his watch. Where was she? She should have been here ten minutes ago. Had she forgotten? No, surely not. She'd been too excited yesterday when he'd let her lead the horse.

He kept his eyes peeled for her. He hadn't seen her since this morning when she'd coerced him into letting her keep a pet in his house. Why had he agreed? He ran his hand through his hair. He knew exactly why.

At that moment, he spotted Katrina bounding across the yard toward him. "Sorry I'm late. We ran into traffic on the way back."

"What?" His brows knitted together. "On the way back from where?"

"Eric took me out to buy some things." She strode past him toward the stable. "I hope I didn't keep you waiting too long."

Jealousy surged in him. "Why did you ask Eric to take you instead of me?"

Her face scrunched up in bewilderment. "I didn't want to bother you. I know how busy you are. All I did was run into the store really quick while Eric waited in the car."

"What?!" Jack's voice almost exploded, and Katrina recoiled backward.

Jack fought to control his voice. He certainly didn't want to frighten her. "You went out alone?" he asked her more calmly.

"Yes," she answered back, eyeing him tentatively. "It wasn't a big deal," she said softly.

Jack thrust a hand into his hair, frustrated beyond belief. "Yes, Katrina, it was a big deal." He'd skin Eric alive the next time he saw him. Eric should have known better! Anything could have happened.

She rolled her eyes and seemed to be getting irritated herself.

He wanted to shake her for her impudence. "You should not have gone out on your own," he repeated.

She thrust her chin in the air. "And why is that?"

He could not restrain himself and grabbed her shoulders. "Because it was stupid!" Did she not realize what she'd done? Moreover, Eric had actually allowed her to go out unaccompanied?

"Eric—was—with—me.   He—was—right—in—the—car," she spoke slowly as if he were an imbecile. "He'd—have—been—right—inside—if—anything—had—happened."

He let go of her shoulders, ignoring her statements about Eric. He'd deal with him later. "Do you realize how careless you were? There's a dangerous man out there probably still looking for you, and you go parading around the city unprotected?" He shook his head. "Bryan aside, there are tons of other people in a big city who could have hurt you! Doing something like you just did is like asking for something bad to happen!"

She'd gone very still during his tongue thrashing and, at his last sentence, her eyes turned dead cold. He realized the error of what he'd just said as she turned on her heel and headed toward the house.

"Katrina, I'm sorry! I didn't mean that!" He ran to catch up with her, but she sped up also. He followed her into the house and all the way up to her room.

"Katrina, stop! Just listen to me!"

He reached her door, only for her to slam it in his face. Before it closed, he saw the tears running down her cheeks and his heart wrenched within him. He hadn't meant to insinuate that she'd welcomed or caused Bryan's treatment of her, but that was obviously the way she'd taken it.

He pressed his forehead against her locked door and cursed himself for what a fool he was. Pounding his hand against the wall, he turned and headed for his own room, miserable.

Katrina threw herself onto the bed, her dam of tears breaking free as she heard Jack slam his fist against the wall. Fine. She didn't care if he was fuming. His anger couldn't compare to hers.

Did he really believe what he'd said? Did he really entertain the notion that she'd encouraged Bryan's advances? Did he really think her so cheap? Her stomach twisted.

How could he even consider that? He'd seen the state she'd been in after Bryan's betrayal. Why would she encourage something like that? More tears fell from her cheeks.

Suddenly, her sobs ceased, her cheeks wet. What if he were right? What if she had unconsciously led Bryan to believe there was more between them than there was? Her mind flashed back to the days before she went to Harvard. The two of them laughing together, taking walks through the courtyard, her arm linked in his, him showing her around his office, dancing with her at her father's boring parties. To her, these had been nothing more than friendly gestures. Yet, Bryan could have seen it all from a different perspective.

Surely not though. After she'd returned from college he'd asked her out several times and she'd always refused. Besides, she'd always assumed he was just trying to be nice to an old friend, not that he was seriously interested in her.

However, she'd finally given into his persistent pleas and went to dinner with him. He was the same Bryan. They'd talked as they always had. Only, when he took her home, he'd kissed her. She'd been so puzzled and shocked, she'd slammed the door in his face. She'd discouraged him every step of the way. Still, Bryan might have thought she was playing hard to get.

Oh no! What if she had brought all this on herself? She sat on her bed, trying desperately to remember every time she might have involuntarily furthered Bryan's pursuit. She hadn't gotten very far when a knock sounded on her door.

No way. Jack could just forget it. She was not going to

open that door. "Go away," she said softly, without venom. After all, she was still living under his roof. And that made her feel even worse. She was truly at his mercy. Technically, if he wanted, he could force her to open the door. It was his door, his room, after all. She hated that feeling and contemplated leaving, but she knew that she couldn't even leave without his help. She'd have to at least use his phone to call her father to come get her, or she'd need help getting a new I.D., so she could travel on her own.

"Katrina?" Elaine's voice sounded on the other side of the door.

Katrina jumped up and glanced at the clock. In her flurry of emotions, she'd forgotten all about her cooking lesson with Elaine. "Um...I'll be there in a minute!"

She ran to the bathroom and washed her red face. While quickly running a brush through her hair, she smiled into the mirror trying to erase all traces of tears. Hurrying back to the door, she opened it to Elaine.

"Sorry," she quickly apologized, "I kind of let the time get away from me."

"It's fine, hon." Elaine peered suspiciously at Katrina's face, but when she opened her mouth to question her, Katrina hastily rushed into the hall.

"We'd better start dinner," Katrina laughed nervously and headed to the kitchen with Elaine following. She certainly didn't want Elaine to know she'd been crying and start asking her questions. Thankfully, the cook took the hint and didn't probe her.

"Okay." Elaine, efficiently taking charge, gestured to the counters covered with various ingredients, "I thought we'd try a simple, homey meal. Baked chicken, mashed potatoes, etcetera. You get the picture. Oh, and for dessert, chocolate chip cookies." She held up the bag of chocolate chips and then added, perhaps because of Katrina's dubious look, "Oh, don't worry. This is the simplest meal there is to prepare. It's almost impossible to mess up. Plus, I'll be guiding you along the whole way."

Katrina took in the items, squared her shoulders, and then nodded. She'd show Eric—and Jack—that she could do things for herself. She might have been attacked, but she wasn't a victim. She could learn to cook, and she could certainly walk into a store by herself.

"You're right," she told Elaine with a shaky smile, her emotions still on edge after her blowup with Jack." How hard could it be?"

Elaine grinned and responded, "That's the spirit!" They both laughed and then set to work. Katrina felt the tension begin to leave her body as she relaxed and actually began to enjoy her lesson with Elaine.

Elaine directed her through each task, intervening every so often to demonstrate exactly how something was done, but mostly Katrina really was cooking the dinner. She basted the chicken and set the timer on the oven. She peeled, cut, and seasoned the potatoes. She likewise prepared the carrots, green beans, and other vegetables and even helped with the rolls.

Once everything was cooking, besides the cookies, Elaine piled the pots, pans, dishes, and other utensils into the foaming dishwater. They worked with a peaceful comradeship. Elaine covered the dishes in suds, scrubbed them thoroughly, and then handed them to Katrina to rinse and dry.

Katrina's heart soared. She was filled with a sense of simple accomplishment. She had actually cooked a meal!

Some might think it silly for her to feel this way, especially after all her strong academic achievements, but she couldn't help feeling extremely proud of her efforts. Suddenly, Saffron's face loomed to mind. A giggle welled up in her throat. Imagine what she would say if she could see her now! She wouldn't believe it.

Her, Katrina, cooking? No way. Katrina smiled.

Katrina glanced above their heads where Elaine had decorated the arches and doorways of the kitchen with holly and began absentmindedly humming *Deck the Halls*. After a minute or so, Elaine joined the humming, until they were both singing at the top of their lungs and laughing hysterically at each other's mistakes and made-up verses.

"Oh my," Elaine's broad chest bobbed up and down with the last of her chuckles, and she wiped the tears from her eyes, "I haven't had so much fun in years."

"Me either," Katrina agreed, and, surprisingly, she meant it. The only time she'd ever laughed so much was with Saffron, and she hadn't seen her best friend since they'd both parted ways for college. An ache filled her as she felt tears prick her eyes.

Although Saffron and she may have been shunned by most of the other kids back in their hometown, they'd had enough fun to make up for their lack of friends. They'd been constantly laughing, often drawing the attention of their baffled classmates, who never could quite figure out how only two people could seem to have so much fun together.

Katrina hastily wiped at her eyes, hoping Elaine wouldn't see her tears, but Elaine was as rapt as an owl in the night. Laying down the dishtowel, she turned to

Katrina asking gently, "What's wrong? Was it something I said?"

Katrina shook her head, then quickly suppressed the woman's feeling of guilt. "Oh no! It was nothing you did, Elaine!"

Elaine studied her fingernails, wiping flour from the side of one, and casually threw out, "Is it Jack?"

Katrina's head swiveled up. "Jack?"

Elaine glanced up. "You two had an argument?"

"How do you know about that?" Katrina asked hesitantly.

Elaine shrugged. "I heard him banging on your door, saying he was sorry."

Oh. Did Roy and Eric know, too? Embarrassment flooded her.

Well, no matter. That between her and Jack, and no matter how much she liked Elaine, she didn't want to talk about it. After all, Elaine had been working for Jack for quite some time now. Whose side was she more likely to take? The side of a man she'd known for years or the side of a woman she'd known for scarcely three weeks? That was a no-brainer. No thanks, but she didn't want to hear Elaine excusing Jack's behavior and insisting on what a good boy he really was.

"I was thinking of a friend who I miss dearly," Katrina confessed, partly because it was true and partly to turn the conversation off of Jack.

Elaine was silent a moment but didn't press the change in subject. Instead, she nodded sympathetically.

Elaine opened her mouth to speak, but they were interrupted by Roy at that moment, "Elaine," he looked frazzled, as he stuck his head in the doorway. "Come quickly, dear. I'm afraid I've made a horrible mess of things," Roy said urgently with a look of dread upon his face, perhaps because of the lecture he knew he was bound to receive from his wife for whatever he'd done. In the short time Katrina had been there, she'd found out that Roy sometimes like to overstep his bounds in the house and "help" his wife, and it didn't always end well. It was actually quite comical, really, some of the fiascos he'd gotten into in his insistence at helping her.

Elaine rolled her eyes and mouthed, 'God give me patience,' to Katrina before she turned to her husband with her hands on her hips and her lips pursed. "What did you do, Roy?"

"Elaine, just come on. We need…"

"What did you do?" she asked threateningly.

When Roy just stood there, she 'humphed' loudly and answered the question herself. "You went ahead and washed the clothes that I told you not to, didn't you?"

Roy's guilt was written all over his face, and Katrina fought a smile.

"You know you don't know how to wash clothes, Roy!" Elaine wailed in frustration.

"I just thought that since I'm finished with my outdoor work that I would help you," he stammered defensively, then went on, "but how was I supposed to know that if you put too much washing detergent in the machine that it would…"

"You did what?!" Elaine whisked past him out the door, yelling at him for his stupidity.

"What? I just thought it would be safer to have too much than too little. And this is what I get for trying to help you! That's gratitude for you!" Roy yelled back at her while following behind her to the laundry room.

Katrina half smiled. She'd heard enough of their arguments by now to know that they didn't really mean anything by it. Still, she couldn't help feeling sorry for Roy. He'd only been trying to help. Though she knew it was more than him just wanting to help his wife. The fact of the matter was he couldn't stand to sit idle. Half the time, they argued because Roy would do exactly as he had today. He would finish his jobs outdoors and then insist on helping Elaine with hers too, usually making things harder for her instead of easier.

The buzzer sounded on the oven, and Katrina hurried over to lift the chicken out of it. It smelled heavenly and was a perfect golden brown. She set it on a platter, then scooped up all the side dishes and put them in serving dishes also. The unopened chocolate chips sat on the counter. Should she begin cooking them without Elaine? From the nature of what Roy had described, she wouldn't be back any time soon. Katrina read the back of the cookie package. The instructions seemed fairly easy, and hadn't Elaine herself said it was almost impossible to mess up?

Katrina took in the prepared dishes spread over the counter tops. If she could do all that, then surely she could make cookies on her own. Bolstered, she pulled bowls and ingredients from the cabinets and set to work.

Eric sat at the table with his head bowed as Jack gave thanks for the food spread before them. The enticing aromas wafted up to greet him. This meal had to be one of Elaine's better efforts, and he told her so.

Elaine waved it off. "Oh, don't thank me. This was all Katrina's doing. I only directed."

"This is delicious, Katrina," Jack was quick to compliment, to which he received a cool nod from Katrina. Eric didn't know what had happened between those two to distance Katrina so, but he couldn't say he disliked it.

Eric stared at Katrina, and he was sure that the surprise he felt was etched onto his face. A smile tugged his lips. "So you really did it, then?"

She blushed but lifted her chin. "Was there ever any doubt I would?"

His smile broadened. "You just had to prove me wrong, didn't you?"

She bit a green bean in half, ignoring him, and he chuckled.

Jack, no doubt hating to be excluded from anything that had to do with Katrina, frowned and asked, "What are you two talking about?"

Eric answered. "I didn't think Katrina could cook a meal, and she was determined to prove me wrong."

Katrina shot him a smug look. "I did, though, didn't I?" she responded challengingly.

Before Eric could answer, Elaine and Roy began a heated dialogue describing the day's earlier misfortune with the washing machine. Honestly, for hired help, Roy seemed to cause more trouble than he cleaned up. Roy's faults, though, didn't stand out as much in Jack's mind as the love Jack bore for him, if his fond smile during their recollections was any indication.

While Jack, Roy, and Elaine were engaged on the topic

of domestic mishaps, he watched Katrina as she cut tiny bites of food, laying them inside her pretty mouth, chewing deliberately. She swallowed, and her mouth stopped moving, drawing his attention to her eyes, which were trained upon him.

"The meal really is wonderful," he told her. To prove his point, he savored a bite of buttered chicken sprinkled with basil. She smiled and must have sensed his sincerity, for her body relaxed and warmth entered her eyes. He exhaled a breath. Although he'd only been teasing her earlier, he was glad she wasn't angry with him. He certainly didn't want her acting as coldly toward him as she was toward Jack right now.

Finished eating, he leaned back in his chair, enjoying her chatter on how she'd cooked each item. The seasoning she'd used, how she hadn't cared how messy her hands got, and so on. Soon, Elaine brought out chocolate chip cookies and announced that Katrina had made them completely on her own, without her even overseeing it.

Eric picked one up, bit into it with anticipation—and almost choked on it. He watched as Jack, Elaine, and Roy all did the same. He knew at once that Katrina must have mistaken salt for sugar, and he also knew from the look on her face that she had guessed the same.

She tossed the cookie onto her plate, flicked her hair back from her face, and pouted, dejected. "I guess you're right, Eric. I can't do anything for myself. The second Elaine left the room I screwed up."

"Oh, hon," Elaine intoned, "it was a simple mistake." She cocked her head. "Come to think of it, I remember making the very same one the first time I made cookies. Only my family knew how touchy I was." She laughed.

"You should have seen my brothers trying to keep from grimacing as my father made them eat the salty cookies." Katrina smiled faintly.

"Everybody makes mistakes from time to time," Jack interjected, though Katrina made no sign she'd heard him.

"Look at me," Roy added with his hands spread helplessly, "I can't even wash a load of laundry. At least you can do that."

Katrina chuckled. "Yes. At least I can wash clothes." She'd definitely done her own laundry at college.

Roy nodded. "That's it. You have to think of the positives."

Elaine nodded her agreement. Jack was silent and downcast.

Eric took that as his cue to enter the conversation. "Yes, think of all the good things. You can wash clothes. You can cook—some things anyways. And you're going out with me tomorrow."

Jack's head snapped up, but Katrina once again paid him no mind. Roy guffawed and elbowed Eric in the ribs. "We told her to think of the positives, not the negatives, my boy."

Katrina laughed, and Eric grinned. He didn't mind being the butt of a joke if it drew such a sound from Katrina. "I call a toast"—He held up his class of tea—

"to the positives in life."

"To the positives," everyone toned in, clinking their glasses, Roy humorously, Katrina and Elaine good-naturedly, and Jack reluctantly.

Eric downed his tea, anticipating tomorrow's dawn like Christmas.

CHAPTER 15

*J*ack didn't sleep a wink. He couldn't stop thinking of Katrina and their argument. He kept playing the scene over and over in his mind, torturing himself with what he could have done differently. He knew he shouldn't have blown up at her like that. But when she'd just done something so dangerous, without even thinking of the risk. The fact was she'd scared him to death. What if something had happened to her? Didn't she realize how big Boston was? Well, technically, she'd only been on the outskirts of it, but still.

He ran his hand over his face, glancing at his alarm clock as he did so. 7:00 a.m. She and Eric would be leaving in another hour or so. Apparently, they were going to make an entire day of their date. It had been bad enough last night at dinner when she wouldn't respond to a word he said besides maybe a curt nod, but whenever Eric had announced their plans for today, it had been like he'd taken a blow to the stomach.

Was she only going out with Eric to get back at him?

He mentally checked himself. That was conceited thinking, and he knew it. Her world didn't revolve around him.

Moreover, no matter how mad Katrina may be, he knew she wasn't the type to toy with men's affections or intentionally cause jealousy. However, it was possible that she was thankful to get away from him for a while. And who could blame her after the way he'd treated her yesterday? Even though his concern was borne of the feelings he harbored for her, he'd handled the situation very badly.

Sighing, he rolled over and pulled himself into a sitting position, his hand moving to the nightstand to flick on the lamp and grab his Bible. He read his routine daily scripture, pausing to muse over certain verses that particularly caught his attention. *A fool uttereth all his mind: but a wise man keepeth it in till afterwards. Proverbs 29:11* He winced. If only he'd have read that yesterday before his row with Katrina. He continued to read the twenty-ninth proverb: *Seest thou a man that is hasty in his words? there is more hope of a fool than of him.* He grimaced, getting the point.

A few minutes later, he returned the holy book to the table, ready to begin the day, if not eagerly, then composedly.

Katrina and Eric walked side by side down the hall toward the foyer, chatting amiably. A few feet ahead, Jack's door swung open and he appeared, freshly shaven and dressed. He halted when he spotted them, and Eric wrapped his arm around Katrina's shoulders as they drew nearer, a gesture she knew did not go unnoticed by Jack. She knew she should pull away from Eric. She shouldn't let him goad Jack so, but then her mind raced back to the hurtful things Jack had said yesterday, and she stayed firmly in place under Eric's arm.

The two men didn't greet one another except for small nods of acknowledgement. Yet, as Eric and she approached the doorway, Jack's gaze bored into her, and she determinedly looked away, refusing to meet it. She didn't want to see what might be reflected in his eyes. She didn't want to feel sorry for him. She wanted to forget he was alive and have fun today with Eric.

As the door slammed shut behind them, Katrina resolved not to think of Jack anymore. She'd promised this day to Eric. Thinking of the city brought excitement, and suddenly she was eager to be surrounded by the hustle and bustle. Ever since she was a child, she'd always loved trips to large metropolises. She liked the feeling of anonymity, of being free to wander in and out of shops at will.

"What is it that's put such a gleam in your eyes?" Eric asked as he started the engine to his sleek, black Mustang and pulled onto the road.

"I was thinking of how much I love cities."

"And here I was thinking that you were just happy to be with me," he joked.

"It'll be nice to get away," she answered truthfully.

"With me?" he prodded.

She laughed despite herself. "You're relentless."

"Incorrigibly," his smile gleamed at her.

"So, where are we going?" she asked him.

"You'll see," he wasn't giving anything away.

"Not even a hint?" she asked.

"Nope." He glanced over at her and grinned. "You'll love it, though."

"Okay," she gave up and laid her head back against the seat, and he couldn't believe he was envious of a seat.

Eric put the car in park and cut the engine. Born with class, Katrina waited for him to come around and open her door. He checked a smile. She fought fiercely for her independence, yet allowed him to assist her exiting a vehicle. Did she know that a true feminist would have jumped out before the male could offer assistance? She was a woman of contradictions. That, along with every-thing else about her, intrigued him.

He took her hand and closed the door behind her.

"Thank you." Her eyes didn't quite meet his as she spoke. She'd been noticeably shier ever since they'd gotten alone.

"Mmmm," Katrina groaned, her head lifted up to the green lettering and logo above the building,

"Starbucks."

He knew by her expression that he'd guessed correctly. She was a coffee shop girl. "You like?"

She turned ecstatic eyes to him. "I love Starbucks. I'd do anything for a fresh cappuccino."

He couldn't help it. His mind took that statement and ran. He raised his brows. "Anything?"

Katrina's cheeks turned a lovely shade of pink, and he grinned. He wanted nothing more than to kiss her right there on the sidewalk but settled instead on locking his fingers with hers.

"Come on." He led them through the door into the quaint setting.

Warmth immediately enveloped them, as did the pleasant aromas of coffees. As they made their way to the line in front of the counter, he noticed the glances and head turns they received. He looked down at Katrina's head, which hardly reached his shoulder, and placed his hand under her elbow. With her dressed in a navy turtleneck, khakis, and matching scarf, and him dressed similarly in a navy sweater and khakis, he supposed they did make a noticeable couple. Not to be conceited or anything, but he rather thought they looked quite nice together.

"May I take your order?" The young man behind the counter looked between them expectantly.

Eric turned to Katrina with intentions of asking what she wanted, but she was already ordering.

"One tall toffee nut cappuccino, please."

The employee punched some buttons on the cash register. "Will that be all?"

Eric didn't know if Katrina had planned on going Dutch, but no woman on a date with him was paying. It just wasn't chivalrous. "And grande one espresso," he added before she could answer.

The cashier totaled up the two drinks, swiped Eric's card, and went to prepare their drinks.

Thankfully, Katrina didn't object to his paying.

Instead, she walked with him to a small round table by the front window after receiving their drinks.

Eric took an appreciative swig of his espresso and

watched Katrina holding the cappuccino up, eyes closed, the steam wafting up to her face. She took a tiny sip, sighed, and then looked up as if just remembering he was there.

"I believe you're in love." He saw her startled expression and could have kicked himself for his bad choice of words. "With the coffee, I mean."

She instantly relaxed. "It's so yummy. And it's been so long since I've sat in a Starbucks," she gestured around the café and trailed off.

His mouth quirked. Did she just say yummy?

Katrina frowned. "What?" Nothing got past her, did it?

"Nothing." He really shouldn't tease her.

She leaned forward, her eyebrows creased. "Really, what is it?"

His smile broadened. The temptation was too great. "Yummy?"

She sat back and shrugged, but her face heated anyways. "I say yummy sometimes. So what?"

He leaned his arm on the back of his chair. "Do you know how childish you sounded? Or how little girlish you looked?"

She raised her chin and took another sip of cappuccino. "I'm not having this conversation with you," she retorted.

He laughed. "It's okay, Katrina. I'm not making fun of you. I thought it was adorable."

She peered up at him suspiciously.

He raised his hand. "I promise."

She sat her cappuccino down and changed the subject. "What are we doing today?"

He downed some more of his espresso. "We're going to

catch the seven o'clock movie later at the Cine. But until then, I thought we'd take it easy and see where the day led us."

She nodded, her crème-colored scarf rippling with the movement.

Eric nodded to her cappuccino. "That your favorite drink?"

She nodded. "Well, one of them." She tip another sip before continuing, "At Harvard, my favorite was the caramel macchiato. Some baristas make them better than others, and the guy who made them on campus made them great."

"So you've lived here before?" he asked in surprise. Jack hadn't told him she'd went to Harvard. He knew she was intelligent, but Harvard? What else didn't he know about her?

She nodded. "I lived in Cambridge."

"So you probably know your way around Boston better than I do," he commented.

"Not really. I didn't get out much. I was too focused on my studies." She set her cup down but continued to palm the sides.

He studied her for a moment.

Catching his look, she hurried to add, "I still had fun. It's not as if I *never* went to the city. I just didn't have much time for it."

He wiped a drip from the side of his cup. "Well, we'll remedy that today. I'll show you the whole city. What do you want to do first?" He downed the rest of his espresso.

"Can we go shopping?" she asked without hesitation.

He took in her eager expression and almost smiled. He'd known that was what she'd want to do.

Katrina almost bounded out the door, she was so excited. Just because she hadn't shopped much in college didn't mean that she didn't like to. She just had different priorities then. She absolutely loved shopping.

It wasn't that she was overly materialistic. It was more the experience of being out and about that she liked. And, oh, the teeming streets looked so wonderful. Billboards and skyscrapers. Nice, quaint little shops. Huge two-story department stores. Designer labels. The beautiful sun lighting up the welcoming city.

She felt Eric's hand close around hers, now so familiar a gesture. She beamed up at him.

"If I'd have known what an affect shopping and a cup of coffee would have on you, I'd have brought you much sooner," he commented.

She flicked her hair, ready to utter a retort when she spotted a familiar flash of blonde hair. The words died on her lips as she stopped short, searching for the figure she knew so well.

"What?" Eric asked, suddenly alert. "Katrina, what is it?"

Her eyes continued to scan the teeming streets frantically. Where did he go? Had she really seen him, or was she just imagining things?

Eric grasped her arm and looked concernedly down at her, heedless to the people rushing past them. "Katrina, what…." he broke off at the expression on her face. "What happened?"

She stared blankly at him until he gave her a slight

shake to bring her back to the present. "Katrina, talk to me!" he commanded her urgently.

She looked up at him, comprehension slowly coming back to her. Eric. He wanted to know. "I thought," she gulped. "I thought I saw someone," she gestured faintly. "I thought I saw Bryan."

"Is Bryan the man who attacked you?" Her face registered a moment of surprise at his knowledge.

"Jack told me," he quickly explained.

She nodded. Or thought she did.

He tensed. "Are you sure?"

She shook her head 'no.' His face instantly relaxed.

He looked up and down the street as if canvassing the area for any sign of danger before he gently took her elbow and guided her onto the sidewalk where they began walking along with the crowds. "There are so many people here that you probably just saw someone who looked like him. Did you get a good look?"

Actually, all she'd seen was a vague glimpse. "I just saw a flash of blond hair and a similar stature," she admitted, realizing how paranoid she sounded.

"Well, it could have been anybody," he offered gently, "Most likely it wasn't him." He hooked an arm around her waist before continuing, "Don't worry. Besides, you're safe with me. I promise I won't let anything happen to you."

Katrina nodded, her heartbeat slowing. Yes, he was probably right. She'd probably just spotted someone with a slight resemblance to Bryan and panicked. The person may not have even looked like Bryan at all. Her glimpse had been from so far away. And she knew Eric was serious when he'd said he would keep her safe. She believed him.

"Are you back with me now?" Eric asked gently. "I thought I'd lost you for a minute there."

"I'm fine now." She smiled shakily up at him. "Thanks, Eric. I'm sure you're right. I probably jumped to conclusions and overreacted."

"You were as pale as if you'd seen a ghost, and then you had this blank look and wouldn't respond to me." Eric shook his head and let out a harsh breath. "Frankly, I was kind of worried about you."

"It's nice of you to be so concerned," she said sincerely.

He smiled now, wistfully. "Isn't that what friends are for?"

"Yes, and trips to the fair," she recalled.

He smiled fondly. "And picnics."

"And tennis matches," she added.

"And now shopping sprees," he supplied with a grimace and shudder.

She laughed. "We don't have to if you don't want to."

He scoffed, "I was just playing. I don't mind doing anything you want to do."

"Maybe next time you'll think twice before taking a girl who just got paid shopping," she suggested coquettishly as they turned into a little boutique off the strip.

"Indeed," he put his hand over his heart and acted as if he dreaded the prospect of shopping all day, but she knew he didn't really mind. In fact, she suspected from how well dressed Eric always was that he enjoyed shopping just as much—if not more so—than she did.

Several hours later, as it was nearing twilight, Eric and Katrina made their way to the car. Eric carried their bags. Though they'd shopped til they dropped as people liked to put it, they weren't laden down with bags. He'd found that Katrina was actually as careful and picky of a shopper as he was, only buying a select few quality items.

He glanced down at Katrina's peaceful expression as he popped the lid to his trunk and placed the bags in it. Although there'd been a few moments when she'd tensed up and seemed to be looking over her shoulder, he'd done his best to keep her distracted, and she eventually relaxed.

As they slid into the seats, Katrina turned to him with a soft smile. "I've had so much fun today, Eric. It's been great."

He savored the warmth of her smile. As she leaned back in her seat, she continued, "You've been great."

His mouth quirked, and he glanced swiftly at her before turning his eyes back to the road. "Except when that waiter was so taken with you at dinner."

She blushed scarlet and turned her head to look out the window. He laughed. He could still see the young Italian man so enraptured with Katrina that he hadn't even noticed Eric and had failed to take his order. Eric had to practically yell to call the waiter's attention—to which the waiter exhibited embarrassment for not even noticing that Katrina wasn't alone.

Eric had been amused at the time, but thinking back on it now, he felt a spark of annoyance when he recalled how the young man had openly flirted with Katrina, even after realizing his presence. The waiter definitely hadn't catered to him as much as he had Katrina. He'd even gone so far as to give him cool coffee whereas Katrina's coffee was so hot the steam could be seen wafting up from it.

It's not that it was the sub-par service that bothered him so much. As long as Katrina was given five-star service, that was what mattered to him. It was more that the young waiter had acted like a fool over her even though he'd been with her. What if they really were an item (as Eric wished they were)? Talk about disrespectful.

He commented on how the waiter had given him cold coffee, and her face turned an even darker shade of red if it were possible. "It was probably just a mistake," she offered weakly.

"It was no mistake. The man was insanely jealous that you were with me and, therefore, had a vendetta against me for making you inaccessible," he clarified.

She didn't deny it because she knew what he'd said was true, but she didn't revel in it either as some women would have. Instead she just said, "Well, I've had a good time and wanted to thank you."

"The party's not over yet," he reminded her. "We've still got the movie."

"Oh, I almost forgot," she sat up and turned to him. "You never did tell me what we're going to see."

"You'll find out soon enough."

"Will I like it?" she asked curiously.

"I sure hope so. It premiers tonight. I checked nearly every theater in Boston before finally finding available tickets. Almost every place was already sold out yesterday."

She looked more curious than ever now, yet she said humbly, "You didn't have to go to all this trouble just for me."

He shrugged that off. "You're worth it, aren't you?"

As he expected, she didn't answer. Instead, she stared out the window as they pulled into the parking lot of the theater. He led her over to the ticket counter with a hand on the small of her back to retrieve their reserved tickets. He watched the emotions flit across her face as he voiced the title.

Recognition and then pleasant surprise. He smiled, elated by her response.

In light of his recent success at bringing a cheerful glow to Katrina's face, he was more than happy he'd opted for the traditional movie date.

CHAPTER 16

*S*he couldn't believe it. Eric was taking her to see Andrew Lloyd Webber's *The Phantom of the Opera*. Although she'd read the book, she hadn't even known of this production by Joel Schumacher. Yet, judging by the mass of people swarming the theater, she assumed the rest of the world had.

Eric tightened his hold on her elbow as they made their way through the crowds into the fourth theater, Katrina holding a soda in each hand and Eric holding a bag of popcorn. They climbed up to the middle of the theater and seated themselves. "It looks as if half of Boston is here tonight," Eric commented.

"Yes," Katrina agreed scanning her surroundings. They were there half an hour early and already the seats were mostly filled.

Eric turned to her with a lopsided grin. "You act as if no one has ever taken you on a date to the movies before."

"No one ever has," she answered, then laughed as his mouth fell open in shock.

"Are you serious?" The look on his face was incredulous.

"Um-hmm," she nodded. "Well, except for my dad, which I don't think counts as a date."

He grinned mischievously. "No, that definitely doesn't count. So I guess I'm the first guy to ever take you to the movies, huh?"

It wasn't a question. It was more of an affirmation, and he looked very pleased with himself.

"Congratulations," she said jokingly. "And I suppose you think you deserve a prize?"

He sobered and his eyes held hers, charging the air with energy. Her breath caught. For several long moments, an eternity it seemed, he stared into her eyes. "Perhaps," he finally answered, then released her by blinking and taking a drink of his Coke.

She felt a prickle of fear run up her spine. She'd been merely jesting when she mentioned a prize, and she certainly hadn't meant it in any way he may have taken it. Surely he wasn't serious. She sipped on her Coke, peeking up at him as she did. This was Eric. He wouldn't hurt her. Hadn't he confirmed that time after time? She shook her head. She needed to relax.

"Popcorn?" His face was warm and caring, squashing any uncertainties she may have been experiencing. He held the bag out to her, and she relaxed, taking a handful.

They sat in silence for several minutes munching on popcorn, watching more people mosey in and out of the theater. Not an awkward silence, but a comfortable, companionable one. After a while, Eric broached a subject they'd never discussed before. "What's your father like?"

Katrina glanced at him quizzically, wondering where

he was going with this. "He's a lawyer with a charismatic personality and a soft heart. He's very affable, but he can be gruff also, especially in court." She smiled with fondness as she described him.

"So you would say that you two get along pretty well?" he prodded.

"Of course we do," she affirmed with some surprise. "Why wouldn't we?" Had he thought that she and her father hadn't had a good relationship?

"I was just asking because Jack told me you had a father you could go home to but that you didn't want to just yet, and I was wondering why." His eyes appraising her were frank.

"I...." she stammered for a reason, wondering why he was asking her all this. Why didn't she want to go home? Because she was afraid? Of her father's reaction? Or of finding Bryan there? Or because of her own pride? Did she want to go crawling home? To turn her father's world upside down with the revelation that Bryan was not the perfect son he'd always wanted? "I don't know," she finished lamely.

"Don't you think your father's worried?" he pushed.

"Yes, but....I can't go back yet," she looked up at him, a thought forming in her mind.

He must have known what she was thinking for he quickly added, with a bit of irritation that she would even think such a thing, "It's not that I want you to leave. I was just curious as to what was going on."

She sighed. "Honestly, I don't know myself. I just know that I need more time before facing my father." She became pensive as she stared unseeing at the black theater screen before them, "I don't know when I'll go home. I know I can't take advantage of Jack's hospitality forever but…." she broke off.

"Hey," he lifted her chin, "if Jack kicks you out, you're more than welcome to come home with me after Christmas." He winked at her, lightening the mood.

She gave him a grateful glance, relieved he'd put things at ease. "That's not what I meant, but thanks. That's very charitable of you."

"Oh, no, I can assure you I have purely selfish motives at heart. I enjoy your company immensely—among others things," he added humorously with a sideways glance at her that swept down her body.

She gasped just as the lights dimmed and the big screen flashed to life. He silenced her with a finger to his lips and a small *shush*, pointing to the previews beginning to show.

She crossed her arms self-consciously and huddled down in her seat, her infernal cheeks still flaming. She hated her body's propensity for blushing. Fortunately, her cheeks began to cool as she was transported to the Opera Populaire of 1870 Paris. The tragic story of the disfigured musical genius who lived in the cellars of the opera had always captured her. His doomed love for the young singer, Christine Daae, had always tugged at her heart. With each scene, each song, she felt a stirring within her soul, especially during *The Music of the Night*. This was the best portrayal of Gaston Leroux's classic tale she'd seen yet. She'd seen the 1925 film starring Lon Chaney as well as a few other film adaptations, but none of them compared to this one. It showed the Phantom not as a monster but as a character to be sympathized with. All that he did was in the name of love. Love for Christine, who represented the purity and beauty he'd always longed for. If only she had not been in love with another.

Katrina's heart wrenched within her as the first strains of Christine and Raoul's famous duet, *All I Ask of You*, began. She'd never been one to cry during movies. In fact, she couldn't remember one time when she'd cried while watching a movie. Yet, as she viewed the deep pain on the Phantom's face as he listened to the young lovers' exchange from his hiding place atop the rooftop of the Opera Garnier, she felt tears pool in her eyes.

She swallowed, blinked several times, and, feeling self-conscious because of her emotion, peeked quickly around the theater. Thankfully, she wasn't the only one touched by the scene. Several people had tears streaming down their faces. She turned her head back to the screen but felt eyes on her. Eric was staring at her intensely, but as she faced him, he averted his attention back to the screen. His solemnity unsettled her. There had been something in his look that she couldn't quite grasp. Pain? No, any pain she thought she saw must be reflected from the movie. She'd probably seen sympathy for the character etched on his face.

A grave expectation, perhaps? What did he expect of her? Realizing she was missing the movie, she put these thoughts aside with one last puzzled look at Eric's profile. She wondered what he thought of the film.

Eric turned his head when Katrina became aware of his attention. His stomach twisted as he watched the Phantom's mouth fall open in the deepest of pain as the object of his love kissed another man. He knew that pain. Hadn't he just days ago stood hidden as the Phantom was now and watched the woman he loved—yes, loved—kiss his rival?

The truth hit him hard. He did love Katrina. Of course, he'd known that he cared deeply for her, that perhaps he was falling in love with her. However, up until this moment, he hadn't known for sure that he loved her already. He hadn't known her long. How had it happened so fast?

But then again, why not? She was everything good and pure and true and innocent. His mind flew back to her timid shyness when they first met. She'd obviously always been sheltered. She'd never even been to a fair and couldn't cook at all. Not to mention the fact that until now, she'd never been on a date to the movies. All of these qualities and more were what made her endearing to him. There was something in her very nature that just drew people to her. Hadn't she befriended Elaine very quickly? Elaine whose heart could take years to soften? And her delight at finding a little kitten had been precious and true. She'd even weaseled Jack into letting her keep it in the house. He frowned. He'd rather not think of why Jack had consented.

Moreover, she'd affected him on so deep a level that he'd changed his life. For once, he wasn't trying to lose himself in parties every night. In fact, he'd been out only once during his stay with Jack. It had been the night after the fair. Sitting at the bar, surrounded by cheap women, suddenly he'd realized something that he'd never thought of in all his years: none of those women loved him. Not one of them cared about him. They were all in just as sad a state as he was, looking for answers and solace where none could be found. At the time, he hadn't known why he felt such discontent at this new knowledge. Soon, though, he came to understand that it had been Katrina's trueness that had brought to light the flaws in his life.

As he got to know her better, the more she was on his mind. At random moments, he would think, hear, or see something and wonder what Katrina would think of it. Her friendship was the most precious thing he'd ever known. And he'd come across a lot of things in his lifetime, many of which he was ashamed of. Of course, he had a great friendship with Jack, but it was different with Katrina. It was as if he had a deep soul connection with her.

After she'd gotten over her initial and understandable mistrust—for how could she not be mistrustful after what had almost happened to her?—she'd abandoned herself to their friendship with an honest, naive freedom.

Just as Christine symbolized goodness to the Phantom in the superfluous, superficial world of the Paris opera, so did Katrina likewise to him in a world filled will hatred and falseness. Yet, as the movie drew closer and closer to the end and he witnessed some of the terrible things that the Phantom did in his desperation for Christine, he was made to remember that just because you yearned deeply for something didn't mean you would always get it. Just because you loved didn't mean you would be loved in return.

He felt a deep foreboding within him. Was he destined to the same fate as the Phantom? Katrina had known Jack longer than she'd known him, just as Christine had known Raoul longer than she'd known the Phantom.

Perhaps Katrina was already in love with Jack, maybe without even realizing it? Had she not wrapped her arms around Jack and gently, but firmly pushed him, Eric, away? Hadn't Jack been the one to save her from danger? Wasn't Jack the good, stable guy who had his life in order, while he, Eric, was rebellious, a little wild, and hadn't a clue where his life was going?

Now that he thought of it, he had many things in common with the Phantom. Although he didn't have a disfigured face, he'd never known love. His parents had both died before he could know them, and his aunt and uncle had only been doing their civic duty to keep him— as they'd often reminded him. Although he could find quick companionship, he couldn't recall the names of any of them. Ultimately, like the Phantom, he was a loner. He loved Katrina in fear of never having that love returned because of his rival. His manner became even graver at his next notion. How could he have forgotten that they even shared the same name? Although not mentioned in the movie, the Phantom's name in the book was Erik, only the spelling making it different from Eric's own.

He watched the rest of the movie in dread, knowing how it would end, hoping that it would hurry up and be over. He was no longer in the mood to do anything but wallow in his self-pity. He knew he would have to summon up a brighter veneer. It would be confusing and unfair to Katrina if he were mute the whole way home. Besides, this movie had only brought to surface his worry of refusal, hadn't it? It didn't necessarily mean that the same thing would happen to him, right?

Yes, exactly. He was just reading more into this than there was. Just because he'd never been loved before didn't mean that it couldn't happen. It was just a movie after all. A movie that was supposed to be tragic and heart-wrenching.

He glanced over at Katrina and the sympathy plainly displayed on her face. One thing could be said in his favor. Katrina was here with him now. She had yet to consent to a date with Jack.

He felt somewhat better at that thought. There was still hope. He wasn't disfigured, didn't live under an opera house, and hadn't been driven to murder by the despair of rejection, though when he thought of the man who'd attacked her, he could easily see himself committing murder in order to protect Katrina. Yet even in the wake of his newfound optimism, in the back recesses of his mind remained a trace of doubt.

Katrina sat beside Eric in a daze, her mind not yet returned from the labyrinthine world of the Phantom's opera. One of the most loved stories of all time. Perhaps because it brought to light the struggles that everyone faces. Or perhaps because it echoed all of mankind's fear of being alone, without love. She didn't know exactly what made it such a compelling tale. She just knew that the scenes played out before her eyes tonight would haunt her for many nights to come.

Yet…not in a bad way.

Eric seemed to be in a similar state of contemplation because he remained silent until she softly sighed.

"Thinking about the movie?" he asked.

"Yeah," she answered absently.

"So, what did you think?"

How could she put it into words? She considered a moment before speaking. "It was deeply moving, romantic, and tragic. It was," she searched for words, one hand splayed toward the air as if waiting to catch the letters, "like nothing else in the world."

She saw him nod briefly, and then silence fell between them once again. Uncomfortable in this new silence, Katrina felt the need to speak, but just as she began to ask his opinion on the movie, he broke the silence himself.

"Who would you have chosen?" he asked so softly she almost didn't hear him.

She didn't have to ask what he meant. She knew he referred to the choice Christine had eventually had to make between the Phantom and Raoul. She was discomfited at how he'd asked the question, though, and wondered why he had.

"I think this is one of those questions you couldn't possibly answer without having experienced the situation," Katrina answered honestly. How could she know which man she'd choose without living through it?

Eric frowned and clicked off the already barely audible radio. At this action, Katrina suddenly felt like a guilty criminal about to face the Inquisition. She knew it was silly. She hadn't done anything wrong. Yet, she couldn't keep her hands from twisting together and her heart from thumping rapidly with nervousness.

He opened his mouth as if to speak, then seemed to think better of it and pressed his lips together. Katrina's agitation grew at his obvious struggle. What was troubling him?

He tapped his fingers against the steering wheel,

ticking down the seconds until her death sentence it seemed. Death sentence? Why was she thinking so grimly? Why did she feel guilty? She wracked her brain in vain. What was wrong?

His sudden outburst caused her to jump, though his voice was low and rapid. "Yes, of course you can't be sure without experiencing it, but who do you *think* you would have chosen? Just try to put yourself in Christine's shoes. Would you choose the Phantom? Or would you choose Raoul?" He paused, and then said more calmly, "Just think for a moment, Katrina."

She stared at the side of his face for a moment instead, wondering why her answer was so important to him. Though she couldn't begin to understand why, another pang of guilt washed through her. Tension hung heavily suspended between them, and, absorbing Eric's urgency, she obliged his request and began to look back once more upon the many opera scenes, only not as an onlooker this time but as the young soprano herself.

For several minutes, she played over the instances involving Christine, Raoul, and the Phantom. Her mind ran through many songs and images. Still, when Eric prompted her the second time, she was no closer to an answer than she'd been the first time he'd asked her.

"Well?" he asked in that same quiet manner.

She cast wildly about, her mind searching for a sufficient answer. Why was it such a hard choice for her? All she had to do was choose one. Whom did she like better: Raoul or the Phantom?

Suddenly, her futile attempts to make a decision were abandoned as, with a screech, Eric's foot slammed on the brakes and his right arm shot out in front of her. Katrina felt her body slam into his arm as they skidded to a stop. Eric managed to maneuver the Mustang onto a gravel road just off the highway, and she saw a red Lexus streak by in a blur.

"Katrina?" Eric was bent over her anxiously. "Are you okay?" He was shaking her now, but she was too mentally numb to care. That car had come out of nowhere and had been heading directly for the left side of Eric's car, only swerving back on the road after it missed them. That had not been a freak accident. That car had meant to hit them. Katrina recalled its model and color and began to shake. She knew whose vehicle that was.

Eric began to curse, and Katrina knew if she didn't respond to him soon, he would do something drastic.

"Eric," she croaked.

"Are you okay?" he demanded.

"How's the car?" she asked back vaguely.

He cursed again and then began to shake her again, gently but insistently. "The car," he gave a half-crazed laugh. "That's not what I'm worried about, babe! *Your* condition is my only concern. Not the blasted car! And if I don't start getting some sensible answers out of you soon, I'm going to be forced to take you to the hospital."

That got her attention. She stared at him in horror before bursting into tears.

He immediately pulled her into his arms, his voice pained at her tears. "Okay, okay. Katrina, don't cry. Come on. It hurts me to see you cry. Look, I'm sorry. I didn't mean to frighten you. It's just that the thought of you being harmed scares me to death. That blank-eyed look you had just moments ago...like you didn't recognize me or your surroundings...don't go into shock," He spoke into her hair now. "How could I live with myself if you were hurt, especially while in my care?"

"It was him!" she cried, ignoring everything that Eric had just said. It was irrelevant, unimportant. She'd barely heard him. "He's found me and now I'll never escape!" She continued to sob hysterically and, in her fear and grief, began to beat her fists against Eric's chest. "I told you I saw him earlier," she babbled on, "and now I'm sure of it. He purposefully tried to run us off the road. I know it was him!"

Eric said nothing. He just held her while she gripped his shirt and let her tears fall. He stroked her hair and back while murmuring comforts to her until, eventually, her shaking began to subside. As her hysterics gave way to calm, her awareness came back.

She pushed away from him, sniffing and wiping at her wet eyes with her hands, trying to summon up what little dignity she could. "I'm sorry," she mumbled, not looking at him. What must he think of her now? Crying all over him like some damsel in distress?

"You have nothing to be sorry for." That was all he said before purposefully settling back behind the wheel and putting the car into drive. He didn't try to dissuade her belief that it had been Bryan who nearly hit them as he'd tried to discount that she'd seen her attacker in the crowds earlier that day. He said nothing. Jaw set firmly, his eyes blazed, and, perhaps in an attempt to calm himself, he switched on the radio.

They listened to an '80s music station for the remainder of the ride. Katrina sat absorbing the words of the music, from British *Duran Duran* and Scottish *Glass Tiger* to Canadian *Corey Hart*. It seemed Eric shared her taste in music. She listened to the songs with desperation, too frightened of Eric's anger and too shaken from what had just happened to say anything. Although she knew his anger wasn't directed toward her, she couldn't help being afraid. His face was murderous, and his hands on the steering wheel were shaking with repressed rage. Of course, she knew that Eric would never hurt her, but in the wake of his newfound anger, he seemed so powerful and capable of anything, almost dangerous. Yet, although it frightened her, Katrina also felt safe and protected knowing that if Bryan were to encounter Eric in a mood like this, he would never stand a chance.

Bryan slammed the door to his suite. He clenched his fist, wanting to pound the wall, anything to release just a fraction of his anger. He stopped himself just in time, slowly lowering his taut arm. He certainly didn't want to be paying property damage costs.

So, she had someone else, did she? Was that man she was with the same one who'd intervened that night weeks ago? He shook his head and began to pace. It didn't matter. All that mattered was the fact that she was with another man. And, judging by how late they'd stayed out and where they had went, they were on very friendly terms.

When he'd spotted her on the streets, he could hardly believe his good fortune. He'd searched all over the city in vain and was on the verge of giving up when she'd finally appeared. His gaze must have attracted her because she'd glanced toward him, and he'd responded by swiftly ducking into the milling crowd. After all, he didn't want to allow her time to run away.

Then he'd noticed she wasn't alone. Well, that had complicated things a bit. He couldn't very well snatch her from that hovering bodyguard. Instead, he'd been forced to wait all day, hoping an opportune moment would arise, always having to keep a careful distance so they wouldn't see him. It had been extremely taxing, especially since that moment he'd waited for had never presented itself. That man never let her out of his sight! She never once left his side!

To top it all off, he'd sat in his car for two and a half hours while they'd watched some sappy new movie that had completely sold out. He didn't dare leave for fear that they might leave early and he'd never find them again.

In spite of it all, he still may never find her again. While impatiently waiting the movie out, he'd tortured himself with images. The little touches and caresses the man had given her throughout the day had not gone unnoticed by him. If their linked hands had angered him before, his rage had been increased ten times when they'd exited the theater, his arm wrapped around her waist possessively.

His mind had screamed in protest. She was his. *His!* After following the black Mustang for several minutes, he lost all vestiges of control. He hadn't planned it or known what it was that he'd hoped to accomplish, but in a blind fury, he gunned the gas and swerved toward the black car. His target had managed to escape at the last moment, and he'd sped off into the night before they could get his license plate number.

He fisted his hands in his hair. *Stupid! Stupid!* He'd

finally found her, but because of his uncontrollable temper he'd lost her once more. He couldn't hold David off much longer. If he didn't bring Katrina home soon, the man would get the police involved, publicity aside. He couldn't give up. Not yet. So things had taken a turn for the worst. It wasn't as if he'd never dealt with unfavorable conditions before.

He had to find her. He *would* find her. He was not going to lose all that he'd worked so hard for, all that he desired, before he even had it.

Elaine watched from her and her husband's bedroom window as a car emerged from the long driveway shrouded in trees. Eric and Katrina were back from their date it seemed. Elaine beheld the sight before her eyes with pity. Eric handed Katrina out of the car just as Jack rounded the corner of the house, back from a long walk no doubt. Her employer stopped in his tracks, and Eric paused also. The two men, once the best of friends, gave no greetings, merely stared at one another until Eric turned away and led the very person who separated them into the house. Of course, Elaine didn't blame Katrina. The poor girl most likely had no idea what she'd unintentionally caused.

She felt her husband's arms encircle her from behind. "Elaine, you've been standing here for ten minutes," he said softly.

She leaned into him and sighed. "Do you realize that both of those men are in love with her?"

Her husband turned her around to face him and

peered into her upturned countenance, crinkled with worry. He opened his mouth to speak, but she jumped in before he could.

"I know what you're going to say. I shouldn't worry about it."

He smiled and softly kissed her forehead. "How do you know me so well?"

Elaine sighed, "I just wish there was something we could do. I don't want to see any of those three get hurt, but it appears to be inevitable."

Roy was quiet, considering what she'd said. One thing that could be said in her husband's favor was that he always listened to her. That was one of the many reasons she loved him.

Finally, he spoke. "No, Elaine, this little love triangle, or whatever you want to call it, has not gone unnoticed by me. And I understand your concerns, dear, because I've had them myself, but there really is nothing we can do—except pray."

She nodded, knowing he was right, but she still feared that this would all end in tragedy.

CHAPTER 17

*T*he very day after Eric had pestered him about throwing a Christmas Eve gala, Jack had sent out many invitations. Previous successes, along with Eric's prompting, had been what had decided him on the matter of having it this year. He'd grieved for his father long enough, much longer than his father would have wanted him to, and it was now time to move on. That Katrina had seemed to like the idea didn't hurt either. Therefore, he'd agreed to host it this year.

The invitations were given on short notice, but by the vast number of acceptance responses he'd already received, he took it that his guests didn't mind the late notice.

Yet, in putting this party in motion at the last minute, he'd also unwittingly heaped a pile of work and stress on his head. Exactly what he was supposed to be getting a break from. Actually, ever since he'd found Katrina trembling in the snow, his quiet, solitary holiday had been discarded.

But who was he kidding? He loved it. Maybe he hadn't liked the idea of being Katrina's unwilling landlord and protector at first, but now he never wanted her to leave. He was even looking forward to having his party this year, even with all the last minute stress. Just as she had wormed her way into his home, so did she into his heart also.

He seated himself behind his desk, bent forward, his hands pressed together and his chin resting on the tips of his fingers, musing. Katrina had awakened a part of him that had died with his father. Although he'd gotten over his initial bitterness at his father's death, he'd never really fully recovered. He'd become a hermit, immersing himself in his work to escape any memories or pain. His life became a routine. He himself was almost a machine going through the motions of living—living his life in solitude.

He knew that pattern wouldn't have changed had it not been for Katrina becoming a part of his life. He would have spent his holidays as he had for the past few years— alone. And before her, that hadn't bothered him. He'd welcomed it, embraced it. He'd made his peace with God but had been too defeated to go back out into the world. So he'd worked and wandered aimlessly. He hadn't even been aware that he was dissatisfied. Then Katrina had led him from his solitude. He'd rescued her, but she'd rescued him too. She'd given him a purpose, a reason to live. He was alive again.

But his lighthearted thoughts took a downward turn when he remembered that Katrina was still angry with him. As well she should be. His conscience had been smarting ever since their ugly blowup. He should never have let his fear take hold of him like that, causing him to yell at her. He knew she was still hurt because she avoided him at all costs. She wouldn't even meet his eyes last night when she returned from her day with Eric. He tried not to speculate on what they'd done all day long. He'd done enough of that yesterday.

He knew he was going to have to make it up to her somehow. But how? Especially when she made herself so unavailable. He dropped his head in dejection. What he needed was some good advice.

Eric stood before the full-length mirror attending to minor details. He straightened his collar and observed his overall appearance. He wasn't fussing or primping, but rather just making himself presentable. Satisfied, he picked up the items he had laid out on the bed in the room he always stayed in when he visited Jack and headed in search of Katrina.

He hummed a light tune as he walked down the halls, sticking his head in various doors. He was still elated at how wonderfully their date had gone. Though he hadn't even so much as kissed her last night, it had been the best date of his entire life. Her companionship was enough.

Eric frowned, though, and his humming began to trail off as he recalled the two incidents that had marred the perfect day. When Katrina had said she'd seen Bryan—how he shook with anger at just the thought of the man's name —he'd tried to pass it off as paranoia. He'd honestly thought that Katrina's mind had been playing tricks on her. Of course, she would be a bit skittish after what happened to her, and the chances of her running into the man in a city as big as Boston were slim at best. Nevertheless, Eric had been even more watchful and cautious after that moment for just in case she really had spotted the man.

Still, he hadn't been prepared for the vehicle that had almost run over them. He could still hear the squeal of tires and see Katrina slumped over, deathly silent and motionless. Thank God she'd been unharmed.

After that run-in, he'd been forced to believe that she had indeed seen Bryan that morning. That move had been calculated. Someone had purposefully meant to run them off the road. Bryan was the only one with motivation to do so.

Had the man been following them all day, ever since Katrina had thought she'd seen him? Had he perhaps not liked what he'd seen? Did it anger him to see Katrina with another man?

Eric knew that it did. The man was obviously clever. He'd chosen not to show himself, giving Eric no evidence as to who he was. He could have confronted Eric and tried to take Katrina from him, but then Eric would have been able to identify him.

No, the man had stayed under cover, silently steaming. That is, until his frustration had become too much for him, and he'd finally snapped and tried to wreck them all. Well, let him steam. Eric was not giving Katrina up. Bryan had best hope that Eric never came in contact with him. He'd rip him limb from limb for ever hurting his precious angel.

Eric stopped walking and closed his eyes. He needed to calm himself. He couldn't be in a rage like this while in Katrina's company. He tried to call to mind pleasant images, most of which included the woman he sought. When he finally felt himself suitably under control, he continued on.

As he turned the corner, he heard a faint melody being played and smiled. She was in the library. Perfect. It seemed luck was on his side today. He'd only hoped to find her alone, but finding her in the library was most convenient. It would serve his purposes well.

Reaching the cracked door, he poked his head inside, affirming that Katrina was indeed the only occupant of the room. He paused before entering, savoring the unfamiliar tune. Katrina truly was talented. He'd always appreciated beautiful music. Though he played no instrument, he could sing exceptionally well.

Eric stepped into the room humming so smoothly and imperceptibly that his voice seemed only an extension of the piano. He inched closer to the piano bench with catlike grace. He strayed from his steady course toward Katrina only once to gently lay his gifts upon the eloquent sofa.

Eric drew even closer as she continued to play that amazing piece. She tossed her head, flipping her hair behind her shoulders and causing him to catch the sweet scent of her shampoo. He stood mesmerized for a moment before regaining his senses.

Katrina's fingers fumbled over the keys as she opened her eyes and saw him standing above her. "Eric…" she breathed out.

He sat down on the bench beside her. "I didn't mean to frighten you," he said. He'd purposefully come up in front of her instead of behind her because he'd been trying not to startle her. After yesterday, it was understandable she'd be on edge.

"It's okay," she said as she flipped idly through the piano book propped up before her. "I tend to become completely unaware of everything around me when I play."

"You enjoy music very much," he stated.

She smiled fondly. "It's one of my passions."

"I'm pleased to hear that."

He smiled at the slightly puzzled look upon her face.

"Why?" Her pretty brow creased. "I mean, how could that matter to you?"

In answer, Eric walked over to the sofa, then turned and presented Katrina with a book of sheet music. He watched unreservedly as a look of surprise crossed her face and then settled into delight as she read the title of last night's movie printed across the front. Next, he handed her a blood red rose tied with a black ribbon. After purchasing the music that morning, he'd gotten the rose to carry with the theme. Why shouldn't this Phantom give his very own Christine a rose? He knew it was a bit eccentric and was glad when Katrina seemed to think only of the sweetness of the gesture, if the softening of her eyes was any indication.

"Oh, Eric, it's wonderful!" she looked up at him with shining eyes. "But why are you giving me such gifts?"

He'd expected her questions and had answers prepared. "Well, after seeing how enraptured you were by the music of *The Phantom of the Opera* last night, I decided that the best Christmas gift I could give you was that music that held you so spellbound. And I can see now that I was correct."

"But, Eric, it's not Christmas yet," she protested with a little laugh.

He was ready for that one too. "Yes, I know, but I thought I'd give it to you early so that you might have time to practice before the talent show on Christmas Day."

He watched her as his words slowly sunk in. Her face was an open book, fascinating to read. "Oh, Eric, this is perfect! I've been despairing over what to play, and now I have this. You've solved all of my problems. This music will be fabulous. Oh, thank you!"

He was extremely surprised when she impulsively threw her arms around him and placed a tiny kiss on his cheek, bounding back over to the piano and losing herself within its chords once again.

Eric stood dumbfounded, rooted to the spot. Katrina had kissed him of her own accord. Had she even realized what she'd done? It didn't matter. He smiled at her lithe form upon the bench already practicing the scores. He decided not to disturb her and left remembering the feel of her arms around his neck and her petal soft lips upon his cheek.

That had turned out much better than he could ever have imagined. He grinned to himself crookedly. If that was how she would receive all of his gifts, then clearly he had some shopping to do.

Hours later, Jack was still in his study. He was so preoccupied with last-minute arrangements that when he heard his door crack open, he immediately snapped a curt dismissal. "Whatever it is can surely wait. Leave me. I'm busy." He didn't even spare a glance for the intruder.

Therefore, he was taken aback when Katrina's voice floated to his ears. "Forgive me," she was hastily attempting to close the door.

He dropped his pen and hurriedly jumped up from his chair. "No, Katrina, wait," he commanded, motioning with his hand for her to stay while maneuvering out from behind his desk.

She obeyed, albeit reluctantly, as her timid stance indicated. He cursed himself for snapping at her. She had enough reason to avoid him as it was without him adding more. "I didn't know it was you," he tried to explain. "I've been working on arrangements for the party, but it's nothing that won't keep. Did you need something?"

"I…I just wanted a pencil," she stammered, wringing her hands together. "I didn't known anybody was in here."

Jack rummaged in a drawer and pulled out the requested item. "Attempting some more writing?"

She stiffly nodded, took the pencil with a 'thank you,' and quickly made to leave, but he detained her.

"Actually, I've been meaning to speak with you." He stood before her in order to face her and to block her exit. "I think you know what about, and you've been avoiding me." She was silent.

He sighed. "Katrina, I was wrong to react the way I did the other day, and I'm very, very sorry. I should never have yelled at you or said the things I did. I'm afraid my horrible temper gets the best of me sometimes."

Still silence.

He despaired. How deeply had he hurt her? He swallowed and drudged on. "I know you may find it hard to do right now, and I know I have no right to ask it, but could you at least think about forgiving me?"

She peeked up at him and then quickly lowered her eyes when she found his focused unwaveringly on hers. He felt like the lowest scum upon the face of the earth. She nodded, and his stomach plummeted. Part of him had dared to hope that she would forgive him right then and relieve him of his misery, but the other part had known that she wouldn't. Not yet. She would need time after the hurtful things he'd implied. At least she'd agreed to consider showing him mercy.

"I need to go," Katrina spoke softly, still not meeting his eye. This time he let her go.

Whoever said that the tongue wasn't a deadly weapon had obviously never had Jack's temper or cut deep wounds with words. A familiar phrase taunted his mind. *Whosoever bridleth not his tongue...* Yes. He was paying for his lack of restraint now. What was more was that he knew he deserved the punishment.

Two pairs of eyes were on Katrina, and she felt very uncomfortable. In fact, ever since she'd entered the game room, Jack's pain-filled eyes and Eric's adoring ones had been riveted on her. The three of them, along with Elaine and Roy, were gathered around a round, dark cherry game table. Katrina tried to pretend that she didn't notice Jack and Eric's attention and watched as Elaine set up the Scrabble board. When Elaine had challenged her to a word game, Katrina hadn't known that everyone else would be playing too. More precisely, she hadn't known that Jack would be joining them.

His plea for forgiveness still burned in her mind. While she wasn't one to hold a grudge, she was slow to forgive. She had struggled with the saying 'forgive and forget' all her life. Personally, Katrina believed you could forgive, but some things you could never forget, not if they cut deep enough. Her thoughts began to wander to past memories before Elaine placed a wooden rack before each of them and bid them to draw seven tiles each from the bag full of letters.

"Who's going first?" Roy asked once the initial preparations had been made and the instructions read.

"Ladies first," Eric opted with a wink. "That way we'll know what kind of competition we're up against."

"Definitely," Roy agreed with a grin, to which Elaine huffed loudly, causing Katrina to smile.

"Of course you need to check out the competition, Roy, seeing as how you can't spell past your own name," Elaine exaggerated sarcastically.

This was met with laughter on all parts and a small grin from Jack.

"Well, would you like to go first, if you're so smart?" Roy countered back to his wife.

"No, Katrina can go first. I'm not ready yet," Elaine said, to which she received another smart comment from her husband.

Katrina didn't really mind being first, seeing as how she'd always had a way with words. While forming words with random letters might prove challenging to some, it was rarely difficult for Katrina, as she soon demonstrated. While Elaine and Roy continued their light banter,

Katrina arranged all seven of her tiles on the board to spell 'fluency.'

When she finished, she looked up to four stunned faces. Eric's mouth was actually slightly agape. "How did you do that so quickly?" he questioned.

"And with all seven letters, no less?" Roy added.

Katrina opened her mouth to explain but faltered when she found Jack's knowing gaze directed at her. Knowing? What did he know? Oh, yes, that day in the garden when she'd attempted writing, he'd stumbled upon her. She remembered their conversation afterwards about her artistic abilities and religion. Jack turned his head, and she suddenly realized that the others of their group were waiting for her answer. When no words came, she just shrugged.

"Well, that was wonderful, hon," Elaine commented before taking her turn.

The game progressed smoothly for several rounds and, aside from the tense moments when Jack's eyes strayed to hers, Katrina enjoyed herself. How long had it been since she'd done something so simple as playing a board game with friends? In fact, had she ever?

Katrina listened as Elaine, Roy, and Eric urged Jack to abandon contemplation and finish his turn already. He was holding up the game, they teased.

All of this was said with the ease of friends who had longevity, familiarity, and trust. What strange twist of fate had led her to this happy bunch? Although the extent of her circumstances still weighed heavily on her mind at times, she often found herself grateful for the company she was in. She honestly didn't know what would have happened to her without these kind people. An unexpected rush of tears sprang to her eyes, and she fought to keep them at bay.

By the time she had her tears under control, it seemed that the others had finally badgered Jack enough. "Alright," he said with a supplicating gesture, "I'm ready, okay?"

They all feigned shows of relief while Jack grumbled and placed his tiles on the board. Halfway through with his task, he looked toward Katrina as if trying to tell her something. *What?* She slightly raised a brow at him in confusion, then looked down at the board as he took a deep breath and laid down his last two tiles.

"Finally!" Eric complained as he proceeded to take his overdue turn. But Katrina stared at the letters Jack had just arranged. 'S-O-R-R-Y.' She looked up into his eyes and saw the true apology and regret in them. Her face softened as her hard feelings left her, and she felt those dreadful tears ready to spill over again. She quickly blinked them back, swallowed, and then sent the slightest of smiles Jack's way.

He smiled a secret smile at her, the relief evident on his handsome face. She felt a moment of guilt herself then, realizing what she'd put him through. Contrite, she thought of asking his forgiveness also, but one look at his expression told her it was unnecessary.

Katrina smiled softly, almost shyly, to Jack, and the mellow cloud that had seemed to hang over the two lifted. Eric, who'd been studying his tiles throughout the whole exchange, obliviously formed his word. And if Elaine or Roy noticed the silent exchange, they made no notion.

Later that night, Roy softly closed the door and turned to his wife with a sigh, a reprimand for her meddling ready at his lips.

Yet before he could utter a word, she was prattling on about her happiness that Jack and Katrina had made up. So caught up in her glee, she was speaking so quickly he was having a hard time following what she was saying. But that's how his Elaine was. Shy and distant in public, but warm and exuberant around those she knew well.

"Oh, Roy, isn't it wonderful? Did you see the way those two looked at each other after Jack's clever apology? They communicated without even speaking. How romantic!" Elaine clasped her hands over her chest, her curls bobbing with the movement.

Roy frowned. Females found romance in the oddest things. "How is not speaking to each other romantic? I thought women wanted you to talk to them?" he asked with true curiosity, his brow furrowed. Elaine disregarded his question, though, and continued with her chattering.

"Once I realized what Jack was spelling, I wanted to get up right then and kiss him myself!"

"Well, I'm glad you didn't," Roy stated frankly but, again, his wife paid him no mind.

"I had planned the game in hopes of their reconciliation but was beginning to worry when the tension between them remained for so long. Then, finally, Jack decided to do something about it, and the rest of the night was perfect after that."

Elaine paused for breath. Roy saw his opportunity and took it. "Nevertheless, Elaine, you should never have interfered. Mark my words. Affairs of the heart are best left alone. You know better. You shouldn't meddle in other people's personal business."

"Ridiculous," she tossed her head, looking him straight in the eye, "I wasn't meddling. Merely prodding. They needed an opportunity to come to terms with one another, and I provided one. There's nothing wrong with that." Her eyes dared him to challenge her.

This was one battle he did not want to have. "My dear, things were hardly perfect after your little scheme." Far from it actually. With the renewed amicability between Jack and his guest had come the renewed strife between Jack and his friend. It seemed that things would never be peaceful between those three with emotions as they were.

He knew that Elaine's thoughts were parallel with his own, and he raised his brow at her. She shrugged. Then, ever one to justify herself, stated firmly, "Well, it certainly wasn't any better when Katrina and Jack were mad at one another."

Roy threw his head back and laughed. He would never get over loving this woman. Just as she made to move away from him, he grabbed her waist and looked down at her. "You are a minx."

"I don't hear you complaining," she retorted.

"No, I'm not," he lowered his head until it was just inches from hers. "You said something earlier about communicating without words being romantic?"

"Without speaking," she corrected as her husband buried his hands in her hair. "Technically, Jack used words. He just didn't speak them…"

"Whatever," Roy cut off her sentence by covering her mouth with his.

CHAPTER 18

*K*atrina startled when the small creature sprang lithely into her lap, and then she smiled, deftly stroking the kitten's furry body as it purred contentedly, flexing its paws against her silk robe. Unable to resist the cuddly bundle, she bent and nuzzled her head against its. It returned the gesture, arching its own head against Katrina's chin.

"Now, Katrina, you are going to have to sit still," Elaine fussed as Katrina's movements threw all of her careful handiwork into slight disarray.

"Lighten up, Elaine. I'm sure a little bump or two won't mess up your masterpiece too much. Besides," she held up the kitten, its purr as steady as the hum of a refrigerator, "who can resist this cute little face?"

Fluffy meowed right on cue, and Elaine laughed. "Clearly I'm outnumbered. What is this—mutiny?" She leaned back, curler in one hand and brush in the other, frowning down at pet and master.

Katrina shrugged and swiveled around on the cush-

221

ioned bench to face the vanity mirror. "Not mutiny but majority," she answered simply. Elaine muttered good-naturedly and resumed her sculpting and shaping of Katrina's hair.

Katrina reveled in the light teasing between Elaine and herself. It reminded her of the constant banter she'd shared with Saffron. Goodness, she thought of her best friend more these past few weeks than she had in all those years at college. Why was that?

Did she simply miss her friend who was a continent away? Was it perhaps because she longed for the way things used to be before any of this happened? Or was it because she felt shamed at knowing that never would Saffron have allowed herself to get into a predicament such as the one Katrina found herself in? Maybe it was a combination of all. She did miss Saffron's strength and vitality. She felt a bit guilty too. It was almost Christmas, and she hadn't contacted her at all. Usually they made plans to see each other at least one day during the holidays. What must Saffron think? Was she worried? Had her father contacted her and told her she was missing? Yes, Katrina was sure that her father would have called Saffron to see if she knew anything of her whereabouts.

She felt a pang at the thought of not spending the holidays with her friend or father, but it couldn't be helped. She wasn't ready to face the real world again.

In fact, would she ever be?

The thought of living out the rest of her life here, snuggly enclosed in the bubble of Jack's manor, was tempting. She had come to love everything about the place and felt completely free. She would be perfectly happy to preside under his kingdom forever.

Yet, she quickly suppressed such thoughts. They were impossible. She couldn't hide here forever. For the holidays at least, she was safe. That was enough for now. And after that… She'd have to wait and see what happened.

"Voila. I'm finished," Elaine announced.

Katrina looked in the mirror and gasped. The reflection she saw was her own, but surely that could not be her! The woman staring back at her was breathtakingly beautiful. She, Katrina Weems, did not look like that.

Elaine had transformed her straight hair into many thick curls and ringlets that cascaded halfway down her back. She didn't know how in the world Elaine had managed it, but every single strand of hair was curly from root to tip. Why, if she didn't know herself, she'd believe the curls were natural.

And her face! Elaine had applied makeup, but with such subtlety that it merely enhanced her features. Her face was a smooth ivory with the slightest blush of pink upon her cheeks, and her eyes were defined with the lightest touches of mascara and brown eye shadow. Katrina lifted a hand to her cheek and said, "Elaine, this is not me! I do not look like this! I am not this pretty!"

Elaine laughed and placed her hands on Katrina's shoulders. "Of course it's you, silly! The mirror doesn't lie. You're radiant," she squeezed her shoulders gently.

"Elaine, you have a gift. You truly do work wonders. I don't even recognize myself."

"I'm glad you like it," Elaine beamed.

And it was true. When Elaine had shown up at Katrina's door earlier saying that she would transform Katrina for tonight's party, Katrina hadn't known just how true that statement had been. Already dressed and styled herself, Elaine had devoted the next couple hours to *creating* Katrina. Perhaps hair and makeup styling really was a form of art.

"I do like it," Katrina assured her.

They both stared at her reflection for a moment more before Elaine announced that it was time to put on her dress.

Katrina watched as Elaine rummaged through her closet, finally debating between a simple white dress that was off the shoulder and flared out at the bottom and the slinky dark blue one with the empire waist and flowing fabric that looked like something from a medieval fairy tale. She recalled the embarrassment she'd felt when the sales lady had ushered her out of the dressing room for Jack's approval. Elaine lifted a hanger and turned to her with a purposeful smile. Somehow Katrina had known she would choose the blue one.

Jack's mouth fell slightly agape, and he almost dropped his glass of champagne as his eyes caught movement at the top of the stairs. Malcolm didn't seem to notice because he kept on talking about the fluctuating stock market that had interested Jack only a moment before. "Last Monday the prices..." his friend and business associate droned on, the words barely registering with Jack.

But Jack's gaze was riveted on where Katrina stood resplendent in the silk dress she'd bought weeks ago when he'd taken her shopping. He suddenly realized that he must resemble a gawking teenager and closed his mouth, but he couldn't tear his eyes away.

He watched, mesmerized, as Katrina descended his ornate and lavishly decorated staircase. Her fingers trailed lightly over the holly and other greenery twisted around the railing, and her dress flowed and swayed with every step. He vaguely noticed Elaine trailing behind her, so intent was he upon the figure growing ever closer to him. Katrina was always so beautiful. He'd thought it impossible for her to be more so than she already was, but tonight it was as if she were an apparition, so pure was her beauty. It wasn't only the flattering dress either. Her long hair was a mass of curls that flowed down her back, and her face bore the barest hints of makeup, just enough to highlight her naturally lovely features. He'd only seen her wear makeup a handful of times and then she'd only been trying to hide her bruises. In short, she was glowing.

She reached the end of the stairs and, at this point, he forced himself to look away. What was wrong with him anyway? He was acting like he'd never seen a woman before in his entire life. He turned back to Malcolm, but not before noticing Eric in much the same state as he himself had been just moments before.

Yet, he also noticed, with not just a little anxiety, that once Eric snapped out of his stunned state, he made a beeline for Katrina. Jack unconsciously curled his hands into fists. Eric's always smooth and ready words floated to his ear, "Ah, Katrina, you are a vision of loveliness." At this, she blushed and lowered her face, murmuring something that he couldn't hear. Jack could feel the blood pounding in his head.

A vision of loveliness? Who did Eric think he was? A silver-tongued suitor of the aristocracy? He was trying to turn her head with pretty words and compliments just like…like he'd planned to do himself, Jack realized with a pang of chagrin.

Well, why shouldn't Eric compliment her? He, Jack, had no claims on her, no right to be angry. Then again, Eric could find any woman, had had many in fact. Why couldn't he just leave Katrina alone?

"Mercy, man, why don't you go over there yourself before you burst?" Startled out of his reverie, Jack turned once again to Malcolm and realized the man hadn't missed a beat.

"I'm afraid I've been ignoring you," he admitted.

"Understandably," Malcolm replied, a thoughtful look upon his face. "You know, I've never seen you like this before, Jack. I'll admit, when we first spoke of her on the phone, I wasn't completely convinced of your feelings, but this must be serious for you to carry on the way you do. In all the years I've known you, I've never seen you react to anyone in such a way. Not one of the many pretty faces that some would sell their souls to have a date with have ever interested you, even when they were practically throwing themselves at you."

Feeling slightly embarrassed, Jack made no reply. Instead, he stated, "I'll be back." Malcolm motioned him on with his hand and raised his glass to his lips.

Frankly, what Malcolm had just disclosed rankled.

Were his feelings so obvious? He certainly hoped not. Perhaps Malcolm just noticed because he knew him so well.

Jack walked over to where Eric had stationed himself beside Katrina like a sentinel guarding his property. Well, not for long. He was not going to allow Eric to keep her secluded in a corner all evening. She needed to mingle with other people as much as a healing process as anything else. She couldn't live in fear forever.

You keep telling yourself that, a voice in the back of his mind taunted. *You just don't want to see her with Eric.* Tightening his jaw, he tried to quell his subconscious. She *did* need to interact with other people. For the past few weeks, she'd only really been exposed to Elaine, Roy, Eric, and himself.

He slowly made his way through the milling crowd, smiling and stopping to extend courtesies along the way. Finally, he reached his destination. Yet, so absorbed in conversation were Katrina and Eric that they didn't even notice his presence at first. After a few 'ahems,' he finally got their attention.

Katrina blinked and looked up at him while Eric glowered.

"Hello, Jack," she greeted him with a sweet smile. "This is a wonderful party. The decorations are stunning," she gushed.

"Thank you. The turn-out was rather well." Jack took inventory of the masses of people swarming the polished floor, refreshment tables, and French doors. Exceptionally well. "

You look splendid," he added.

While she blushed and thanked him, he turned and greeted Eric with a calm voice. He had to admit that one thing he'd always prided himself on was his control. Surely no one could guess the storm brewing just below the surface of his forced gaiety.

Eric responded with barely a nod, and Jack's heart knew a moment of heaviness. He truly regretted the tension that now seemed ever present between the two of them. He missed their times of easy friendship and wondered if they would ever have that again or if hard feelings and suspicions would always remain between them.

"Would you forgive me if I stole Katrina away for a moment, Eric?" He tried to make his voice light and jovial in order to avoid a confrontation with Eric. Yet, Eric's eyes darkened dangerously anyways. Perhaps he hadn't used a wise choice of words. "I would like to introduce her to some of our guests," he explained.

Eric shrugged and matched Jack's happy air. "I don't mind if she doesn't." However, his expression contradicted his statement.

"Oh, I don't mind," Katrina chimed in, her eyes wide.

A moment of disappointment showed on Eric's face. "I'll find you later then," he spoke to Katrina, of course. Heaven forbid he even spare a glance for Jack, his rival. In his insolence, Eric told her, "Save at least ten dances for me."

Katrina laughed. "As if you would allow me to do otherwise." Eric winked and finally retreated into the crowd. Jack watched Eric stop to speak with Mr. Firmin and his wife and then the orchestra crew as they were setting up.

Silence was suspended between Katrina and Jack as he fought the urge to pummel Eric for his swagger. In control once more, he motioned to Katrina, "Shall we?"

She took his proffered arm, and they left the shadowed arches. He could sense Katrina's nervousness at the curious looks and stares she received. Her grip on his arm was gradually tightening, his suit bunching beneath her fingers. He instinctively placed his hand atop hers, attempting to put her at ease. Apparently, it worked because she loosened her grip, her arm going lax. She didn't stay that way for long, though.

When a young man suddenly appeared before them, her fingers dug almost painfully into his arm. Jack didn't recognize the man but guessed him to be a few years younger than he. Jack's party wasn't exactly an open event, but he did permit his guests to bring their own guests. Consequently, he wasn't familiar with all the faces around him, but that had never been a problem in years past, so he allowed it.

Not surprisingly, the man, probably not knowing Jack to be the host, spared barely a courteous nod his way before addressing Katrina. He flashed a smile that was meant to be charming as a lock of blonde hair fell across his forehead. His voice inquisitive, he cut to the chase, "Excuse me, Miss. The orchestra's nearly set up, and I was wondering if you would honor me with a dance?"

Jack automatically disliked the fair-haired man. What made the boy so sure that Katrina wasn't with him? Was it so unthinkable? Jack was miffed. He looked the boy up and down. He reminded him of an over-eager puppy, tongue lolled out, begging and pawing at an unwilling lady's skirts. And unwilling is exactly what Katrina was. She seemed to be shrinking back from the attention. He could just imagine her hands up to fend off the exuberant lap dog.

Still ruffled by the man's earlier assumption, Jack intervened, "She won't be dancing just yet, thanks." He watched the boy's eyes shift from Katrina to him and back again, trying to gauge what they were to one another. Jack knew what he must have concluded when he seemed to deflate, his tail between his legs. "Oh, well, when you're ready…" he smiled apologetically and left them.

As for Katrina, she seemed as if she didn't know whether to be grateful for his rescue or outraged at his arrogance of answering for her. Before she had a chance to decide, he went ahead and explained, "You looked like you needed a little help."

"I could have managed," she stuttered, though it was said in a mild and unconvincing tone of voice.

He chose not to debate the issue and tactfully changed the subject. "How about some refreshments? The champagne is a fine vintage."

"Sure," she relented. It seemed gratitude won out over any resentment at his audacity. He realized he was stalling his initial purpose of presenting her to other people, but perhaps a drink would help calm her some.

No matter what she said to the contrary, she'd frozen back there when that boy had spoken to her. "Jack, can I ask you something?"

"You just did," he pointed out lightly.

She gave a tiny smile, "Clever. But, really, I'm serious." They neared the cloth-covered tables laden with delicate hors d'oeuvres and fine drinks.

"I'm kidding. Of course. Ask me anything." He selected two glasses and handed one to her. "Would you care for anything to eat?"

She quickly finished her sip, then shaking her head said, "No, thanks. This is fine."

Jack steered them out of the line of traffic near a vacant wall. "Now, what was it you wanted to ask me?" He proceeded to take a sip of his own champagne, savoring the dry taste.

"Well," she ran her finger along the rim of her glass, "I was just wondering about something," she glanced up at him hesitantly.

He swallowed. Did she know how tempting she looked with one long curl falling in front of her shoulder like that? "Yes?" he prompted.

She wiped the bead of moisture on her fingertip against the side of her glass, then looked him square in the eye. "What's going on with you and Eric?"

He almost choked on the sparkling white wine. He didn't know what he'd expected her to ask, but it certainly hadn't been that. "Pardon?"

"It just seems as if you two have been a bit...estranged lately. I know it's really none of my business, but when Eric first came here, you seemed almost like brothers, yet now you hardly speak to one another. I can't imagine what could have happened," her eyes were innocent and questioning, concerned about his relationship with his friend. She really had no idea.

"Can't you?" he countered softly before he could stop himself. Her brows furrowed in confusion while he silently cursed himself. He desperately hoped she wouldn't grasp his meaning.

She did, though. He knew the moment comprehension dawned on her. Her cheeks flushed, her lips parted, and her eyes swirled with too many negative emotions: understanding, guilt, shame, pain.

Why could he not just keep his mouth shut when he was around her? Better yet, why could he not just stay away from her since lately it seemed as if every time he got near her, he hurt her?

"Jack," she fumbled for words, "I don't know what to

say. I feel terrible." And self-conscious, he could tell. Well, what woman wouldn't feel that way after having a man insinuate that she had come between him and his best friend? He may as well have boldly declared, *Oh, yes, Eric and I dislike one another now that we're rivaling for your affections.*

Talk about pressure.

Chastened, he grasped her hands with his own and willed her to meet his eyes. "Look at me, Katrina." She obediently did. "Don't worry about it. Eric and I are not your concern. You are not in any way to blame for how we act. I'm sorry. I don't know what came over me. I'm a fool."

She looked extremely uncomfortable. "You were only telling the truth."

He squeezed her hands. "Let's just forget about it, okay? Please?" He certainly didn't want a rehash of a couple of days ago when they hadn't been on speaking terms.

She seemed relieved to do just that and nodded in assent. Just then, Jack glanced up to find Malcolm hailing him from across the room. He held up a hand in response and began moving them in that direction. "I'd like to introduce you to Malcolm. He's a close friend and business partner of mine."

"You were his translator?" she appeared interested. Glad she was back to normal, he answered eagerly,

"Yes, and traveling companion."

"But isn't that his wife standing beside him?" she inquired.

"Ah, yes, that's Sophie, but this was before he was married. It was when he was a missionary," he observed her reaction to the word *missionary*. She looked surprised but only said, "Oh."

"It took you long enough," Malcolm jested. "This must be your young friend, Katrina," he appraised.

"How's my girl?" Jack asked as he gently tickled Malcolm's three-year-old daughter, who squealed in delight.

Jack made the rounds of introductions, including Malcolm's wife and daughter, Sophie and Melanie. Although a bit shy, Katrina got on well with Sophie, and Jack felt himself relax for the first time that evening.

"She is a bit flighty," Malcolm muttered to him after several minutes, "which is understandable considering…" he trailed off as Jack's eyes flashed at the reminder of the injustice done to her. "Anyway, I find her quiet modesty and shyness charming and wish you the best of luck, Jack, but she needs more than you can give her, if you get my meaning. Just remember that."

Jack recalled their earlier telephone conversation about unequally yoked relationships. He knew that was true, but surely he could teach her of Christ's love, and in time, she would come to see the truth. "I know, Malcolm, and I will remember."

At that moment, Melanie, who'd been studying Katrina in typical childlike curiosity, wriggled her little hand free from her mother's restraining hold, tugged on Katrina's dress, and piped up in a sweet little girl's voice, "Are you an angel?"

Jack laughed at the precious little girl along with the proud parents, while Katrina blushed and looked down at the child peering up at her. Clearly flustered, Katrina answered, "Um, no. No, I'm not."

Melanie was unconvinced. "But you look like an angel," she insisted. "You have yellow hair," she stated as if that explained everything.

Jack and Malcolm watched in amusement as Sophie tried to reason with her daughter. "Katrina's just a very pretty lady with blonde hair, honey. Lots of people have blonde hair. Like your friend, Anna. Remember Anna's yellow hair?"

"But, Mommy," Melanie whispered loudly, "she looks like the angel in my picture book."

Sophie smiled and pointed to Katrina, who appeared embarrassed at the attention she was receiving. "Yes, but she doesn't have wings or a halo."

At this Melanie paused and studied Katrina, her little head cocked, before persisting stubbornly, "Where are your wings and halo?"

Katrina, at a loss for words, just smiled kindly at the girl.

Melanie took another step closer to Katrina. "Did you leave them in Heaven?"

By this time, the music had started, and people were already moving across the dance floor. Perhaps noticing Katrina's discomfort, Sophie intoned, "Malcolm, I think it's time we took her back to the room."

"Yes. It's getting late," Malcolm agreed. "That's probably a good idea." He turned to Jack and Katrina. "If you'll excuse us, we'll be stepping out for a short while."

Once they were gone, Jack said to Katrina,

"Melanie's an adorable little girl."

"Yes, she is," Katrina agreed, watching as Malcolm and Sophie spoke with Elaine while Melanie looked back at her. The child waved animatedly, and Katrina waved back.

Jack smiled. He guessed Katrina hadn't been around children much. She seemed unsure of how to respond to the child, yet Jack bet that she was pleased that Melanie liked her so much.

"You know," he stated. "they say that children and animals are very perceptive about a person's true character."

"Yes, I think I've heard that," she commented as the first song died down and a new one began. "Though I would have to say that I am far from an angel."

"*Au contraire,*" Jack contradicted, "I would have to say that you are everything angelic."

He had only a moment to admire the delightful blush that stained her cheeks before he spied Eric making his way slowly but surely toward them.

Jack looked back down at Katrina. He would have to make this quick if was going to bed Eric. "Katrina, would you care to dance?"

She assented, and he led her onto the dance floor. He glanced up and saw Eric seething from across the room at being bested. Putting Eric from his mind, he deftly led Katrina through the motions of the waltz, all the while noticing how graceful she was. With one hand engulfing hers and the other clasped around her tiny waist, he was once again struck by her delicateness. It would not take much for him to crush her. The thought both excited and frightened him. She was so fragile, so much in need of protection. He unintentionally pulled her closer to him.

After he did, she suddenly pulled out of his arms. "I'm sorry, Jack. Please excuse me for a moment." With that, she began moving toward the doors with purposeful strides, her face a mask. Had he offended or frightened her so badly that she was returning to her room? Stunned, he could only stare after her as she left.

Regaining his senses, he asked in confusion, "What? Katrina, wait, I..." She ignored him and disappeared into the hallway that led to the rooms. Feeling slighted and very much a fool, he stood alone in the middle of the dance floor as pairs of dancers continued to swirl around him in a blaze color.

CHAPTER 19

atrina raced into the hallway, hoping to quickly catch up with Elaine before she lost track of her. She hadn't meant to be rude, but the whole time she'd been dancing with Jack, she hadn't been paying a bit of attention to him. Her eyes had been glued to Malcolm and Sophie leading a resistant Melanie out. She felt responsible for the little girl's unhappiness because she knew that her parents were putting her to bed for her sake.

As the child had looked back at her with undisguised adoration, her heart had wrenched within her. True, she'd never been around children much and wasn't sure how to act around them, but she was flattered that the little girl seemed to attach herself so innocently to her.

When Malcolm and Sophie were intercepted by Elaine, who spoke to them with many smiles and glances at Melanie, finally taking the little girl's hand and relieving the parents of their duty, Katrina saw her chance and sprang for it.

Quickly excusing herself from Jack, she'd hurried after them, struck with inspiration. She knew something that would surely cheer Melanie up from her banishment. She entered the hall just in time to see the pair turn right at the Gothic statue of a lion's head at the end of the hall. She quickened her pace until she was almost running and called out to Elaine.

Elaine turned to her in surprise, while Melanie's face lit up with glee. "Katrina?" Elaine asked.

"It's the angel I told you about," Melanie cried excitedly as she rushed to Katrina's side and wedged her hand into hers. Katrina found herself smiling at the sensation of Melanie's small palm pressed against her own. It was infinitely sweet and touching and made her wonder if she'd ever have her own child. It was a strange thought, for she'd never really been the kind of girl who dreamed of having children—not seriously anyway. Of course, she and Saffron had played pretend they were mommies were they were kids, but as she'd gotten older, a family and children had never really been at the top of Katrina's list of goals. A career and success had been her focus. She'd always thought the other could come later on after all that.

Katrina glanced up to see Elaine smiling broadly at them. "Is it alright if I come with you for a few minutes?" she asked, knowing that Elaine wouldn't deny her.

Her face held a knowing look. "Of course. I've agreed to watch her so her parents can enjoy themselves longer and also so she doesn't have to go to bed just yet," Elaine explained as they walked.

"We're going to the game room to watch movies.

Aren't we, Melanie?" she asked, looking for feedback. Melanie nodded emphatically, "Yes!"

Katrina squatted down to Melanie's level and told her, "I have a surprise for you that will be really fun." Elaine's eyes were questioning, and Katrina silently mouthed 'kitten' to her, to which she received a 'genius' and thumbs up.

"Su-prise?" Melanie mispronounced the word sweetly.

"Uh-huh," Katrina nodded. "Let me go get it, and then I have to go back to the party with the other grown-ups."

Melanie's lips formed a pout. "But I don't want you to go back to the party. I want you to play with me."

Katrina was debating on just how to answer when Elaine rescued her from the sticky situation. "She has to go back, Melanie. There are a couple of young men who are counting on her to be there to dance with them."

Katrina's eyes shot to Elaine who only winked at her. "Besides," she continued, "if she doesn't go, she won't be able to give you your surprise. You want your surprise, don't you?" Elaine imparted this last information with the utmost seriousness.

Eyes wide, Melanie nodded. "Okay," she said slowly, "but hurry."

Katrina laughed, "I will, sweetie."

And she did. She went straight to her room and got Fluffy, careful not to get the cat's hair on her dress. One very rambunctious and purring kitten in tow, she made true to her word and hurried to an equally rambunctious and awaiting child.

When she entered the game room where Elaine already had a Disney movie playing and presented her gift to Melanie, she was very glad that she did.

"A kitty!" she squealed, running over to the kitten, which basked in the attention.

Mission accomplished, Katrina left Melanie giggling as Elaine dangled a string above the playful, pouncing kitten. Katrina's idea was successful because so taken with the kitten was Melanie that she didn't even notice Katrina's exit.

Heart full and satisfied that Melanie hadn't been punished on her account, Katrina returned to the ballroom. She skimmed the edge of the room still smiling to herself, all of her earlier nervousness at the number of people gone. There was nothing to fear here. Jack's house would protect her. Jack would protect her. As people walked by, they only smiled at her and politely greeted her. There were no leering eyes or unkind faces. Completely content, Katrina leaned lightly against the wall and gazed at her surroundings.

She was so absorbed in her daydreams that she didn't notice Eric standing beside her until he spoke.

"Hello, there."

She jumped with a gasp. "Eric, you startled me!"

"Sorry," he replied lowly. Leaning closer, he added, "You're spending a lot of time in fantasy worlds here lately." He traced a finger along her jaw line. "Would you mind telling me what's in them?"

She pulled her face back. "Nothing," she answered.

Eric sighed. "You think of nothing?"

"What were you expecting me to say?" She asked with furrowed brows as she stepped back as a waiter passed before her with glasses of wine precariously balanced on a silver tray.

Eric followed, causing her to retreat until her back was

pressed fully against the wall. "I was rather hoping that you'd say your thoughts are filled with me as mine are with you," his eyes darted between hers, searching for some sign of light. Katrina only bit her lip and looked away. Eric stared at her bottom lip as she chewed on it nervously, turning it redder and fuller. He could feel his blood running hot and quickly stepped back from her.

As for Katrina, her mind was thinking of Jack's earlier confession that she was what stood between him and Eric. He hadn't meant to say it and had later denied its truth, but Katrina knew otherwise. She knew the truth when she heard it. She truly felt horrible, and her heart was torn in two between the two men.

Eric shook his head, trying to clear it. "I believe you promised me many dances, yet I have yet to receive even one." He held out his hand to Katrina.

She stared at his waiting hand for several moments, then looked up to see the open affection in his eyes. "So I did," she replied, stepping away from the wall.

After a few moments of silence, Eric spoke softly with twinkling eyes, "Then may I have your hand, please?"

"Oh, right," a tell-tale blush crept up her cheeks. "Sorry," she said as she placed her hand in his.

"It's certainly nothing to apologize for. I flatter myself that the reason for your momentary lapse was due to the prospect of dancing the night away with me."

"Actually it was," she watched Eric's eyebrows shoot up in astonishment. A grin came over his face.

"I am simply overwhelmed," she continued with a teasing smile. "How ever will I survive it?"

Eric feigned hurt, placing his hand over his heart. "That was cruel, Katrina. And just for that I will not release you for the remainder of the evening." He took her waist in his hands. "You are mine tonight."

Her breath caught, and her heart quickened at the look in his eyes. She made an attempt to step back and put some distance between them, but he was having none of it. "Dance with me," he commanded deeply. He was darkly handsome and commanding, his voice irresistible, smooth silk.

His eyes held hers captive, and, entranced, she obediently placed her hand in his. Strangely spellbound, she wordlessly followed his every footstep and silent command, as all the while he kept his green eyes trained upon her.

When a waltz began, Eric pulled her daringly closer and transferred his hand from the side of her waist to her bare back. Katrina gasped and stiffened slightly, but he made no indication that he noticed.

He leaned close to her ear and spoke for the first time since they began dancing. "Do you remember that little red number I tried to convince you to buy?"

Katrina felt her face heat. Oh, yes, she remembered. They'd had great fun that day shopping at many stores with her modeling different outfits for Eric's approval. Eric had an eye for fashion and picked out many of her final purchases. When he'd handed her a slinky red dress to try on, she'd taken it without question, barely even glancing at it. Once she'd gotten in the fitting room and actually put it on, though, she'd regretted it. Cut extremely low and extremely short, it had left her feeling *extremely* exposed.

After several minutes had passed and she still hadn't come out, Eric had called to her quite loudly and quite insistently through the door. To prevent making a scene, she'd very nervously and grudgingly emerged—to almost immediately put herself back behind doors and away from Eric's devouring and unsettling gaze. He'd begged and pleaded with her to buy the dress, but she'd firmly refused. It was enough that he'd even swindled her into trying it on.

"Yes, I do recall that." Although she was blushing furiously, she plowed on. "Why do you ask?"

He smiled triumphantly, and she realized that she'd played right into his hand. "Because," he splayed both of his hands fully against her back and traced them slowly up and down her spine as he spoke lowly into her ear, "as wonderful as that one was, I find I like this one much, much better."

Katrina swallowed and focused on maintaining even breathing. No man had ever said such things to her, and, therefore, she was at a loss of how to react.

"What? No witty comeback?" Eric chuckled. "Can it be that I've stricken you speechless?"

Katrina stared straight in front of her at his chest to avoid looking at his eyes. "I don't know what to say," she admitted. She could feel his intense gaze on her, coaxing her to turn her eyes to him, yet she kept her gaze fixed straight ahead.

"Hmmm," was the only response he gave as he continued to twirl them around the dance floor. A few seconds later, so smoothly was the action made, Katrina was stunned to find herself outside standing on one of the many balconies that led from the room they'd just been in.

Eric discreetly pulled the doors closed, blocking out all sound but that of the night. Katrina skimmed her fingers along the railing as she gazed up at the stars. She'd almost forgotten how sometimes nighttime could be even more appealing than daytime. Although it could be dangerous and frightening, it could also hold beauty untold. For so long now, night had held only nightmares and terrible memories for her.

When her hand reached the end of its trail, Eric's descended upon it. He held their hands pressed against the smooth surface for several moments before slowly lifting them and entwining his long fingers with her petite ones, his emerald eyes, made blue by the moonlight, holding hers. Unsettled, Katrina tried to speak, but Eric held a finger to her lips, tracing it slowly back and forth over their shape.

She shivered and turned her head downward away from his burning, soft caress.

"Are you cold?" His voice was concerned.

Though that was not the initial cause of her shiver, the winter chill was freezing against her exposed skin and even through her evening gown. She nodded in the affirmative and wrapped her arms about herself but needn't have for Eric removed them only to replace them with his own. He pulled her close into his warm embrace and whispered into her ear, "Are you warmer now?"

Yes, she was considerably much warmer and blushing at his boldness. She gave an attempt to escape by wiggling around a bit but gave up when she realized her efforts were to no avail, and he only resettled her against him, pulling her closer if it were possible. "We shouldn't be out here. People will begin to wonder where we are." She was mortified to hear how her voice shook.

Eric chuckled softly, a rumbling that she felt against his chest. "Ever the proper lady, aren't you, Katrina?"

She realized he was waiting for a response and laughed nervously. "Once again, I don't know what to say."

Eric considered this comment just as he had when she'd stated it earlier, only this time his response changed. "Why don't," he spoke very slowly, "you just say what you feel?"

Katrina looked away. What if she didn't know what she felt?

Eric reached out and, with two fingers under her chin, guided her face back to him. "Katrina," his voice was still low, but more serious than before, "do you remember the night when you told me that you felt free and accepted for who you are here?"

The first and only time he'd kissed her. She nodded, and he continued.

"Good, so you know that you don't have to be shackled by restraints. You can be yourself with me." Still holding his fingers under her chin, his eyes took on a burning intensity, and he whispered. "Now then. What do you feel right now at this moment?"

Katrina could do nothing but tremble and stare back into his eyes—those eyes that wouldn't allow her to look away. They bored into hers with a look that no man had ever given her before.

"You're trembling," Eric stated. "Why?" His eyes searched hers, and his voice held a hint of desperation, "Why?" He shook her shoulders lightly at the repeated question, sending her curls bouncing around her face.

She could not face these questions! With all her might,

Katrina pulled herself from his grasp and sharply turned her back to him, her chest heaving with uncontrolled emotion.

Eric allowed her her space. Her breath fogged in the air rapidly while her heart raced. After a time the puffs became less frequent as her breathing calmed and regained normalcy. She felt Eric's presence close behind her and inclined her head slightly to the side as he placed a hand on her shoulder.

His other hand, he held before her face, his arm resting at the nape of her neck. "Look, Katrina," she felt his breath close to her ear while the hand that was on her shoulder traveled up and along her neck to bury itself in her curls. The other hand he kept positioned before her eyes. "See what you do to me? I too am trembling."

Katrina focused on the masculine hand before her and saw that what he'd admitted was true. His hand shook ever so slightly, as did his body when her legs seemed to give way beneath her, causing her to lean back into him. He enfolded her in his arms from behind with a tremulous sigh.

She felt him press a kiss to the top of her head before resting his own head against hers. His actions were deeply moving, and she hadn't the heart to deny him. Actually, she wasn't sure that she wanted to.

"Katrina," he breathed, still stroking her as if she were the most precious and delicate of all possessions in the world, "I love you."

She stiffened in his arms, and he, sensing the change in her, turned her to face him. "Wh-what did you say?' she stammered.

He looked right into her eyes, unblinkingly. "I love you," he stated.

Katrina stared at him completely stunned. His eyes were open and honest. What he spoke was true, she knew. It was mirrored in his eyes, his voice, his actions.

This was the time when she should return the declaration. But could she? Dare she? Her heart was in a muddle, confusion reigning supreme.

"I have never known a love like this before," he continued, his features begging her to understand, pleading with her to return his affection. "You fill my loneliness, my emptiness. We are linked to one another somehow. There is a connection, an energy between us that I can't explain. I've felt it since the day I first met you." He paused and watched his words register with her before continuing even more adamantly. "You feel it too. I can see it in your eyes." He reached out and tightly grasped her hands. "Our souls are one."

Katrina could not speak, and he stared at her strangely for a moment before releasing her and putting a hand in his coat pocket. What he removed was small and square. A black, velvet box. Katrina felt her heart stop within her.

"Katrina, will you marry me?" he asked as he opened the tiny box revealing the most beautiful ring she'd ever seen. It was of a modest size with several diamonds sparkling and gleaming in the shape of a flower. Eric slid it onto her finger as she stared at him wide-eyed. She looked from him to the ring and back again, her heart and mind both racing frantically. Dear God, what could she say?

Eric, who'd been waiting patiently throughout the

whole interval finally expelled a nervous breath. "Say something, Katrina. Please."

She answered honestly. "I don't know what I feel for you."

That seemed to revive his hope, for he grasped her hands once again. "In time, you will learn to love me, if you don't right now." He squeezed her hands reassuringly. "If you married me, I would make you the happiest of women. There is no end to all we could share. I would protect you. You'd be safe. You'd never have to worry about a thing. Katrina, please."

He moved one hand to the side of her throat and appealed once more, "Please. I've never needed anyone and have always scoffed at the idea, but I need you." There was the tiniest trace of vulnerability in his voice, a sound Katrina never would have believed possible of him.

She knew in that instant that Eric truly did love her— much more than she deserved to be loved by him. She wished she could tell him what he so desperately wanted to hear, but she did not know her heart. "I cannot answer now, Eric." She removed the ring and tried to give it back to him, but he refused.

He enfolded it in her hands. "Keep it. It doesn't matter what your answer is. It's yours either way."

She started to protest, but he interrupted her. "Let me love you," he said hoarsely, his mouth descending upon hers as the extreme control he'd been exercising broke, and he could hold back no longer.

This kiss was much different from the other one Eric had given her. It bespoke of his love and promised of things to come if only she would allow it. It was heart-breakingly tender, yet at the same time held more passion than she'd ever known before. A tiny whimper escaped her before his mouth claimed hers a second time, harder than before.

"Say yes, Katrina," Eric coaxed as he rained tiny kisses across her cheeks, her eyes, and her forehead.

Her defenses were growing weaker in the wake of his attentions. She almost heard herself agree to his proposal when a sharp voice rent the air.

"Katrina," Jack's deep voice cut like a whip. Katrina sprang from Eric guiltily but not before Jack had guessed what was going on.

"Y-yes?" she answered.

His eyes flashed between her and Eric, and his voice, when he spoke, was wound tightly with fury. "Come back inside."

It was then that Eric emitted a low growl and pulled Katrina back to his side. "She's with me right now, Jack. And I believe she's capable of deciding where she wants to be herself."

Jack looked at Eric coldly before fixing his eyes on Katrina. He was a fearsome figure, standing tall and authoritative. Holding out his hand, he commanded, "Come here, Katrina."

She looked between the two men, sensing the power struggle between them, her being in the center of it. They both watched her expectantly, and she stood uncertainly between them.

"Come to me, now, Katrina," Jack bid her once again, his eyes catching and holding hers. They were dark with anger but also filled with some indefinable emotion that bid her expressly to obey him. She felt herself drifting toward him, mesmerized, almost in a daze, and did not see Eric's clenched jaw or fist behind her as she placed her hand in Jack's.

His eyes continued to hold hers as he led her back inside and wordlessly pulled her into a dance, only breaking contact when he returned a passing comment from a fellow dancer. All of Katrina's earlier gaiety was gone, though, and she found she wished nothing more than to be alone in the comfort of her room. Although when she begged Jack to be excused, he stiffened and commented sardonically, "You want to walk out on me again, then?"

Katrina stumbled in her dance steps, so completely caught off guard was she. "What? Walk out on you?" When had she ever walked out on him?

His eyes held a blazing hurt as he began to rave quietly. "Is my company so intolerable that you cannot even suffer through one whole dance with me?"

"Maybe you want to run back to Eric's arms again and leave me standing in the middle of this bloody floor like a fool a second time?" he continued, his voice low and bitter.

Katrina stared at him in horror as he rained accusations down upon her. He dragged them into a deserted corridor in his frenzy and rounded upon her, his whole form trembling with jealous rage. "Are you so taken with him that you could not bear to be parted from your lover for a moment longer?"

Katrina had never seen Jack in such a temper, and it was even more frightening than his usual manner.

She'd always been an easy crier. It did not take much to set her tears in motion. She was trying unsuccessfully to fight them now.

"Jack, I don't have a clue what you're talking about. I never went to Eric. When I left our dance earlier, it was to follow Elaine and Melanie." She didn't bother trying to wipe away the tears that stained her cheeks.

Jack was quiet for a moment, then. "Why were you following them?"

"I thought Melanie would enjoy playing with the kitten," she answered.

He was silent again, his eyes boring into her. When he took a step closer to her, she jumped back and yelped when her back hit the wall.

Something in his eyes softened and then became pained at her show of fear. She was visibly shaking as he reached out and touched her arms. "Don't be afraid of me. Don't." His eyes were supplicating as he embraced her frail body. He was so very warm and strong, and Katrina melted against him in relief and allowed him to comfort her. Of course, she knew he would never hurt her.

He stroked her hair while saying, "I'm sorry, Katrina. It's just that when I found you outside with Eric, I automatically assumed…" He trailed off as if he couldn't bear to finish the thought.

She heard him suck in a ragged breath as he pulled back and looked down at her with renewed fervor in his eyes. "The thought of another man holding you drives me insane," he growled, his brown eyes filled with fire at his admission.

She barely had time to blink before he clutched her between the shoulders with strands of curls tangled in between his fingers and kissed her deeply, possessively. His arms closed around her as his mouth moved from her lips to her neck, and she sucked in a sharp breath. But he didn't stop. His hands moved seductively down her stomach and the sides of her hips before trailing back up to capture her quivering hands.

He claimed her mouth again, more slowly than before, his urgency giving way to gentleness. He silently cherished and worshiped her. While rubbing the pads of his thumbs across her fingers, he tenderly kissed the tears from her cheeks while whispering to her to cry no more.

He released her after one last kiss to her forehead and walked her to her room. He knew her well enough to know she was ready to leave the party. Too much had happened, and she wanted to be alone.

He allowed the silence between them, and Katrina made no effort to break it. After turning the doorknob, before allowing her to enter the haven of her room, he gave her one last lingering kiss, his eyes smoldering. She didn't resist at all, instead giving in to the wonderful, yet confusing sensations his kiss conjured within her.

When he finally released her again, she walked into the room as he leaned his arm on the door frame. "Goodnight," he whispered as she clicked the door shut. On the other side, Katrina slid down the door and buried her head in her hands hopelessly.

CHAPTER 20

*J*ack couldn't sleep. His mind kept replaying the night's events over again and again. He saw Eric kissing Katrina and was immersed in the overwhelming urge to throttle him. He was shamed at how he'd scared her with his jealous anger. He remembered how warm and soft she'd felt in his arms when he'd kissed her himself.

He groaned. The party had died down long ago, and he'd been the last to retire and was probably the only one still awake. He tried to empty his frantic mind, but his thoughts would not stop turning to Katrina. He thought of how she'd looked that night and how her lips had tasted when they'd met his. The desire and wanting he'd felt earlier encompassed him until sleep became impossible.

Images unbidden entered his mind, and he jumped out of bed and paced furiously, ordering himself to stop this madness. Outside the warmth of his sheets, he noticed how cold the night was and thought of how he wished he were keeping a certain someone warm. He rammed his hands into his hair as he cursed his treacherousness. He needed to purge his body of such lustful and sinful thoughts.

He was sitting on the edge of his bed, head in his hands, when he heard the cries. Reacting on instinct, he leaped from his sitting position, raced down the hallway, and burst into Katrina's room to discover with relief that she was in no real danger. She laid thrashing on her bed, though, obviously plagued with some nightmare.

Hoping to release her from her terror, he laid a hand on her shoulder and gently shook her awake. She bolted upright, gasping, and gave a small cry when she saw him standing beside her bed. Pulling the covers close about her, she eyed him uncertainly but did not speak.

She was visibly trembling, and Jack, finally letting loose his reservations, abandoned thought and let his actions lead him. He sat on the edge of her bed, feeling it sink beneath him, while she sat unprotestingly motionless, barely awake, probably still in that medium between dream and reality.

He took her hands and contemplating speaking, but wordlessly gathered her to his chest instead when she began to cry. Her shoulders shook with her silent sobs, and he stroked her hair and murmured into her ear, trying his best to soothe her.

His heart wrenched when her head burrowed into the crook of his arm in a self-protective gesture. No one should be reduced to feeling as frightened as a hunted animal. Would she forever hold such fear inside?

"It's alright," he cooed as he ran his hand along her

face, damp with perspiration and tears. "I'm here. Nothing can harm you."

She continued to sob, and he began to hum softly, hoping to relax her with the timbre of his voice.

Eventually, her shudders passed, and she pulled back, wiping the remaining tears from her cheeks.

"Would you like to talk about it?" he ventured when she seemed to have pulled herself together. She shook her head, and he sighed, wishing she would open herself up to him. "Very well, then. I suppose I'll go now and leave you to rest."

He stood to go, but she halted him when she slipped her arms around him in a hug.

His body reacted as a match to kerosene at her touch. His mouth immediately devoured hers as he crushed her to him. To think that she would initiate such close contact with him made him lose all semblance of rational thought. God help him, but he could not stop his kisses, nor could he quench the overwhelming urge to touch her, to caress her perfect, delicate skin.

Surprisingly, she didn't dissuade him. True, she didn't encourage him exactly, but she didn't pull back or push him away either. Instead, she lay lax in his arms like a contented cat with its master.

Although every siren and warning bell in his head was going off, he pushed against her until she was lying back down with him halfway on top of her. Still, she didn't protest, and he knew he was pushing the limits of his endurance.

She had to be half asleep to allow his behavior. He knew that were she fully in possession of all of her senses, she wouldn't condone his conduct right now. His kisses were bordering on indecent, and the fact that he was lying on a bed practically on top of her *was* indecent. He knew he would never compromise her, but how could he force himself to pull back from her sweetness?

Her hair was so incredibly soft, and her skin was so warm beneath his fingers. She was the ultimate of desires, beauty personified, innocence exalted. He loved her, and he was drowning in that love right now.

It was when she finally, drowsily, returned his kiss that he snapped back to attention. He jerked away from her as if electrocuted. Her face showed mild bewilderment as he swung his legs off the side of the bed and dropped his face in his hands. He was behaving like a selfish brute, a mindless animal that could not control itself. He'd never given into temptation this much before, but with Katrina he seemed to lose his head. He couldn't think properly in her presence.

Oh, and this other part of him was cunning. *Just a little more,* it would say. *What harm would it do, really? This is what you ought to do...* Soon this new part of him would cleverly twist his morals, blurring right and wrong, until he caved into his wants.

"Forgive me, Katrina," he muttered, shamed at himself, but she was already sleeping soundly again.

He stood gazing down at her still form. It was many minutes before he quietly made his way out the door, his heart and mind ablaze with a newly occurred thought that would have to wait until morning.

Katrina woke slowly, stretching languidly, until the startling events of last night came rushing back to her memory in full force, and she bolted up abruptly. She remembered with perfect clarity the nightmare that had set it all in motion.

She was standing on a ledge. It was pitch black, yet somehow she could make out the two shapes before her and recognized them as Jack and Eric. They were arguing about something, and true to the nature of nightmares, in a flash of motions, like skipped scenes, both men were hanging off the edge of the cliff. A cavernous hole of black flames roared below them and lightning split the sky above her. She found herself standing before them, quaking like a timid little mouse at the darkness and the rumble of the storm.

Both were pleading with her to help them, but she couldn't help both.

"Katrina!" She immediately ran to Jack at his supplicating call, but stopped short when she heard Eric's anguished cry.

"Katrina," Eric's voice came out as a faint sob at her betrayal.

She turned toward Eric but hesitated again at the hurt sound that came from Jack.

She was caught between them indecisively and began to sob hysterically as the ledge began to crack and they both slipped. Each looked at her expectantly, but she couldn't choose! The ledge cracked once more and still she hesitated. She would lose them both if she didn't do something soon. A third and final crack rent the air, and she screamed as she saw their forms plummeting below.

Katrina was shaking violently now as she recalled all

of this and vaguely remembered waking up in Jack's comforting arms. She remembered his soothing kisses and caresses and blushed at the intimacy. She also recalled with mortification how in her dreamlike state she'd responded to him and was utterly grateful that he'd been such a gentleman as to not have taken advantage of her as he most surely could have.

She stretched once more and snuggled back into the covers when it suddenly hit her that this was Christmas morning. All previous thoughts forgotten, she crawled out of bed and turned on the shower.

As she got dressed, she thought how strange it was to not be at home with her father on this holiday, to not be waiting excitedly for Saffron to show up on their doorstep. Even stranger, it did not bother her that she wasn't. She knew how worried they must be and felt sadness for them, but she didn't feel any on her behalf. She was actually content where she was. Just as she began to worry over these abnormal reactions, a series of knocks sounded on her door.

"Jack," she was surprised to see him standing before her, completely decked out in coat, boots, and gloves.

"Merry Christmas," he leaned against the door jamb with his eyes trained on her appreciatively.

"Merry Christmas," she returned, and then blushed as she realized he was staring at her robe. It seemed they'd come full circle back to the way he'd found her the first morning she'd spent in his mansion.

He grinned devilishly as if he knew what had made her blush. "I have something for you," he stated.

"Oh," Katrina said, feeling awkward.

He seemed to be completely at ease, though. "May I

come in?" He asked the question as he entered.

"I'm not dressed," Katrina stammered.

He quirked an eyebrow at her as his eyes roamed her figure once more.

Her cheeks burned.

He positioned himself in a chair near her bed. "I'll wait while you dress."

She turned to obey him, going to her wardrobe. She could feel his eyes on her and hesitated before retrieving her undergarments from the dresser. She quickly stuffed them in between the sweater and pants she was holding, hoping he'd not seen her frilly intimates.

As she entered the bathroom and turned to shut the door, she happened to look back at Jack. His eyes were trained on her and his fists were clenched, but he relaxed and smiled when he saw her watching him.

She blushed again and closed the door. As she donned her clothing, her brow furrowed in interest. What did he have in store for her?

Jack brought the tiny hand that was wrapped in his own to his mouth and kissed it. Katrina was blushing again, unsure of how to respond, he knew. When he'd seen her this morning, all thoughts of the night before had overwhelmed him, threatening to consume him with his repressed urge to kiss her. He was becoming less capable of resisting those urges and had been forced to fist his hands together earlier to maintain control, so powerful was his need to touch her.

Yet, somehow he'd managed it because now they were

tromping through the fresh snow toward the stable. He could hardly wait to see her reaction once they reached their destination. He knew she would be overcome with wonder and awe at what he'd prepared.

He stroked her fingers. "We're almost there." He saw the curiosity mounting in her eyes and hastened their pace.

He was by no means disappointed in her reaction. In fact, it was more than he'd expected. Her eyes widened and her mouth fell open as she clapped her hands together in delight like a child.

"A sleigh!" she exclaimed, her eyes shining as she took in the carved wood and reigned horses.

"I take it you've never ridden in one before?" he questioned.

She shook her head, "No, but I've always wanted to." She looked at the sleigh eagerly, and he smiled at her innocence.

"Well, now you shall. Come on," he seated her before climbing in behind her and taking the reins. He was instantly gratified that he'd purchased one modeled after those from the nineteenth century. It lay low to the ground like a sled and had room enough for two people seated vertically rather than side-by-side. Due to its small size, Katrina was enclosed safely in his arms, leaning against his chest.

"Are you ready?" He glanced down at the top of her head, which was resting on his shoulder.

Her head bobbed up and down emphatically. He closed his eyes and drew in a deep breath as her hair brushed against his cheek. She would be his undoing.

"Alright then," he slapped the reins and they were off.

He guided them through the frozen orchards and gardens where icicles gleamed and sparkled on the brittle branches, scattering rainbows of incandescent light all around them.

Katrina's eyes sparkled themselves, and Jack's heart swelled with love each time she exclaimed over some particularly beautiful sight and each time her hand found his. As astonishing as it seemed, the things that he took for granted as a child, Katrina was just now experiencing. It was as if she were truly experiencing life for the first time, and he found himself reveling in her discovery with her.

All too soon, it was over with, although it had taken them a good hour to completely cover his grounds. Katrina nimbly hopped out of the sleigh and moved to pat Rose and Caesar who were standing stolidly, still reined. Jack fought the urge to snatch her back to him. "That was wonderful, Jack. Thank you," her little mouth curved into a warm smile. "A perfect way to begin the day."

He shrugged. "I guessed that you'd never been on a sleigh ride as a child and thought you'd enjoy it."

She nodded quickly, sadness passing over her features.

Jack was instantly alert. "What? Have I said something wrong?"

"No," she hastened to assure him. "I just—I never want it to end," she sighed.

Somehow, he didn't think she was talking about the sleigh ride. A bit hesitantly, he stepped closer behind her and laid a hand on her shoulder. If this wasn't the perfect opening to what he wanted to ask her, he didn't know what was. "It doesn't have to end," he stated.

"Doesn't it?" she smiled sadly as she continued to pat

Rose. "I'll miss not seeing you every day," she spoke to the horse while nuzzling its neck.

Jack stood in contemplation for a moment before taking a deep breath and forging ahead. "You know, Katrina, I had planned on giving you another gift, but it depends on your willingness to accept it."

She appeared startled. "Jack, I would accept anything from you! How silly!" The wind caught a strand of her hair, sending it flying behind her head, and he reached out to bring it back to her face.

"Perhaps you should hear what I have to say first," he said gently. Her eyes were questioning, and he took her hands in his, looking down at them. "What if I told you that you could see Rose every day?"

Her brow furrowed. "The only way that's possible is if I never left."

"Exactly." He watched her take his statement in.

She shook her head. "I don't understand."

"Katrina," he gripped her hands tighter, "What if I told you that I wanted you to stay here with me forever—as my wife."

She pulled her hands away from him and wrapped them tightly about herself as she walked away a few feet, then turned back to him with a frightened look. "I can't," she whispered, but the way she said it was unconvincing.

"Why not?" Jack could not stop the rapid pounding of his heart as he advanced on her. She was silent as he turned her around and pressed his mouth to hers hungrily before gently planting touch-and-go kisses on her neck. She melted in his arms, and, in response, he tightened them around her possessively.

"I love you," he breathed as he continued to kiss her.

"Stay here with me. This is where you belong." He held a ring in his hand, and when she didn't protest, he lifted her left hand and slid a simple, round-cut diamond on her finger. It looked beautiful on her, though the diamond didn't do justice to her lovely hands. He leaned down to kiss the ring, and when he looked up, she had tears in her eyes.

She was still shaking her head indecisively, over-whelmed. He simply couldn't believe that she didn't care for him. The way she responded to him was all too real. And the way God had orchestrated their meeting was surely a sign that they were meant to be, right? But what if he was reading it all wrong?

"Katrina, I love you," he managed to croak again. He certainly knew how he felt. He was head over heels in love with her.

She was silent for so long that he almost believed her tears to be those of pity for him. His hands clenched tightly at his sides, he waited as she licked her lips and then said so softly, he wasn't sure she'd actually said it or if it was the production of his deluded senses, "I love you, too."

It took several moments for her confession to process to his brain. She loved him. She truly returned his love. Overcome with joy and desire at her statement, he pulled her to him and whispered lowly into her ear, "Then say you'll stay with me."

She nodded timidly against his shoulder to which his willpower finally broke way and he lavished her with affection. She was smiling the most beautiful smile he'd ever seen as he twirled her around in the air, her musical laugh resounding around them.

After several minutes of thoroughly expressing his love for her, he released her, and she smiled impishly up at him and asked, "So what's this other present I get?"

"Well," he kissed her lightly on the nose, "besides the fact that you get to marry me," he turned to her as she laughed at that statement and lifted her astride Rose, "this mare is now yours."

"Really? Oh, Jack! Thank you so much!" She was brimming with happiness while fawning over Rose, and he commented playfully. "Hmm, obviously a man can't hope to compete with fine horseflesh. Here I thought the way to a woman's heart was to surrender your own, but…"

"Are you jealous?" she interrupted while planting a kiss atop Rose's head. The tease.

"Yes. Especially so. *I* am your fiancé," he growled playfully as she continued to adore the horse. He plucked her from the horse and kept his hands on her waist, making no move to add to the space between them. "What are you going to do to assuage this situation?" he asked deeply.

She lowered her eyelashes modestly before slowly leaning toward him, her pink lips parted, silently beckoning to him. His eyes slid shut in anticipation, and he shuddered as he felt her warm breath pass across his lips. Her lips barely brushed his as she whispered softly, "Nothing."

Laughing, she bolted away from him just as he reached out to drag her to him. He stood grinning for a moment, admiring the sight she made running through the snow, her boots spraying snow from the ground and leaving tiny prints behind like that of a lithe doe. He would let her enjoy her short-lived victory. He could easily catch her any time he pleased. *His* Katrina. Soon to be *his* wife.

CHAPTER 21

*T*he day flew by in a blur for Katrina, and before she knew it, she found herself standing before Jack and Eric, presenting them with their Christmas gifts before they all three left for that night's performance as Elaine and Roy had already done. She was extremely nervous about it. She'd never performed in front of an audience before, but she tried to put that out of her mind for the time being.

In truth, she'd been pretty much by herself all day beyond the *Merry Christmases* passed her way that morning at breakfast. It was the one event that the whole household had shared together, and then they'd all gone their separate ways to prepare for the night's festivities.

She produced the scarves she'd made for the two men and wrapped each around his neck in turn. Eric reached for her left hand, but she quickly pulled it back to tuck a strand of hair behind her ear, forcing him to settle for kissing her right hand instead. Somehow, she'd managed to skillfully keep the ring she now sported on her hand hidden from him all day.

Thankfully, though he hadn't been at all pleased, Jack hadn't protested when she'd insisted on keeping their engagement secret for a while.

Part of the reason why she dreaded confessing her engagement to Eric was that he'd asked her to marry him first. She'd not even given him an answer before she accepted Jack, though she'd not consciously done so. She'd been so caught up in the moment that she'd honestly forgotten all about Eric's proposal when she'd consented to marry Jack. She guessed that was evidence of her true feelings for Jack, that he had the power to make her forget all others when she was with him. Nevertheless, she needed time to talk to Eric and give him an answer before she announced that she was engaged to another.

But it was so much more than that, too. Eric was her friend, and she didn't want to hurt him. She needed the right time and place to make him understand. And there were so many other factors that she didn't even—couldn't even—realize herself.

Now she watched Jack's reaction as Eric kissed her hand and complimented her debonairly. "Thank you, Katrina." Eric smiled crookedly as he continued, "As much as I would love wearing this, though, maybe I should surrender mine to you for the time being. Otherwise I fear you may be too chilled in that lovely little dress of yours." She saw Jack's fists clench as his one of Eric's hands moved to caress her throat.

She hastily moved out of his reach while suggesting,

"Perhaps you wouldn't mind fetching me my shawl then. That way you won't have to surrender your gift."

"I live to serve," Eric joked as Katrina directed him to its whereabouts and sagged in relief when he left the room.

Jack's eyes bored into hers knowingly as she wound his scarf around his neck. "He is the reason you don't want our engagement announced," he commented with some resentment.

She braced herself. "Yes, Jack, but not for any of the reasons you may think. I can't tell you why right now, but just trust me." Jack didn't know of Eric's proposal and, while she wasn't going to keep it hidden from him forever, it was hardly fair for Jack to know the answer to it before Eric himself knew. While she didn't want to cause suspicion in Jack, she didn't want to hurt Eric either and felt she owed him that much.

When Jack opened his mouth to protest, she pleaded. "Please, Jack. You have nothing to worry about. I love *you*." She kissed him lightly. And she did. The words had poured unbidden from her mouth after his proposal. After a moment of consideration, he nodded stiffly, and she was thankful his stubbornness hadn't won out for once.

"By the way," he added, "Melanie thought you an angel last night, but she'd really be convinced tonight. You look divine."

"Do you really think so?" She was wearing the white dress tonight, and Elaine had curled her hair and done her make-up again.

"I know so," he affirmed as Eric returned with Katrina's white fur shawl. He insisted on draping it across her shoulders for her, and Katrina tried to quell Jack's jealousy with her eyes.

"Shouldn't we be going then?" Eric prompted. Looking over at Jack he said, "The audience will be awaiting our prima donna."

Eric winked at Katrina, not knowing the knots of anxiety his statement had just put in her stomach. Dear God, what was she doing? She was far too shy to be subjecting herself to the stares of a hundred people.

Neither Jack nor Eric suspected her reservations as they all filed out the door. They were too busy making small talk about past performances and the ones they believed she would surpass. It was too late to turn back now. She just hoped she didn't freeze on stage tonight.

A hush fell over the audience as the lights of the community hall dimmed, signaling the beginning of the first act. It was a group of children performing a skit of some sort. Eric sat with his elbow on the side of the chair, his head propped up on his hand, bored out of his mind, counting down the acts until Katrina's performance.

He was sitting on the first row of the far left side of the hall, the closest seat to the piano where Katrina would be playing. The families behind him tittered with excitement over their little ones' performances while he glanced around curiously trying to locate Jack and the others. He was not surprised to see them also in the front on the other side of the building, surrounded by friends who they occasionally made comments to with broad smiles on their faces. This was one setting that Jack, Roy, and Elaine fit into that Eric did not. That's why he sat silently by himself, though that didn't bother him.

When they'd first arrived, he'd barely had time to wish Katrina good luck before she was directed backstage, and he and Jack had been pressed to seek out empty seats among the already very filled ones. In fact, it seemed as if all day Katrina had been in a state of being ushered away from him. Every time he'd tried to talk to her, their conversations had spanned no more than a couple of minutes. She'd been so busy that day. He was anxious to speak to her and put his troubled mind at ease about her answer to his proposal. It was all he'd thought about all last night and all day today. He had to know her answer one way or another or he'd go insane.

Surely she wasn't toying with him. He flexed his fingers and looked at his watch. Katrina's act was the last, and they had to be nearing it soon. She had to know the state of waiting he was in to be maddening. He didn't want to rush her. He wanted to give her plenty of time to consider her choice, but if she still hadn't answered him by night's end, he would approach her.

"And now," Mrs. Firmin spoke into the microphone with excitement, "we are proud to present our last and newest performer, Miss Katrina Weems."

Eric straightened as Katrina took the stage, her steps slow and timid. She was beautiful with the lights shining on her pale skin and hair.

Katrina cast frightened eyes to the crowd of onlookers as she seated herself at the piano. Mrs. Firmin positioned the microphone and exited the stage. His poor girl was shaking. Eric longed to comfort her and willed her eyes to meet his. When they did, she smiled tentatively at him before launching into the *Overture*.

It was magnificent to say the least. She played with all the skill of a seasoned performer, and Eric was the first, but not the only, one to rise to his feet when it ended. Katrina smiled prettily amidst the applause, her eyes shining with her success, and Eric's heart swelled with pride for her.

As she stood from the piano bench to leave, though, she was halted by Mrs. Firmin who scurried on stage and speaking into the microphone said, "That was marvelous, dear, just marvelous. Don't you agree?" She looked to the crowd, which roared with applause once more. "Do you sing?" Mrs. Firmin put her on the spot. Katrina blushed and stammered, "Well, yes, a little…"

Mrs. Firmin's eyes lit up. "Well, then you must sing us a song!" The crowd agreed with her if their claps of approval were any indication. Eric smiled widely at the positive acceptance of Katrina's talent and nodded at her to accede to their request when she looked at him.

She seated herself once more and began to play the opening chords of *Think of Me*. When she began to sing, quietly at first, then louder as her confidence grew, he felt as if he'd been transported to heaven. She had the most exquisite voice he'd ever heard. When her voice rose flawlessly on the cadenza, his heart almost stopped within him, so pure was the sound.

The audience was on its feet once more, begging for just one more song.

"Really, I can't," Katrina told Mrs. Firmin. "All of the other songs require a male voice type."

Mrs. Firmin was undaunted as her eyes scanned the crowd. "Jack can sing with you," she proposed. Eric froze at the suggestion, and his smile faded as he watched as the people around Jack immediately begin to nudge and encourage him. "Oh, come on, Jack," Mrs. Firmin continued, "Everybody here knows you can sing. Come accompany Katrina in just one more song, and then we'll leave her alone."

After much prompting, Jack rose and stepped onto the stage. Eric fought down the rage that coursed through his body at the thought of Jack singing a duet with Katrina. *Curse all of them,* he thought darkly. As if being graced with one song was not enough for their ungrateful ears.

A lead weight settled in his stomach, and a feeling of doom washed over him as the two smiled at each other and Katrina began to pluck out the familiar chords of *All I Ask of You.* Jack played his part well, for as he sang his lines, his face wore all the expressions of love that the song denoted. Eric's fingers gripped the arms of his chair tightly. He didn't know how much more of this he could stand.

Katrina's sweet voice filled the air, and then he saw it. A shift of her hand revealed a diamond on Katrina's finger —a diamond that was too small to be the one he'd given her. His heart plummeted within him. How had he not noticed it sooner?

Suddenly it all made sense. He hadn't seen the ring because she hadn't wanted him to. The aversions all day had been planned. She'd been avoiding him because she didn't want him to find out that she'd accepted another man's hand before even refusing his.

He'd offered her everything. Everything! And she had betrayed him!

He looked over the mass of people with disdain, gathered to praise a merciful being who surely didn't exist. If there was a merciful God, he would allow him the one and only thing in life he'd ever wanted—love.

His knuckles were white with his grip on the chair arms, and he felt as if he were going to explode at any moment. When Katrina and Jack's voices melded together in climax, his soul filled with angst, and he could endure it no longer. Standing abruptly, he slipped down the side aisle of the building, his heart and mind beating in furious tempo with the condemning music that Katrina continued to play.

Katrina stepped into one of the private dressing rooms backstage, the applause still ringing in her ears. She needed a moment to collect her bearings before joining the others in the casual festivities of eating, conversing, and fun and games that were now taking place.

She couldn't believe that it had all gone so well. They hadn't scoffed or ridiculed her. They'd truly loved her performance—enough to give a standing ovation and an encore! It was greater than she could have imagined. To be praised for her musical abilities was elating.

Still riding the cloud of her success, she threw her hands up in the air and twirled about, humming the tunes from her performance, her thick white skirt billowing out around her. Her carefree dance was broken when she knocked haphazardly into a chair that was set before a lit mirror. She quickly steadied herself and was surprised to see a rose with a black ribbon tied around it sitting atop the table.

Eric. She looked up to see him half hidden within the shadows of the corner of the room. He came forward at her notice, and she blushed when she realized that he'd seen her childish display. "I didn't know you were in here."

He nodded and his eyes darted to her left hand. She felt her stomach drop within her. When he looked at her, she knew he could read every expression in her eyes. "Can we go someplace to talk?" he asked quietly.

She stared at the collar of his shirt, knowing she must grant him this one request. When she nodded her assent, he led her outside through an exit that she didn't even know the dressing room had. She wrapped her arms about herself to fend off the chill and thought about going back to get her shawl, but Eric was already a step ahead of her. He'd apparently grabbed it for her on their way out because he draped its heavy warmth around her shoulders now. She tried not to notice how his hands lingered or the sigh he gave when he moved away from her.

They got in Eric's car, and he revved the engine to life. As soon as they were on the road, he wasted no time in speaking what was on his mind. "I wanted to talk to you because I'm going to be leaving soon." He was looking straight ahead, but it made no difference because it was so dark that Katrina couldn't make out his expressions anyway, except for when the streetlights added a brief illumination to his features.

"Where are you going?" she asked cautiously.

She saw his shoulders move in what she supposed was a shrug.

She tried another avenue. "What will you do when you leave?"

He expelled a breath. "Probably go back to selling condos."

She debated over what to say to him. He was in a tenacious mood, and she didn't want to be the one to send him tattering over the brink. She didn't want him acting like this at all. She wanted him to be the same as he'd always been. Not as solemn and somber as he was being now.

She tried for a cheerful veneer. "You'll make loads of sales with your personality. You're very persuasive."

He was silent before answering, "I'm obviously not persuasive enough."

Her smile fell, and she gripped her hands more tightly in her lap. "W-what do you mean?"

"I'm your phantom, aren't I, Katrina?" he asked her with such a tone of despondency in his voice that her heart tripped within her.

Katrina was silent. Actually, she thought Jack was more of the phantom type, but she knew what Eric meant. He was referring to his unreturned love.

"Katrina," he whispered and took her left hand, looking at the ring Jack had given her in a heartbreaking gesture.

Katrina felt tears spring to her eyes when he struggled for words and then dropped her hand when none came, turning his focus back on the road. She truly did love both of them, only in different ways. They were so alike in some ways and yet so different in others. They were both tall, dark, and handsome, of course. Yet, Jack was the brooding intellectual with imposing power, strength, and surety, whereas Eric was the eccentric wanderer with self-assured masculinity and wild abandon. Eric loved her with desperation and slavish devotion, whereas Jack loved her with a steady, raging fire, a promise. Most importantly, while she was drawn to Eric by *his* need, she was drawn to Jack by *her* need.

Katrina glanced out the window. "Where are we going, Eric?"

He gave a choked laugh. "I don't even know. Back to the mansion, perhaps?"

His behavior was beginning to frighten her, and, thankfully, five minutes later they did pull up to the gates of Jack's grounds. When Eric parked the car, Katrina made no move to get out. She intuitively knew that their conversation wasn't over.

"Katrina, why?" Eric asked, his voice broken.

She swallowed nervously before attempting to explain. She felt like the lowest of women on the face of the earth. "Well, he loves me and I…" she stammered but was interrupted by Eric's burst of outrage.

"*I* love you!" He turned his head and cursed softly before turning back to her. "Can't you see that?" His eyes were pained, and Katrina realized once more to what extent his feelings for her went. They were deep, very deep, and she was shamed at that knowledge.

He reached out and cupped her cheek. "I would do anything for you. Anything!" His eyes implored her.

"There is nothing I would not do to make you happy," he reiterated. "Do you understand? Nothing."

At this point, he broke off and fresh tears flowed from

his eyes. Katrina watched in horror as he openly cried before her. She'd never seen a man cry like so before, and it was not a pleasant sight. Katrina was grateful then that he'd interrupted her earlier because she'd been about to confess that she loved Jack, and she now felt that confession would kill him.

Katrina found herself with doubts once more in the midst of Eric's grief. What if she was meant to be with Eric? She shook off those thoughts. She had promised herself to Jack.

She longed to reach out and comfort him, but she didn't want to encourage false hope. He would take it as permission to hold her and that could not happen now.

Her voice shook when she spoke, "Two broken souls cannot make a complete one." His eyes became desolate as comprehension of her statement set in.

As inadequate as it was, she offered him all she had left to give him. "I'm sorry," she whispered.

Oh, yes. Bryan followed the black Mustang from a sizable distance but still close enough to discern its direction. A wide grin spread across his face that he couldn't erase if he tried. All these weeks of searching had finally paid off. He'd found her at last—again.

He had to admit that after that last mishap when he'd temporarily lost control, he'd agonized of ever finding her again. In fact, just now he'd been on his way to the airport ready to concede that Katrina was as good as dead to him when he happened to drive by this little community gathering and see a vehicle that appeared to be very similar to the one he'd been searching for.

And sure enough he'd been right. Katrina had appeared with the same companion she'd been with the last night he'd seen her. Though his blood boiled at the sight of the man, he tempered his rage. There would be no mistakes this time. No losing her again.

He almost laughed. The odds of finding her once were slim to none, much less twice. Fate had worked in his favor tonight. Soon all would be well. He would have Katrina back soon. All in good time. All in good time.

Where could she have gone? After thoroughly searching the building from top to bottom, Jack had been forced to conclude that Katrina wasn't there. His worry now was if she was all right or not. Had she left, or was she taken involuntarily? Jack frowned at the trees as he searched for her outside. Surely she wouldn't just leave without telling him. Besides, she had no mode of transportation.

His heart began to beat rapidly as there was still no sign of her. He returned to the front of the building and scanned the parking lot. Eric's Mustang was gone, he noted, as was Eric. Now he remembered that Eric had asked Elaine and Roy to drive his car when he left earlier with Jack and Katrina so that he would be able to leave whenever he wished. The couple had, of course, had no problem with the arrangement since they would stay until the event was officially over and could always ride back home with Jack.

Jack would never have believed he would feel this way,

but he desperately hoped that Katrina was with Eric right now. Better that than her being in some kind of danger. At least she would be safe with Eric. Perhaps she'd chosen to leave early with him. But if so, why didn't she inform him? Didn't she know he would worry?

He had to find her. He worked his way through the groups of merrymakers until he found Roy and briefly summarized the situation to him. Alarmed at the news, Roy hurried him on, promising that it was fine. He and Elaine could indeed enlist someone else to bring them home.

Jack jumped in his car and sped back home, guessing that to be the most likely place they would be. At least, that was where Eric would likely be. Whether Katrina was with him or not still remained to be seen.

He skidded to a stop behind Eric's vehicle and raced into the house, taking the stairs two at a time. He slowed as he heard voices drifting from Katrina's room and closed his eyes in relief as he recognized one of the voices to be hers.

Moments later, his relief turned to anger at her insensitivity. He heard Eric speaking lowly but couldn't make out what he was saying. He rounded the corner and barged into the room to find Eric's hands around Katrina's as he implored her to "reconsider." When he reached atop her dresser and pulled down a ring, Jack suddenly understood what was going on. A growl of fury emerged from Jack's throat.

"Jack," Katrina's surprised tone only served to incite him further.

He paid no heed to Eric's suddenly hostile stance as he approached Katrina and addressed her. "Why did you disappear without telling me?" His voice was icy even to his own ears.

She cowered before him. "I forgot. I wasn't thinking."

"That's an understatement."

She winced.

"Did it ever enter your mind how worried I would be when I couldn't find you?"

Eric stepped in front her protectively, enraging Jack all the more. "It was my fault, Jack, so leave her alone. I made her come with me."

Jack balled his fists and spoke through clenched teeth. "Do not push me right now, Eric."

"Push you? Push you!" Eric's voice was outraged. "You have absolutely nothing to be angry about, Jack!" Eric gave a hysterical laugh and wagged the elaborate diamond ring Katrina couldn't wear because of Jack's ring in his face. "You won. How classic. Once again the good guy gets the girl."

Eric's face twisted in pain for a moment as he studied the ring. He went on to lick his lips and harden his face, masking the pain for his pride's sake if nothing else. "Congratulations, Jack," his voice dripped with sarcasm.

Jack was stopped from launching into a heated argument with Eric by a small cry from Katrina. She looked between them and covered her mouth before running, sobbing, from the room.

There was only silence after that as both debated over whether to follow her. The choice was made for them when her sharp scream rent the air. They both bolted out the door and down the stairs into the frigid night. Acting on a hunch, Jack made a quick detour into his office and grabbed the small handgun that he kept hidden there. He didn't know why he felt compelled to get it, but he did.

He wasn't far behind Eric, who halted abruptly on the stone steps right outside the door. The sight that met Jack's eyes explained why and stopped him cold in his tracks.

A man stood behind her with one arm wrapped around her arms and waist in a firm and captive embrace while the other one waved a gun over her shoulder. Jack instantly knew who the man was, and his blood boiled. He glanced at Eric and noticed his hands were white with the force of his clenched hands, his stance rigid, and his face hard as stone.

"Oh, so you have two of them, my dear?" Bryan spoke into Katrina's ear, never taking his eyes off of Eric and Jack. "I had not taken you to be *that* kind of woman, Katrina. But then I've entertained many misconceptions about you, haven't I? Still, I must say this is sorely disappointing."

Katrina's face was even paler than usual, and she was quaking in his embrace. For all their sakes, Jack fought the urge to act immediately. It would be all too easy for Jack to pummel Bryan, the man's stature being much smaller than his own, but Bryan wielded a weapon that could at any moment end any one of them, including Katrina.

"Release her," Eric commanded.

Jack ground his teeth together at Eric's impulsiveness and prayed that it didn't get them all killed.

The blond man cast a disdainful look at Eric before continuing as if he hadn't spoken. "Do you know how much trouble you've put me through?" He peered down at

Katrina and pulled her hair, causing her to whimper in pain, a sound that sent a knife through Jack's soul.

"Do you know how long I've been looking for you?" the man Jack knew to be Bryan went on. "How long I've waited for you?" His voice was ironically incredulous. "Thinking you were all perfect and innocent and now I find out that you're really nothing more than a common…" He called her a name that infuriated Jack. Jack watched as the man continued to rain a procession of obscenities upon her now. Katrina was hysterical and sobbing in fear.

Jack's vision turned red, and he felt himself getting ready to charge at the man, but Eric beat him to it. With a cry of inhuman rage, Eric lunged while Jack's body tensed in suspension.

Bryan swiftly flung Katrina aside. She hit the ground several feet from them, but seemed to be unharmed. Jack turned his attention back to the scene playing out before him, anxiety mounting as he saw the stranger's gun lift.

"No!" Jack's cry, accompanied by Katrina's, was lost amidst the sound of gunshots firing simultaneously. He watched in horror as Eric went down. The smoke curled up from his own gun as his bullet found its mark, and Katrina's attacker fell silently to the ground seconds later, his gun smoking as well.

The gun fell from Jack's hands with a dull thud as he watched the blood seeping through Eric's white sweater.

Eric looked at Katrina and rasped, "I love you."

She crawled over to him, sobbing, and knelt beside him, rubbing his hands, tears flowing freely down her chapped cheeks, her hair askew. "I love you, too, Eric," she whispered, her voice catching. "I do."

He seemed to smile at that, true happiness lighting his face.

His head turned to Jack. "I'm sorry," he managed to say. Jack felt tears gather in his throat as he nodded that all was okay. With that, Eric's eyes closed, never to open again, and his breathing stilled. Jack was bleakly staring down at his friend's lifeless body when he heard the sound of tires against the pavement.

CHAPTER 22

*A*fter enduring several hours of air travel, Katrina entered the familiar foyer of her childhood home and sat on the bench beneath the fountain as she used to do when she was a child. After everything that had happened at Jack's, she'd finally decided to come home. She'd called her father, and he'd pulled a few strings to get all the documents she needed to travel, just happy to know she was alive. She hadn't told him everything that happened yet, certainly not about Bryan. Not only could she not talk about it yet, but she didn't want to break his heart. She'd promised him they'd talk in person when she got home, but she dreaded doing it. She had no energy for talking or anything. She was just so disconnected from everything at this point.

She ran her hand through the water, blindly, mechanically. One of the servants scurried by and then returned with concern and asked if she could help her.

"Is my father home?" Katrina asked in a voice she

didn't recognize as her own. It was strange how every-thing was unchanged and different at the same time, from the tiled floor to the sculpted ceiling.

"Excuse me?" The woman's voice sounded odd now, but Katrina didn't notice.

"My father," she continued to swirl her fingers in the pool, "is he home?"

The servant cleared her throat nervously. "Miss, your father is dead," she informed her cautiously.

Katrina stilled and looked up. "What?" Her whole being went cold. Her heart felt as if it'd stopped beating. A few moments of no breath, and then her breath returned with rapid heartbeats, bringing her painfully back to life.

"I'm sorry, Miss. I thought you knew," she seemed truly sorry for her. "He had a heart attack two days ago."

Katrina had been in a stupor ever since that awful night at Jack's. She'd cried nonstop it seemed for days, and then she'd finally shed all her tears. Then, she'd felt noth-ing, no emotions, nothing, since then. It had actually been a welcome change to not feel so much.

Now that feeling came back to her in an icy rush as pain washed over her. She was snapped harshly back to life as the reality of what she'd been told sank in. If only she would have come home two days ago.

She thought she'd spent all her tears, but she was wrong. A new wave surfaced and overtook her. *Why? Why?*

The woman stood by wringing her hands, obviously at a loss of what to do. *Go,* Katrina motioned to her. *Go and leave me* . She was now completely and utterly alone.

Three. Three people were dead now because of her. Her father. Bryan, who she'd once counted as a friend. And Eric. What had Eric been? A friend certainly, but perhaps he'd been something more too.

And now she would never know.

She stared at the cold, hard ground as the coffin was lowered into it. She didn't cry at her father's funeral. Her tears had finally run dry, and her soul was now as bleak as the winter day she found herself in.

Funeral directors always expected the closest family members to be first row, front and center. They thought it was a comfort, but it wasn't. Katrina didn't like being in full view of the prying, waiting eyes. She could feel the sympathetic stares of those around her. Poor girl, they thought, watching for some hysterical display of grief from her.

They would be disappointed. She'd been through that already. Now there was nothing. Nothing.

Someone had taken care of the funeral arrangements, but she didn't know who. She was grateful, but actually, it didn't really matter. She didn't care who'd done it, just that it had been done. God knew she couldn't have done it herself.

Contrary to custom, she didn't stay and mingle with the crowd of sympathizers and well-wishers. She didn't want to hear comments of what a good man he'd been, how they were sorry for her, what he would wish. She just wanted to be alone.

After hours of laying on her bed staring at nothing, someone entered her room. She didn't move to see who. She didn't have the will or the strength.

Saffron. It was Saffron. She saw her out of the corner of her eyes. She'd missed Saffron and had been longing to see her but not like this.

When Saffron slowly sat next to her and laid a hand on her arm, Katrina felt the tears well up. A damn of emotions that she'd been holding back broke free, and she told her best friend everything. About Bryan and how Jack had rescued her. About Eric and Elaine and Roy. And Saffron listened and cried silently with her.

"So what happens now?" she asked as Saffron hugged her. "What do I do now?"

Saffron pulled back and looked at her with all the determination of their teenage years. "Move on." Said with grief but also with purpose and strength. *Move on.*

Jack couldn't move on. He'd tried. Oh, how he'd tried. But it was all to no avail. He couldn't forget her.

He'd made his peace with God over that night. He'd repented of his own actions when it came to Katrina, the times he'd displayed less than Christ-like behavior to her. He hung his head in shame at the thought. He hadn't been a good witness of Christ's love with all his jealousy concerning Eric.

He missed his old college buddy, and he grieved for him. But he had somewhat come to terms with that simply because he knew there was no going back to undo what was done, though at first he'd blamed himself for his part in Eric's death, wishing he'd just stepped aside and let Eric pursue her, keeping his own feelings for her unknown.

But Katrina…Try as he might he could not get over her.

The kitten Katrina had rescued jumped onto his desk, meowing for attention. He absentmindedly stroked the beast. He hadn't had the heart to get rid of the animal after Katrina had left. It kept him company and was like a piece of her was still with him. Now that Katrina was gone, the cat had taken to following him all around. He scratched behind its ears. "I know I'm a sorry substitute for Katrina, little cat, but I'll have to do."

As if agreeing with him, the kitten flicked its tail and then jumped off the desk, sauntering away.

Jack thought back to when he'd first found Katrina cold and shivering on the side on the road. He hadn't wanted to be responsible for her then. She'd been a nuisance, a crimp in his plans. Yet, all that had changed as he'd gotten to know her, as she'd unknowingly, unintentionally made her way into his heart.

He worried about her. She was so full of tenacious life. She was such a child at times. She needed protection. He smiled. Yet, she so fiercely tried to prove how grown up she was. She was so timid at times, and at others she could be stubborn and defiant.

Most of all, he worried for her soul. With all she'd been through, she needed God. Jack desperately wanted to be there to comfort her himself, but it didn't seem like that was in God's plan, so he prayed for her almost incessantly, that God would protect her and draw her to Him.

God knew how much he wanted her to come back to him and how many times he'd fought getting on a plane and going to her. Every time he thought about doing it, something held him back. He knew it was God telling him 'no,' and as much as he didn't want to listen, he did. It was hard, though.

Tears stung his eyes, and he dropped to his knees in his office, head bowed, his own soul tormented. He couldn't get her off his mind. He couldn't let go. But he knew he had to. She was God's—not his—and he suddenly knew that he had to release her in order for God to do His work. It was time to love her unselfishly—to love her enough to let her go forever if that's what it took for God to reach her.

Lord, Jack prayed silently with a lump in his throat, *I think I hear what you're telling me. I'm turning her over to You. I'm going to trust You to take care of her—even if that means it's not Your will for me to ever be a part of her life again. Just comfort her as only you can.*

It had been almost a year now. It was Christmas Eve, and as Jack walked the streets of Boston, all he could think of was how last Christmas had been.

His scarf whipped out behind him as the wind howled fiercely and freezing cold raindrops fell on his head. Seeking shelter and warmth, he made his way into the nearest shop.

Passing the group of readers seated on plush sofas and chairs, he began to browse through the bookstore while waiting for the icy storm to die down. He looked through the bestsellers, selecting a paperback by one of his favorite classic authors. He almost dropped the book he was holding when he came to the new releases and saw a book of poetry by an author with the name of Katrina Weems.

He reverently picked up the volume, studying the simply stated, elegant cover. Could it be that Katrina had written this? He tried not to jump to conclusions. There could be another woman with the same name, or someone could have chosen this name as a pseudonym, but his heart told him that 'yes' it was her. He knew without a doubt that this was his Katrina, the very same.

His heart was beating with excitement, but he paced himself, buying a cup of coffee before settling down in an isolated chair. Forgetting about the storm and all else, he read until the store closed and he was asked to leave, so captivating was her work. He purchased it and hastened home to continue reading. Her poems were the mirror to her soul. They told her every thought and feeling. He could just picture the look upon her face at the time she'd written some of these. He devoured the book like a starving man, reading all through the night.

He could sense a change in her as he read her writing. She seemed almost at peace. He closed his eyes. The last image he had of her was shadowed with the sadness and grief of her leaving. And the thing that had frightened him most—the dead look she'd worn, as if she'd finally been beaten down by life. He'd begged, pleaded with her to stay, told her they'd get through it together, but she'd still left, stating that nothing could ever be the same again.

The pieces were masterfully done. They were so beautiful that he re-read some several times. The one that held him the most and lingered in his mind was *Planting the Rose*.

He was still pondering it as he walked through his frozen gardens just before dawn. He passed through the many orchards and stopped just as the sun rose into the sky when he reached the rose garden. Its bright glory shed rays of light on a most peculiar phenomenon.

There in the center of his rose garden was one bloom in the dead of winter, dewdrops sparkling from its petals. Even more astounding than the fact that it was there, vibrantly alive in winter, was its appearance. The petals were the purest of whites, outlined with deep hues of red, and the center burst into a soft pink. Jack stood in awe of its entire splendor. *It's impossible. No, it's a miracle,* he thought.

Does this mean what I think it does, Lord?

In the next second, he held the rose in his palm and was preparing for the next flight out of Boston.

Katrina had just seen Saffron out not five minutes ago and sighed with a smile at the knock on the door. She and Saffron had grown much closer over the last year, and Katrina looked forward to her visits. Saffron had been staying with her on and off for weeks on end sometimes, and Katrina had become quite accustomed to her ways. "What did you forget this time, Saffron?" she asked as she opened the door, failing to look out the peephole.

Only it was not Saffron who stood on her steps this night. It was Jack. She hadn't seen him in a year and was shocked to find him on her doorstep. They stared at each other for several moments before he cleared his throat and asked, "May I come in?"

"Oh," she stammered, "yes, of course." She stood back, remembering her manners, and allowed him to cross the threshold of her home.

Her mind was awhirl with questions. How did he know where she lived? What was he doing here? Much less on Christmas? Yet, she didn't know how to begin to say anything to him, so she waited for him to speak first.

They stood in the foyer in silence before Jack removed his hands from his pockets. He was still as tall and handsome as ever. His hair still had that penchant for falling into his eyes. His eyes…his eyes were still the same too. Katrina just stood drinking him in until he finally spoke.

"Look, I'm not going to 'beat around the bush' as you say down here," he ran a hand through his hair," I just had to see you."

Her heart began to beat rapidly, but she didn't say anything, instead just listening to him.

"I read your book," he went on.

Her eyes widened. He'd read her work?

"It was wonderful," he continued. "Words cannot describe how I felt when I read it. I felt as if I knew you completely at last. I saw the real you, Katrina. Not only the frightened, terrified victim, but also the vivacious, life-loving dreamer."

He took a step toward her, and for once, she didn't step away from him, a gesture that didn't go unnoticed by him, she saw. His brown eyes flamed with a flicker of hope, piercing her soul.

"And I wondered how?" he mused aloud. "How could you have gone from terrified to peaceful after everything that has happened? What could have inspired such a change?"

His look was knowingly inquisitive, and she couldn't stop the smile of joy that spread across her face. "Well," she began, "I'm peaceful now because...I found God—or rather, He found me. And it is just as you explained back in your garden when we first spoke of it."

Jack looked at her in wonder before his face broke out into the widest smile she'd ever seen on him.

"That's great, Katrina," he hugged her exuberantly, and she laughed. "God is good," he whispered softly into her hair.

"When did this happen?" he asked pulling back and gripping her hands gently.

His touch felt as good as ever, only now when he touched her she didn't feel even the tiniest flicker of fear. She realized he was still waiting for her testimony, so she began, "One night while I was in bed..."

She recalled to him her feelings of despair and hopelessness and how she'd prayed—really prayed—for the first time since childhood. "Because of Him, I have finally moved on from that night," she finished. "I couldn't have done it without Jesus, Jack. I was dying—both inside and out. I couldn't eat or sleep or *feel* anything. I'd just become a shell."

Jack nodded knowingly and listened to everything she had to say, often shaking his head. His eyes sparkled with tears a few times as she spoke, and he said 'thank God' many times.

After she was finished, they both sat in silence together for a moment before Jack said softly, "I have something to show you."

He removed his gloves and very cautiously pulled

something that was wrapped in a handkerchief out of his coat pocket. She gasped softly as he revealed the most beautiful rose she'd ever seen.

His eyes were watching her very closely as he gingerly held it up for her view. "As I was still thinking about one of your poems this morning, I happened to find this in my garden."

Katrina's eyes went wide as she beheld the delicate blossom. It was beautiful. She'd never seen a rose like it before.

He leveled his eyes at her and spoke as if he knew what she was thinking. "I know. That's what's so magnificent about it."

He studied it, twirling its stem between his fingertips before kneeling before her and handing it to her. She gently grasped the smooth stem in her fingers. He had removed the thorns.

"This rose, planted by Heaven, symbolizes all that you are, Katrina. Beautiful and enchanting, yet pure and true with the perfect balance of each. I call it *Maiden's Blush*."

Tears slipped down her cheeks, but she made no move to mask them. Jack stopped and gently wiped them away with the pads of his thumbs, and she closed her eyes at his gentle touch.

When he was finished wiping each tear from her eyes, he pulled her to her feet and clasped his hands behind her waist. "I couldn't forget my love for you, Katrina. No matter how hard I tried."

He dropped his hands from the small of her back and gently captured her own hands in his, threading his fingers with hers. "I don't want to pressure you. You might already have someone else, or you might not even want a relationship at all, but I just need to you know that I still love you as fiercely as ever."

Katrina hesitated only a moment before responding, "I love you, too. That's never changed, Jack."

Jack nodded knowingly and revealed his revelation, "But I couldn't be your Savior. Only Jesus could fill that role. That's why He had you leave."

Katrina nodded in agreement. She saw the truth in his words. If she had stayed with Jack and let him help her through everything, he'd have been her savior, her everything. Would she ever have accepted Jesus then? No, God knew she had to reach that totally broken point before she could turn to Him, having nowhere else to turn. She had to totally hit rock bottom to find His light.

Her mind marveled at how the Holy Spirit worked. Even when she didn't really know Him, God had been working in her life to bring her to Him, and her heart overflowed with gratitude. She might not have her earthly father anymore, but she had her Heavenly Father, and she trusted that she would see her father and mother both again in Heaven someday. She'd never really, truly, believed in Heaven before, but now she did with a deep-seated conviction. She had that hope and reassurance true Christians spoke of, and the peace that had flooded over her like a blanket when she'd met Jesus still rocked her to her core in amazement.

She gave a tiny laugh of wonder. "But now I am whole again. Isn't it wonderful, Jack?" She couldn't stop the smile that spread across her face. It was amazing knowing that Jack truly understood how she felt about her newfound relationship with Jesus because he'd once been there too.

Jack's eyes glistened with true happiness for her. "I am so glad he answered my prayers for you, Katrina. I prayed for you every day you were gone. Yes, I wanted you to come back to me, but more than that I prayed that God would reveal Himself to you and watch over you, and He did," Jack confessed.

She felt a lump in her throat at hearing his confession of how he'd prayed for her every day, and tears pricked her eyes again.

"I truly love you, Katrina," he told her again, his voice and eyes full of that love.

"And I you," she answered back, realizing that only now that God had healed her troubled soul could she love him in return the way he deserved to be loved. She'd been too broken to love him properly before, but now she could love him with all that was in her, and her soul soared.

She thought he would squeeze the breath from her with the possessive embrace he pulled her into.

When he kissed her, he did so more passionately than she'd ever been kissed before. When he moved from her lips, he rained kisses all over her: her face, hands, shoulders, arms. She was drowning in his affection until he pulled back to stroke her cheeks. His eyes and voice were deep with emotion when he asked, "Marry me?"

This time she had no hesitation and there was complete peace in her answer, for she *knew* it was right. "Yes, Jack."

She blushed when he just stared into her eyes lovingly for several minutes.

"Ah, there it is," he smiled softly as he pushed a strand of hair away from her cheeks.

"What?" she asked, smiling back at him.

"Your maiden's blush," he answered before his lips touched hers again.

ABOUT THE AUTHOR

Kayla Lowe has always held a passion for writing and has been doing so from an early age. At age 15, she attended the Tennessee Governor's School for the Humanities where she began honing her craft. At age 16, she began writing her first novel, the Christian romance, *Maiden's Blush*. An avid reader herself, she enjoys novels about the Phantom of the Opera as well as an eclectic mix of fiction and nonfiction.

Kayla became a professional freelance writer in 2007. In 2011, she was one of the Top 100 Writers on Yahoo! Voices. In 2017, she became an editor and hobbyist blogger.

Kayla loves hearing from her readers. You can find out more about her and how to connect with her on social media by visiting her website: www.kaylalowe.com.

www.ingramcontent.com/pod-product-compliance
Lightning Source LLC
La Vergne TN
LVHW040959160425
808804LV00002B/9